COME
TWILIGHT

OTHER TITLES IN THE
LONG BEACH HOMICIDE SERIES:

COME TWILIGHT

A Danny Beckett Novel

TYLER DILTS

THOMAS & MERCER

Text copyright © 2016 by Tyler Dilts

Published by Thomas & Mercer, Seattle

www.apub.com

Amazon, the Amazon logo, and Thomas & Mercer logo are trademarks of Amazon.com, Inc., or its affiliates.

ISBN-13: 9781477827673
ISBN-10: 1477827676

Cover design by David Drummond

For Jeff and Kim

Napalm smells best in the evening
It's not worth believing what you heard

Thirty-one hours before my car exploded, I was at Julia's condo on the Promenade downtown. I still hadn't gotten used to spending so much time in a place that once would have made me uncomfortable in its luxury, but Julia made it feel like home.

It was a Thursday night and we were getting an early start on a weekend-long *Downton Abbey* binge. She'd been wanting to watch it for a while but hadn't ever managed to make the time. I'd never seen it because it was *Downton Abbey*.

We were three and a half episodes in when my phone rang. I was next up in the homicide rotation, so that meant I was on call. There was an apparent suicide in Belmont Heights.

I told Julia that I had to go to work. I'd been a homicide detective for nearly a decade, and she'd been a social worker for several years before she became a photographer, so she had some understanding of my job. But she still wasn't quite used to death being so ever-present in my life, and I could see the sadness in her eyes.

"I'm sorry," I said as I got up. "Why don't you go ahead and keep watching."

"You don't like it?" she asked, surprised.

"No, I do." It pained me to admit it, but I did.

"Then I'll wait for you."

"Okay, thanks," I said, glad she'd offered. I would have made the request myself, but I wasn't sure if we'd reached the point in our relationship when it was appropriate to ask her not to watch something without me.

The last time I'd been called out while staying at Julia's, I'd needed to go home to get a fresh suit. When I told her about it later, she suggested I leave a spare in her closet. So the charcoal Men's Wearhouse special that was number five in my work rotation was waiting for me. After a quick shower, I brushed my teeth and dressed.

She handed me a travel mug filled with fresh coffee when I went back into the living room.

"Thanks," I said. "I'll probably be all night."

"I know, Danny."

"I should still be able to make tomorrow night, though." Julia had a few photographs in a show at a small gallery in the East Village. We'd planned on dinner after the Friday-evening opening.

She kissed me good-bye and I looked into her green eyes, crinkling at the corners with her smile, and I touched the single dimple in her left cheek. For the first time in years, I would rather not have gone to work.

When I started my Camry and drove out of the parking garage, something didn't sound right. The engine was running rough and the car seemed sluggish. I drove for a block and decided I could probably make it to the crime scene. It was only two and a half miles. I felt a twinge of the chronic pain in my wrist creeping up my arm.

When I got there, my partner, Jennifer Tanaka, was already waiting.

"That was quick," she said. "I thought you were going to be at Julia's tonight."

"Just came from there," I said.

She looked at what I was wearing. "Fresh suit."

"So?"

"You have that in your car?"

"No."

She raised her eyebrows and smiled.

• • •

A little before nine, someone had reported a gunshot. Because it was a slow night, a patrol unit arrived less than ten minutes later. The responding officers investigated and found the body.

The crime scene was in an eight-unit apartment building near the corner of Belmont Avenue and Second Street. It was one of the old, well-maintained, pre-WWII buildings that were in high demand on Long Beach's booming rental market.

"The call came from a woman upstairs in the back," the uniform told me on the sidewalk. "She said she only called because the noise sounded like it came from the apartment below her, number six."

I looked at the building. There were four units in front—two on the first floor, two on the second. Probably two bedrooms each. "Four apartments in front, four in back?"

"Two in back, two over the garage." He looked curious. "How'd you know how many?"

I pointed at the mailboxes. They were numbered one through eight. Number six had a small label beneath it that read "MANAGER." He nodded.

"You talk to any of the other neighbors?"

He gestured toward the lower-left door. "The couple in this one asked what was going on."

"What did you tell them?"

"Just that we had a crime scene and were investigating."

"Good," I said.

He walked me along the south side of the building to a small porch, three steps up. There were two doors—the one on the right led up a staircase to the top floor, the other directly into apartment number six.

"You go inside?" I asked.

"Yeah. We came downstairs, knocked. There was no answer, but the door was unlocked. I opened it, saw him there, went straight to him to see if he needed an ambulance, checked the bedroom and bathroom to make sure no one else was here, then came right back out and called it in."

"Thanks," I said.

I went up to number six and looked inside. The victim's body lay slumped on a couch that divided the large living room in two. In front, a flat-screen TV, an upholstered chair with a matching ottoman, and a coffee table. A big bookcase and a desk tucked into the corner. On the far wall were two doorways, one leading into the kitchen and the other into the hallway to the bedroom and bathroom. From the porch I took several photos on my phone before heading back to the front of the building to find the crime-scene technician.

I looked around. It was a slow night, even for a Thursday, so we had at least three cars more than we needed. Because of the location of the victim's apartment in the back of the building, it was easy to contain. We just needed a few people at the front gate and one or two in the alley in back.

"How's it look inside?" Jen asked.

"Seems pretty straightforward. Give me a couple of minutes with the body, then come in and take a look before the ME gets started."

I went back inside. The first pass through had been to get an overview. This time I'd look closer and start picking apart the details.

First, the body. We had a preliminary ID. The apartment belonged to William Denkins. DMV records told us he was a fifty-two-year-old white male, five foot ten, one hundred ninety pounds. The victim seemed to fit the description. I squatted at the corner of the couch, careful not to touch the coffee table, and looked him in the face. He had graying brown hair, a little thin on the top. His upper body had fallen against the arm and backrest, and his head was resting on his shoulder, a lime-green pillow wedged between his elbow and the dark-beige fabric of the couch. There wasn't much blood. One thin line ran down from his temple, collected in the corner of his closed left eye, then continued on to the edge of his mouth, stopping at his slightly parted lips. His left arm hung down to his side, a Smith & Wesson Chiefs Special still gripped loosely in his hand.

On the coffee table in front of him was a nearly empty bottle of Glenlivet scotch and a single glass. The only other things on the table were a phone and two remote controls.

I stood and went to the desk in the corner. He kept it neat and well organized. The screen on his notebook computer was dark, so I tapped the backslash key with my latex-covered index finger. It lit up and displayed his Gmail inbox. No unread e-mails.

A wallet and a set of keys sat in a shallow tray on the upper-right corner of the desk, and on the opposite side were two lined yellow notepads, a smaller one on top of a full-sized eight and a half by eleven. Without moving them, I could read the grocery list on the top pad and a good portion of what looked like a building-maintenance to-do list underneath.

I looked back over my shoulder at the body, then back down at the writing on the pads.

"Fuck," I said out loud.

I went outside, found Jen, and brought her back.

"What am I looking for?" she asked.

"Check out the body, then look at the desk," I said.

She studied him for a few moments, then went to the desk. She saw it even more quickly than I had. "That handwriting doesn't look left handed."

"No, it doesn't," I said, bracing myself for a longer night than I had expected. "I think we might have a murder here."

• • •

The sky was brightening with the first hints of the sunrise when I hit the drive-through at the Dunkin' Donuts on Seventh Street and picked up a dozen assorted and two large coffees. Up until a few months ago, I'd spent most Friday mornings having breakfast with my friend Harlan, a retired LA County sheriff's deputy. Like me, he was an early riser. Unlike me, he was an excellent banjo player. Several years earlier, my left hand had been nearly severed while apprehending a suspect. The incident left me with near-constant chronic pain that stretched from my hand all the way up to my shoulder and neck. When a physical therapist suggested I take up music to help alleviate the pain and recover the dexterity in my injured hand, Harlan had given me a gift, a Deering Saratoga Star. It was a much finer instrument than I needed or, in fact, deserved, and when my learning curve had proved to be a bit shallower than he and my therapist had hoped, Harlan had bullied me into lessons with him. We traded our Friday breakfasts for donuts and banjos.

My car was still across the street from the crime scene, where I'd left it, hoping I'd be able to get it to a mechanic later in the day. I parked the unmarked cruiser I'd checked out at five that morning in front of Harlan's house, and he opened the door and started barking at me before I even made it to the porch.

"Where's your banjo?"

"Caught a case last night. I can only stay a few minutes."

He eyeballed me through the screen door while I balanced the donuts in one hand and coffee in the other. "You going to open up for me?"

"Depends. What kind of case was it?"

"The callout was for a probable suicide."

He pushed the screen open and stood back to the side so I could squeeze past.

"Poor soul," he said, his voice weighted with sadness. "He hear you practicing?"

I refused to give him the satisfaction of my laughing, even if I had to fight the urge.

We sat at the table and opened the box of donuts. Buttermilk for him, cruller for me.

"Probable, you said?"

"Yeah. GSW to the left temple, Chiefs Special in his left hand."

"Ten percent of people are left handed. They never shoot themselves?"

"His handwriting didn't look left handed."

"In the suicide note?"

"No note. But he had a bunch of stuff with his handwriting on it piled all over his desk."

He finished his donut and took a long pull from his coffee cup. "Doesn't sound very 'probable' to me."

"I know. I'm on the way to make the notification to his daughter. I'll find out for sure."

I took my coffee and another cruller for the road. He walked out onto the porch with me. Any other time he would have given me shit or tried to get in a dig of some kind. Instead, he just patted me on the shoulder and gave me a nod. He was an old cop and he knew where I was going.

• • •

Jen and I were waiting in an unmarked cruiser outside Lucinda Denkins's house at a quarter past seven. Jen had squeezed in a few hours of sleep while I was finishing up at the scene. Back at the station, I had spent twenty minutes on a cot and showered before putting on the fresh suit I keep in a locker for all-nighters.

The house looked like a small three-bedroom. Spanish style, with a nicely maintained drought-tolerant yard in front. An Altima parked in the driveway. We planned on giving her until eight, unless she came outside and looked like she was heading out for the day. It's awful to ambush someone in their driveway first thing in the morning with devastating news, but it's slightly less awful than having to break it to them at work.

My phone buzzed and I looked at the screen. "Hey, Lieutenant," I said.

"You're making the notification?" Ruiz asked.

"Yeah. Did you get my message?"

"You think maybe it's not suicide?"

"Got a red flag I have to check out with the daughter."

"Keep me posted," he said.

I looked at my watch.

Jen said, "Time to knock?"

"Yeah." I checked my hair in the mirror, got out, adjusted my tie, and buttoned my jacket. We walked up the drive and onto the porch, where we paused to listen for a moment. I heard what might have been a TV or a radio on the other side of the door. Things usually went better if the person being notified was already awake.

I rang the doorbell. A few seconds later a shadow moved behind the peephole. Then a woman opened the door. She was dressed in business clothes—slacks and a cream-colored blouse. Her blonde hair was pulled back, and she had a curious but pleasant expression on her round face.

Holding up my badge and ID, I said, "Lucinda Denkins?"

"Lucy," she said.

"I'm Detective Danny Beckett of the Long Beach Police Department, and this is my partner, Jennifer Tanaka. Is there some-place we could talk?"

"Yes, of course." She took a step back and pulled the door open wide for us. "Please come in."

The door opened into the living room. The furnishings were nice but not too expensive. It looked like mostly secondhand and vintage stuff, the kinds of things someone with good taste but not a lot of money would choose. Jen and I sat on a brown sofa that reminded me of the one in my childhood family room, and she took a seat in a chair that didn't quite match.

By the time we were all settled, her expression of curiosity had been replaced by one of worry.

"What can I do for you?" she asked.

"Your father is William Denkins?"

She nodded. "Is he all right? Has something happened?"

"I'm very sorry to tell you this," I said. "He died last night."

An almost inaudible sound came from her throat. If she hadn't been trying so hard to contain it, it might have become a gasp. She brought her hand up to her mouth and held it there for several seconds. Then she said, "How? What happened?"

"At this point, we're not sure. It may have been a suicide."

"No, it couldn't—he wouldn't do that." There was hope in her voice. If we were wrong about how the victim died, we might be wrong about his identity, too.

"Had he been depressed?" Jen asked. "Was anything troubling him?"

"No, nothing." She paused. "Are you sure it was him?"

"Yes," I said. "I'm afraid so."

She sank back into her chair. "There must be some mistake. He wouldn't kill himself. He just wouldn't." Her tears were beginning to flow.

Jen offered her a tissue. I hadn't even seen her reach into her jacket for one of the pocket-sized packets we always have with us when making a notification.

I heard some shuffling noises from the back of the house. "Is anyone here with you?"

"Yes, my husband." As if on cue, a door opened in the hallway and a tall, lanky man in gym shorts and a T-shirt came into the room. He had dark, shaggy hair and a soul patch under his bottom lip.

"What's going on, babe?" he asked Lucy.

She stood and hurried over to him. "My dad's dead."

He pulled her into his arms. "Oh my god," he said. "I'm so sorry. I'm so sorry."

We let him comfort her. As she buried her face in the crook of his neck, her back and shoulders rose and fell with her sobs.

After a few moments, he looked at us with accusation in his eyes.

"They say he killed himself," Lucy said.

"What?" he said. "That can't be."

The two of them were still standing behind the chair Lucy had been sitting in. We stayed seated. With only the couch and the chair available, the two of them would have to separate, and I was trying to decide who I'd rather have on the couch next to Jen.

"What happened? How did he . . . ," Joe said.

As his words trailed off, I said, "A gunshot wound. To the head."

Lucy buried her face in Joe's neck again.

"I know this is a very difficult time, but we need to ask you a few questions," I said.

They chose the seats themselves. Lucy on the couch, her husband in the chair.

I had a much better view of him, so that's where I started. "I'm Danny Beckett and this is Jennifer Tanaka. We're with the LBPD."

"I'm Joe." He tried to reach across the length of the coffee table to shake my hand. I leaned out and met him halfway. "Joseph Polson." He started to lean back and realized he hadn't shaken Jen's hand, so he awkwardly shifted toward her. She gave him a quick shake and let go.

"As I told Lucy, we're very sorry for your loss." I watched him while I spoke.

"Thank you," he said with a nod.

Jen asked Lucy, "Did your father have any history of depression?"

"Yes," she said. "But never anything serious."

I let Jen continue. Sitting next to Lucy, she'd be able to build a stronger connection with her. "Did he receive any treatment for it?"

"A few years ago. He went to a therapist and took an antidepressant for a while."

"How long ago?"

"I'm not sure," Lucy said. "Four or five years?" She looked at Joe.

"It was before we met," he said. "So at least five."

"Nothing since then?"

"No," Lucy said.

Jen continued. "Had you noticed any changes in his behavior recently?"

Lucy shook her head.

Jen asked a few more standard questions. It was clear that Lucy had no reason to suspect that her father might have wanted to hurt himself. There was a pause in the questioning, and even though Jen didn't look at me or give me any other signal, I knew it was an invitation for me to join the interview.

I said, "Was your father left handed?"

"No," Lucy said.

Joe looked puzzled. "Why would that matter?"

"It probably doesn't," I said. "We just need to check everything out." That seemed to answer the question well enough for him. I looked at Lucy. She was slowly sinking into the new reality of her life. Her father was gone. Nothing for her would be the same again.

We asked several more questions and fingerprinted them so we could eliminate their prints from those we found at the crime scene, and then we wrapped up the interview.

"What happens now?" Lucy asked.

"There'll be an autopsy this afternoon and we'll be in touch as soon as we have more information for you," I said.

"Do we"—she paused, as if she were rehearsing her next words in her head—"have to make arrangements?"

"Yes. The medical examiner's office will contact you to help with that. You'll probably hear from me before that happens, though."

Joe slid next to her on the couch, and we listened to her crying as we walked out and shut the door behind us.

. . .

The night before, Jen had done a preliminary canvass of the apartment building's tenants while I was working the crime scene. No one had answered her knock at either of the two studios above the garage. I was particularly interested in talking to the occupants of those units, because of the way the building was laid out. The garage and the studios, along with a small laundry room, made up a second structure separated by ten feet or so from the main building. The foot of the stairs up to the two small apartments was perhaps two yards away from Denkins's porch, and the landing looked down on his apartment with a clear view of its side door. From there, it was only a few steps to the gate leading into the back alley. That would be the logical escape route.

"Let's see if anyone's home," I said to Jen, tilting my head toward the stairs.

As we climbed the steps, I saw one of the slats on the miniblind fall back into place behind the window next to the closest door. I'd planned on starting with the farther apartment, but went to the first door instead.

I fought the urge to use my standard cop knock and gave the glass a few light raps with my knuckle. "We're with the Long Beach Police Department," I said, my voice only slightly raised. "Can we talk to you?"

We heard nothing from inside.

"I know you're in there. I saw you peek through the blinds."

Something shuffled on the other side of the door.

"Please," I said. "We just need a few minutes of your time."

There was more muffled noise, and the door, secured by a safety chain, cracked open.

The man who answered showed me only a single bloodshot brown eye under a large forehead topped by a mess of disheveled salt-and-pepper hair. "Yes?" he said.

I held up my badge and introduced myself. "My name's Danny Beckett. We need to talk to you about what happened last night."

"Okay, I guess." He didn't move, just kept staring through the crack.

"Can we come inside?"

His eye twitched and I could feel his anxiety seeping past the edge of the door. "Um, no?"

"That's okay," I said. "Would you mind opening the door or stepping outside for a minute?"

He nodded and the door closed. I expected to hear him undoing the chain, but there was only silence. I looked over my shoulder at Jen.

She made a hand gesture asking me if I wanted her to check the back of the building.

I shook my head. Unless he was going to squeeze through one of the tiny windows in back and jump fifteen feet to the alley below, he wasn't going anyplace.

He kept us waiting long enough for me to think I might have made a mistake. Then the door opened just wide enough for him to slip through and pull it closed. His hair was neater, and he seemed slightly less agitated. He was short, maybe five-seven, and his thin frame made his gray T-shirt look too big. I couldn't tell how old he was. Maybe forty, maybe sixty.

"Thank you, sir," I said, extending my hand. "I'm Danny."

"I'm Harold," he said. It looked like it took a significant act of will for him to shake my hand. "Harold Craig."

"Are you all right, Harold?" Jen asked.

He nodded. "I have an anxiety disorder," he said. He took a deep breath. "I didn't sleep last night."

"We apologize for the disturbance," I said. "Do you know what happened?"

"Bill's dead."

"Yes." I nodded. "He is."

Harold looked unsteady. "Let's sit down," I said, motioning to the top step. He put his hand on the railing and eased himself down. I sat next to him. Jen stepped halfway down the stairs and turned so her face was on the same level as his.

"Tell me about Bill," I said.

Harold told us how he'd lived there for twelve years, ever since he'd been laid off from his job as a high-school math teacher. While he spoke, he held his hand in front of his chest and shook it up and down in a small arc. He didn't seem to be aware of it. Bill had been a good friend to him, he said, not like a landlord at all. They'd go to lunch sometimes. Second Street or the Belmont Brewing Company if Harold wasn't having a bad day. Bill even got him a faster Internet connection when he needed it to work from home. Never once raised his rent or anything.

"Do you think they'll let me stay?" He noticed his hand then, and held it in his lap to keep it still.

"I don't know, Harold," I said.

He looked at his feet.

"What can you tell me about your neighbor?" I tilted my head toward the door of the other studio apartment.

"Kobe?" he asked.

I nodded as if I recognized the name.

"He seems like a nice kid. Asian."

"Kid?"

"Well, early twenties or so. You get old enough, everybody seems like a kid."

"Can you tell us any more about him?"

"I don't think he came home last night."

"That's unusual?"

"Yeah. He's usually home. Playing his Xbox."

"He bother you with that?"

"No. It's a thin wall, though."

"When did you see him last?"

"He went out not too long before everything started happening."

"Did you hear the gunshot?"

"No. Someone shot Bill? That's how it happened?" His hand was off his lap and shaking again.

I nodded. "When you say 'before everything started happening,' what do you mean?"

"Before you all started showing up."

Jen and I exchanged a look. Did Kobe leave before or after the shot was fired?

We talked for a few more minutes. I gave him one of my business cards and asked him to call me when Kobe came home.

When Harold was back inside, Jen and I went downstairs and let ourselves into Denkins's apartment. The crime-scene techs had scoured the place for any potential physical evidence, but we needed to go through it one more time for anything else that might provide useful information before we released the crime scene to the family.

"What do you make of Harold?" I asked once we were in the living room with the front door closed.

"I feel sorry for him," she said.

"Think he knows more than he's saying?"

"Everybody knows more than they're saying."

Most of what I was interested in was in the desk or file cabinet—rental agreements, financial records, legal documents. Jen searched the rest of the apartment while I dug into the paperwork. An hour later, I had a box full of files and Jen had searched the place from top to bottom.

"Find anything?" I asked, snapping the lid closed on the large plastic evidence container.

She shook her head. "Not really. Nothing out of the ordinary. Don't think Bill was a big drinker, though. No alcohol containers in the trash and only one beer in the fridge, on the bottom shelf, pushed way in back."

I looked at the coffee table where the Glenlivet bottle had been before it was collected as evidence. "Last night must have been an anomaly."

"So, why did Bill get shit-faced last night?" she asked.

"And who was he with?"

• • •

Jen offered to take the autopsy so I could get some sleep before Julia's show. I wanted to make a good impression, because I hadn't met many of her friends yet. But when we got out to the curb, I saw my Camry, still parked halfway up the block.

"Shit," I said. "I forgot I need to get my car to the repair shop."

Jen took pity on me. "Give me your keys. I'll get a tow for you."

"Thanks," I said, working the ignition key off of my key ring.

"Still take it to that place up on Cherry?"

I nodded, handed her the business card I keep in my wallet for the mechanic, and started for the cruiser.

She read the card. "See you tonight."

That stopped me. "You're going, too?"

"Your girlfriend sent me the event invite on Facebook, so yeah."

"We're not, I mean she's not—"

"Go sleep." I heard her laughing as she walked away.

CHAPTER TWO

THE BOY IN THE BUBBLE

Three hours in bed wasn't enough to make up for the sleep I'd lost the night before, but I was feeling rested and, honestly, a little bit nervous. I was certain Julia had anticipated this and invited Jen so I wouldn't feel quite so fish-out-of-watery.

After a shower and a shave, I spent too much time deciding what to wear. I went with khakis and a blue linen button-up with vertical stripes that I knew from experience would do a good job of concealing my Glock in its inside-the-waistband holster behind my right hip.

When I was as ready as I was going to get, I headed out to the gallery. It was in the East Village, which was really just the eastern edge of downtown Long Beach. Several years ago someone thought rebranding the area might be a good idea, so they hung a new name on the neighborhood and watched the gastropubs and retro-cool dive bars and art galleries sprout and blossom. I'd been spending a lot more time there since I'd been with Julia. The truth was that I was beginning to enjoy the neighborhood more, and that left me feeling conflicted. I worried about becoming so comfortable with the curated authenticity of the hipsters and gentrifiers that I'd lose my sense of the actual authenticity I needed on the job whenever I ventured out of the comfortable pockets of privilege where I found myself spending more and more of my time.

When I mentioned this to Julia, she just smiled at me. "What?" I'd asked her.

"That's a good thing to be worried about."

As I circled the block a second time looking for parking, I thought about pulling into a loading zone or a short-term spot. Nobody would ticket an unmarked police car. I decided against it, though, because I thought one of Julia's friends might see me do it, and I didn't want the first impression I made on anyone to be of a cop exploiting the perks of his job.

I found an empty space two blocks over on Elm and checked my watch. Five minutes to seven. Perfect timing. As I turned the corner onto Broadway, I could see Julia and Jen on the sidewalk up the street in front of the gallery. I picked up my pace.

Jen saw me first. She said something to Julia, who turned and smiled as I got close.

"They're just about ready," she said, giving me a quick kiss on the cheek.

I looked inside. A young guy with a thick hipster beard and waxed mustache was adjusting a cheese tray and lining up bottles of wine on a folding table. No one else was inside.

"And I was worried I'd be late."

Julia laughed. "I should have mentioned that no one shows up to an art opening on time."

"No one except the cops, apparently," Jen said.

Julia laughed again. Her easy calmness impressed me. I hadn't expected too much nervousness or anxiety from her, she was always steady that way. It was one of my favorite things about her. She never seemed to rattle. But I knew this show was a big deal for her. Things were really taking off with her photography. Not only was the show more exposure for her art, but she was hoping to sell, too. On the advice of the gallery owner, a man-bunned guy named Trev, she'd increased the asking prices for her new works. From what I could see, though, I was more concerned about how the evening would go than she was.

"Come inside," Julia said. "I need to show you something."

I followed her toward the back corner where her work was displayed. It looked good. She'd shown them all to me a few days earlier, when she was deciding which ones to include. She had a dozen photos of various sizes, some color, some black-and-white. Street photography, she called her style. She liked to find a subject, a person, and to photograph him or her in a way that situated the particular person in a particular place. Whether it was a homeless person downtown, a gangbanger in North Long Beach, a rich guy on Naples Island, there always seemed to be something that pulled me into the moment she'd captured. My favorite of the lot was a black-and-white that she'd taken on Belmont Pier. There were about a dozen people in the photo, but its subject was unmistakably the bearded man in running clothes sitting on a bench and focusing intently on a running shoe he was holding up in front of himself. It was only after studying it for a moment that I realized it was not just a shoe, but his own prosthetic lower leg.

As we got closer I saw one I didn't recognize—in the center of a dark rectangle was a bright square of light, in which stood a man facing away from the camera on a balcony, looking out at the city. It took me a few seconds to realize the photograph was taken from deep inside a room, and the dark frame consisted of the walls around a sliding glass door. It took a few more seconds to realize I was the man and the balcony was Julia's.

"What do you think?" she asked.

"You got my good side," I said.

"Is it okay? Do you mind me including it?"

I looked her in the eyes. Honestly, I wasn't sure how I felt about the photo. Part of me felt flattered to be one of her subjects, to be part of a piece of her art. But I also felt a certain uneasiness. I had no idea where it came from or why I felt it, but the idea of that photo hanging on a stranger's wall bothered me.

"I like it," I said. "But do we have to sell that one?"

She pointed at a small, round red sticker on a bottom corner of the frame's glass surface that I hadn't noticed before. "I'm way ahead of you. That means this one's already spoken for."

"Look at you," Jen said, approaching us. She had a small paper plate with cheese and grapes in her hand. "She got your good side."

A few more people had arrived. Julia introduced us to Trev, the owner, and to one of the other artists. We made some small talk, and by then the crowd had begun to grow.

"I should probably start mingling," Julia said, giving my hand a quick squeeze.

"Go ahead," I said. "I'll try not to break anything."

I watched her greet a small circle of women. They looked like old friends—hugs and smiles all around. Then I noticed Jen watching me.

"What?" I asked.

"I like her," she said. "And I like you with her."

"You don't like me otherwise?"

She didn't take the bait. "She's good for you."

"That she is," I said. Julia had moved on to a group of two couples and she seemed just as happy to see them as she had the others. I couldn't help but wonder if I was good for her.

• • •

As soon as I had the chance I pulled Jen into a corner to talk about the case. "How'd the autopsy go?" I asked.

"No surprises." She took a sip of bottled water. Neither of us had opted for the wine. "Blood alcohol was point-one-nine, with more in his stomach."

"And if he wasn't a heavy drinker," I said, "he was probably close to passing out."

"If he wasn't already unconscious."

"GSR on the left hand?"

"Yeah, but inconclusive."

"So someone could have put the gun in his hand and manipulated it themselves?"

She nodded and eyeballed the picked-over cheese tray. "We're going for food after, right?"

"That's the plan. Reservations at James Republic."

"Should have worn your fancy pants."

I laughed and stepped away to call the crime lab to check on the preliminary results from the scene. It was nearly eight, but it wasn't unusual for them to work late processing evidence. The phone was still ringing when I saw Julia waving me over to where she was standing. She was chatting with a young guy, maybe midtwenties, who looked happy to be there but seemed a little out of place in his Dockers and long-sleeved plaid shirt.

"Danny," Julia said. "This is Terry Wright."

I slipped my phone in my pocket and reached out and shook his hand. He had a solid grip that made him seem stronger than he looked. He had his shirt cuffs turned up and I noticed a tattoo on his forearm. It was only partially exposed, but I could see what looked like an old aerial bomb over lightning bolts and a wreath of some kind.

"It's a pleasure to meet you, sir."

"Likewise."

Julia looked at me expectantly, as if she thought I might recognize him. "He's in the Belmont Pier shot you like so much."

"Shit, I'm sorry. You shaved." I tried not to look down at his prosthetic leg.

"It was time for a change," he said.

When I'd told her that photo was my favorite of the lot, Julia had mentioned that she'd actually met Terry a few years earlier, when she'd worked at the VA hospital. She didn't mention in what capacity they'd met, so I assumed it involved some sort of counseling situation.

The gallery manager came up and put a red sticker on a bottom corner of his picture and gave Julia a subtle thumbs-up sign. Then he motioned for her to follow him.

"Somebody likes it," she said to Terry.

"I don't think it's me they're buying," he said as we both watched her walk across the room to another group of patrons.

I wondered how much it had sold for. Julia often gave the subjects of her photos a cut of the money if their photos sold. She said it was unusual, but not unheard of. Many of the people she took pictures of were struggling in one way or another, and she never wanted to feel like she was profiting from their misfortune.

My phone vibrated in my pocket. I wondered how long it would be before I could check it without looking like an asshole.

"How do you know Julia?" he asked me.

"From work," I said. We'd met when I was investigating the murder of a homeless man who'd been burned to death by a group of aspiring gang members.

He looked curious, but I didn't offer any more. We stood there for a minute and I could sense he was feeling awkward. I was, too, but one of the things I'd learned in my years of detective work was how to project a kind of pleasant disinterest no matter what I was feeling. I found it at least as useful in social situations as it was in the interrogation room. No matter how out of place I felt at a party, I could pretty much always make the person I was chatting with feel like they were the source of the awkwardness between us. It was kind of a dick move, but that never stopped me from using it.

Terry looked at me with a polite expectation in his eyes, and when I didn't speak, he said, "I'm going to go grab a glass of wine. Can I bring you something?"

"No, thanks," I said. As he walked away, his limp was almost imperceptible.

A twinge of embarrassment lodged itself in my gut. I looked at the scar that encircled my wrist, almost hidden by my watchband, and felt the familiar tightness grabbing at my arm and shoulder.

I went outside to check my phone. Ethan, the crime-scene technician who'd collected and cataloged the evidence last night and this morning, had returned my call and left a message. So far the only news was that fingerprint evidence revealed there had been at least three people other than Bill Denkins in his apartment recently. If Lucy and Joe were two, who was the third?

When I went back inside, I saw that the gallery had filled. There must have been three dozen people crowded into the space. As I checked out the other artists' work, I felt a trickle of sweat run down the small of my back. I found Jen studying a photo of some kind of purple flower. The richness of the color stood out against the duller and less focused tones of the background.

"That's not as good as Julia's," I said.

"Not that you're biased or anything."

"Objectivity is the bedrock of my existence."

"Yabba-dabba-doo."

• • •

As things were winding down, Julia found Jen and me back at her section of the exhibit. All of her photos had been red-dotted.

"A few people are going to Thai District across the street," Julia said.

"I made reservations at James Republic."

"What would you think about canceling?"

"I don't know." I put on my best faux-disappointed face. "I was really looking forward to the grilled octopus and heirloom gazpacho."

Twenty minutes later, Julia, Jen, and I were sitting by the window with Trev, whose name unsurprisingly turned out to be short for Trevanian rather than Trevor, and two of the other artists.

After the wine came and the server worked her way around the table to me, I said, "I'll have the chicken fried rice."

Julia and Jen shared a laugh.

"What's so funny?" I asked.

Julia looked at Jen. "You're right."

I wasn't sure if I was irritated or pleased that the two of them were bonding over their shared enjoyment of making fun of me. Probably both. "Right about what?" I asked.

Julia turned to me, put her hand on my knee, and said, "About your amazing ability to find the whitest, most Americanized dish on any ethnic restaurant's menu within ten seconds of opening it."

The server had finished taking everyone's order and was leaving the table as I tried to catch her attention. I didn't succeed.

Julia said, "Did you need something else?"

"Yeah," I said. "I wanted to see if I could add a side of fries."

Trev clinked his wine glass with a fork to get our attention. He held it up in a toast. "What a wonderful, wonderful opening. We sold almost everything tonight. Old friends, new friends"—he paused to make eye contact with Jen and me—"thank you all so very much." His gratitude was so sincere that I felt happy for him. And for Julia. And maybe even a little bit for myself.

It was after eleven when we got back to Julia's condo. She put her bag down on the kitchen counter just as her phone rang. She dug it out of her purse, looked at it, and sent the call to her voice mail.

"Who was that?" I asked.

"Unknown caller," she said and turned to me. "Did I mention that Trev asked me to teach a workshop on street photography?"

"No," I said. "Are you going to do it?"

"I told him I would. It sounds like fun."

"How long do you have to get ready for it?"

"A couple of weeks. It's right after Buskerfest. We're still going, right?"

"Sure," I said, reminding myself to check out the festival's lineup and try to familiarize myself with some of the local musicians who'd be playing. Julia had told me that the first local event she'd gone to after she quit her old job, took up photography full time, and moved to the East Village was Buskerfest. As she watched the succession of bands play, she knew she was home and had made the right decision. I was looking forward to sharing it with her this year.

"Thank you for tonight," she said.

"You're welcome," I replied, reaching for her hand and pulling her close. "I had a good time."

Her eyes searched mine. "You did, didn't you?"

I nodded and she kissed me deeply.

She pulled away and reached up to my face to brush the hair back from my forehead. "You're exhausted, aren't you?"

I wanted to lie, to tell her no, not at all. But I knew she'd see the truth, that the effect of the three hours of sleep I'd had in the last two days was more than I could hide, no matter how badly I wanted to.

"Why don't you go to bed? I'm still pretty pumped up from everything. I think I'll work for a while."

"No, I—"

"It's okay, Danny. Go get some rest."

After changing my clothes and brushing my teeth, I kissed Julia goodnight and, for the first time, got into her bed by myself. I felt the weariness pulling me down, but for some reason I couldn't quite grasp, I fought the urge to sleep. I didn't want the night to end. Had I any idea what the following days and weeks would bring, I would have fought so much harder.

I woke to the sun bright in Julia's bedroom window. Reaching across the bed, my hand found the empty space where she should have been. I rolled over. For a few sleepy moments I thought she must not have come to bed. But the sheets were pulled back and her pillow crooked against the headboard. She'd come and gone while I slept so deeply that I'd missed her presence entirely. A small wave of disappointment flitted through my mind.

In the bathroom I swished some Freshburst Listerine around in my mouth and tried to make my hair presentable. It didn't work.

Julia was in the kitchen making omelets. She'd put some music on. A sad song was playing softly, a familiar voice singing in French. Nina Simone?

I walked up behind her, put my hands on her waist, and kissed the back of her neck.

"Morning," she said. "How'd you sleep?"

"Good. I didn't even hear you come in."

"You were really out."

"Did I snore?"

"Not too bad."

I wasn't sure, but I was inclined to believe that meant I'd been going like a buzz saw all night.

"Sit down," she said.

I looked out the window next to her dining table. It was just after eight, and the Promenade four floors down was starting to see some foot traffic. During the week the people started earlier, hustling off to work. But weekends were different. The days would start slow and gradually. The street below would become more and more crowded as the urbanites and gentrifiers came out of their caves hunting for brunch.

The omelet was simple. Cheese and fresh tomatoes. She'd held back on the onions without even having to ask. After she put our plates down, she poured us each a cup of coffee from the French press. I wouldn't admit it to her, but it put the Keurig machine in my kitchen to shame.

"You have to work today?" she asked.

"Not until later. Just going into the squad to review things."

As if on cue, my phone rang, and before I even saw Lieutenant Ruiz's name on the screen, I knew my plans were changing.

I answered and Ruiz said, "How soon can you be in my office?"

"Half an hour. Why? What's up?"

"I'll tell you when you get here." He ended the call.

"Shit," I said.

"What's going on?" Julia asked.

"I don't know. But if the lieutenant is there on a Saturday morning, it's got to be serious."

●　●　●

When I got to Ruiz's office, Patrick Glenn, another member of the homicide detail, was already inside, as was another detective who I didn't recognize. I'd stopped downstairs for a coffee on my way in, but when I saw the seriousness on their faces, I looked down at the cup in my hand and regretted that I'd spent the time while they were waiting.

"Danny," Ruiz said, his voice neutral.

There were only two chairs facing his desk, so Patrick got up and gave me his with a nod. He moved over and leaned against the edge of a dark-wood file cabinet that matched the desk.

I didn't like that. Whenever we crowded into the office, the chairs were always first-come, first-served. We didn't give up our seats unless we were deferring to someone of a superior rank. Or to someone who had bad news coming.

My coffee was finally cool enough to drink, so I took a big sip and swallowed.

"This is Neal Walsh," Ruiz said. "He's with LASD Bomb Squad." Long Beach didn't have its own, so when we needed to, we worked with the team from the Sheriff's Department.

"What's going on?" I asked.

Walsh eyeballed me like I was a suspect. "Where's your car?" His voice was hard and confrontational.

"It's at the mechanic," I said. "Why?"

"What mechanic? Where?"

He was grilling me. I didn't know why, but I didn't like it. I bit down my rising anger. "North Long Beach. Place on Cherry."

"Where were you at ten o'clock last night?"

"Eating Thai food."

"With who?"

"Your mother," I said. "What's your problem?"

"Danny." That one word was all Ruiz needed to back me off.

I drank more coffee. It was too sweet.

"Your car," the lieutenant said, leaving the sentence unfinished.

"Somebody blew it up," Walsh added. "With a bomb."

• • •

When I went back into the squad, Jen was at her desk.

"What was that all about?" she asked.

"Someone put a bomb in my car," I said. "How come you're here? I thought you had the barbecue today." Every two or three weeks, Jen had her parents and brother over for a family meal. Unless there was an emergency, she never worked on those days, taking the morning for shopping and preparing.

"Patrick called me."

I sat down at my desk and opened my e-mail. There were a lot of new messages. I looked at the senders and subject lines. None of them seemed to make any sense.

"What are you doing?" she asked.

"Trying to get back to work."

"Really?"

I clicked on a random e-mail. It was something from Admin about repairing the plumbing in the locker room.

"Stop it," she said, her voice soft but weighted. "Look at me."

I did.

"Tell me what happened."

Not everything the lieutenant and Walsh said had really stuck. So I did the best I could relating what I knew to Jen. Someone had placed a bomb on the undercarriage of my car beneath the driver's seat. Whoever had done it had known what they were doing. It was designed to send the blast upward and kill or seriously injure whoever was behind the wheel. It had been triggered remotely by a cell phone, and it looked like whoever had done it didn't want to kill anyone but me. The working theory was that when the car unexpectedly wound up at the mechanic's shop and the bomber figured the device would be discovered, he waited until the garage was empty and triggered the device. Or something like that.

"Why was Patrick with you?" she asked.

"They're opening an attempted-murder investigation. He's working it with the bomb guy from the Sheriff's Department."

"Shit," she said, worry in her voice.

"Yeah."

"Somebody who knows what they're doing wants to kill you."

"Yeah."

"Who?"

"No idea."

"What are you going to do?"

"Figure out who killed William Denkins."

• • •

I'm only really good at two things—investigating homicides and denial. After a worthy but failed attempt at trying to engage me in a conversation about my feelings, Jen had asked what she could do to help. I sent her to go pull the files we'd collected at Denkins's apartment from evidence, then dug into my e-mail. After searching through my account for a while, I found one that mattered. I'd missed it initially because the return address, hc@hcconsulting.com, gave no indication of the sender's identity, and the subject line just said "Information." It turned out to be from the witness who lived in the studio upstairs from Denkins. **Dear Detective Beckett,** it said, **I thought you might want to know that Kobe, my next door neighbor, still hasn't come home. Sincerely, Harold Craig.**

Yes, as a matter of fact, I did want to know that. My plan for that afternoon had been to comb through the files I'd booked into evidence from the apartment, looking for, among other things, information on Kobe. We didn't have quite enough to officially consider him a suspect yet, but Harold's e-mail had made finding him our top priority.

I checked the time. Patrick was still working with the bomb-squad guys. He'd asked me to meet him at noon so he could do the preliminary interview for the attempted-murder case. My attempted-murder case. That gave me almost two hours.

When Jen returned with the file box, I told her about Harold's e-mail. "There's a folder of rental agreements in there. Can you find it for me?"

She did and handed it across the desk to me. I flipped through them quickly. Kobe's wasn't hard to find. There were only seven marked "Current Residents."

I opened it and saw his full name at the top. "Kobayashi Maru," I said to Jen. The name sounded familiar, but I couldn't place it. "That ring any bells for you?"

Jen shook her head. "No. Should it?"

"I think I've heard it before, but I don't know where."

Running his name didn't help. No criminal record. Not even anything from the DMV. The name had to be an alias. I shook my head and sighed.

"Nothing?" Jen asked. "What about the phone? If he was planning on moving in he'd have to give Denkins a working number."

"True," I said. We couldn't call it, though. The only way that would pay off would be if he was just an innocent neighbor happy to help out in the investigation. What were the chances of that, if he was renting the apartment with an assumed name and disappeared immediately after the death? No. The phone might be our only connection to him, and if he had any idea we were using it to find him, he'd dump it as soon as he could. Hell, he'd probably already dumped it. "I'll start working on a warrant request for the phone records."

Jen nodded. "You want me to do one for his apartment?" Our normal procedure was for the lead detective on an investigation to do all the warrant requests.

"I know what you're trying to do," I said.

She tried to play it off. "What?"

"If I wanted to be thinking about my car, I would be."

With a shrug she let it go.

On my computer I opened the template for a phone-records warrant. As I started filling in the specifics, though, I felt a rising queasiness in my stomach. I tried to push it back down, but it wouldn't quit. When it reached the back of my throat, I leaned over and puked into my wastebasket.

Maybe I'm really only good at one thing.

• • •

"You want the meatball or the chicken Parm?" Patrick said, opening the bag from Modica's, an Italian deli a few blocks from the station.

It had been almost half an hour since I'd left my breakfast in the trash can, so I decided I'd eat. "Surprise me," I said. He slid one of the sandwiches across the conference-room table to me.

"You catch the Keith Richards interview on *WTF* yet?" Several months earlier, when I was bitching about an NPR pledge drive, he'd suggested a few podcasts to me, and, while I was reluctant at first, I'd since become an obsessive listener.

"No," I said as I unwrapped the chicken sandwich. The marinara sauce had leaked out from the inside and coated the edges of the bread. "Got any extra napkins?"

Patrick reached into the bag and handed over half a dozen. "I love it when Maron goes all fanboy on the guest."

I took a bite of the sandwich and for a moment considered the possibility he was trying to loosen me up and build a rapport with me like I was a suspect. Walsh's accusatory tone from the meeting in Ruiz's was echoing in my head. Was Patrick setting me up for an interrogation?

"You should check it out," he said. "It's good." Then he bit off a big chunk of meatball sub and I watched him chew. After he swallowed, he sucked some iced tea through a straw and said, "You have any idea who wants to kill you?"

I told him I didn't, and he laid out what they knew so far. The bomb had been constructed out of an antipersonnel mine—like a claymore, he said, but a smaller version, made in South Africa. It wasn't complicated, but the bomber clearly knew what he was doing. And, more alarmingly, had access to black-market military-grade hardware.

"Why detonate it at the mechanic's shop?" I asked.

"That's a good question," Patrick said. "Maybe he figured they'd find the bomb and knew it would be harder to trace if he detonated it."

I thought about it. "Maybe he hadn't planned to set it off while I was in the car. Could it have been a warning?"

"Maybe. Walsh and I talked about that, too. We just don't know yet."

"Do they have any idea how long it had been there?"

"Not yet," he said. "Walsh thinks they might be able to narrow down a window with more analysis."

Patrick kept eating his sandwich as he spoke, taking small bites and chewing and swallowing in between sentences. I had lost my appetite.

"He says they might be able to get something that will help identify the bomber, but we shouldn't hold our breath."

"He actually say 'don't hold your breath'?"

Patrick took another bite, and a glob of marinara plopped down onto the table. "Yeah, he actually did." He wiped up the sauce with his finger and licked it clean.

"What's your take on him?" I asked.

"He's a complete asshole." Patrick sucked some more tea through the straw. "He's supposed to have a good squad, though. Ruiz asked for him personally."

"So how do we do this?" I asked. "I've never worked a bombing before."

"Neither have I."

"Well, then, I won't worry."

Patrick laughed, but I felt like a dick as soon as I said it. He was a good cop. I'd been working with him for more than long enough to know that. The only person I'd trust more than him to have my back was Jen. "I'm sorry. I shouldn't have said that."

"Dude," he said, examining me. "You okay?"

I nodded. "Why?"

"Because that crack was barely even passive-aggressive and you're apologizing. You're worse than that when there's no more Splenda by the coffee machine."

"There's a giant Costco-sized box right in the cupboard," I said.

"See?"

He was right. I didn't want to admit to anyone, least of all myself, that I was rattled. And I didn't want to be. But I could feel a ball of anxiety roiling in my gut. I imagined it spinning and growing like a cartoon snowball on its way down a hill. It wasn't that I hadn't come face-to-face with the idea of my own death in the past. I had. Many times. When my hand was nearly severed, I came very close to bleeding to death, and in the year I spent recovering, hardly a day passed when I didn't contemplate my own mortality. That was the darkest period of my life. Even darker than the time I spent mourning my wife. I learned what the muzzle of my gun tasted like and made a list of songs to play at my funeral. When I came back from that, though, I thought I'd lost the fear of death once and for all. I've been in a handful of potentially fatal situations since then. In none of them, nor in their aftermaths, had I felt anything shake loose.

"So what do we do?" I asked Patrick.

"We let Walsh and his crew do their job and we do ours. Let's start digging through your cases and looking for suspects."

On the table was the two-thirds of the sandwich I'd left uneaten. I wished I'd had the other one. Meatballs save a lot better than chicken Parmesan does. Still, I went ahead and wrapped it up for later. I knew I'd be hungry again before long.

"How you feeling?" Jen asked when we came back into the squad room.

"Okay," I said.

"You eat something?"

"A bit."

I hadn't told Patrick about throwing up earlier. He was right there with us, so I expected him to ask what she was talking about. Then I expected Jen to tell him. Then I expected them to laugh at me and turn my weak stomach into a running joke. When none of that happened, I was afraid the nausea was going to return.

When Walsh had treated me like a suspect in Ruiz's office that morning, it pissed me off. Still, though, that was better than what seemed to be going on here. If Patrick and Jen started treating me like a victim, I wouldn't be able to take it.

My arm and shoulder had been tight and stiff all morning. So instead of telling them my concerns like a grown man, I turned to my desk and started trying to stretch some of the ache away.

"Why don't we get started?" I said.

I pulled my files going back two years and we started sorting them, giving the highest priority to open files and the closed cases for which I knew I'd be testifying in court in the near future. There were six, and five of those were gang related.

Before we could start reviewing them, though, Patrick's phone rang. He answered and listened for a few seconds. "Yeah," he said. "He's right here." Whoever was on the other end talked some more, then Patrick said, "Okay, we're on the way," and ended the call.

"On the way to where?" I asked.

"Your place. They're bringing the dogs."

CHAPTER FOUR

PRIESTS AND PARAMEDICS

For several years, I'd lived in the lower unit of a duplex on Roycroft that I moved into after my wife died in an automobile accident. I'd gotten very comfortable there. Only once had that comfort been shaken. A suspect in a case I'd been working found my house and tried to ambush me. He was involved in the murder of a homeless man who had been burned to death by three teenagers trying to score street cred. Untangling that mess had also brought me into contact with a gang lawyer who we suspected had been connected to the murder.

"You're quiet," Patrick said, turning off of Seventh Street. "What are you thinking about?"

The attorney, Benicio Guerra, was better known by his street name. "Benny War," I said.

"Think he'd be involved in something like this?"

"No," I said. "It's not his style." If he'd come for me, it would have been quiet. Maybe even looked like an accident. And I'd almost surely be dead.

An LA County Sheriff's SUV and matching patrol car were parked in front of my house. Patrick drove past them, made a three-point turn, and parked across the street. As we were getting out of the car, my phone rang. Julia.

"Hi," I said.

"How are you doing? Think you'll be able to make it tonight for round two of *Downton Abbey*?" she asked.

I hadn't even thought about that. Or about how to tell Julia what was going on. "I'm not sure yet." I felt like I should say something else, but didn't have any idea what it should be. "I'll give you a call later, okay?"

"Sure," she said. "Don't work too hard."

"I won't." I ended the call and crossed the street.

Patrick was on my drought-brown lawn with two bomb-squad deputies in tactical uniforms. Each had a German shepherd at his heel. Walsh wasn't there. I was glad for that.

Patrick introduced us. He'd met them the night before at the mechanic's shop. The thick, dark-haired deputy who looked like an Olympic power lifter was named Kevin Farley, and the shorter, wiry one with the long scar that ran down from his temple to the corner of his mouth was Steven Gonzales. He was the senior deputy and did most of the talking while Kevin nodded and looked stalwart.

"The outside's clear," Gonzales said. "But we still need to check inside the house and the garage. Could I get your keys?"

I showed him which key went to which lock and handed them over. "Should we just wait here?"

"Might want to wait across the street by your car," Gonzales said. "Just in case."

We watched them go up onto the porch and work the key into the lock.

"He was joking, right?" I asked Patrick.

He shrugged his shoulders and we both headed back onto the asphalt.

"Hope you didn't leave anything embarrassing lying around."

"Like what?" I said. "Bondage gear?"

"I was thinking of all your banjo stuff. But whatever floats your boat."

Twenty minutes later Gonzales gave us the all-clear and motioned us back across the street. "What about upstairs?" he asked me.

"It's vacant," I said.

"Can you call the landlord for us?"

"Don't need to. He's got a Hide-A-Key in the backyard."

I led them around to the small backyard and picked up a fake rock from the planter along the back fence. "Here you go," I said, handing it to Gonzales. He led Kevin and the dogs up the back stairs.

"They got you showing the place to prospective renters?" Patrick asked me.

"No," I said. "Worse. The guy I let in was a contractor."

"Remodeling?"

"I don't know. I'm a little worried. The big thing in the neighborhood right now is to take these prewar two-story duplexes and turn them into single houses and sell them for a million and a half."

Patrick and Jen had both moved out of rentals in the last few years. Patrick bought a condo in Signal Hill and Jen, with the help of her parents, had lucked into a fantastic house in the Heights before the real-estate market had bounced back from the recession. I didn't even want to think about moving, let alone that kind of major change.

Only when Gonzales and company came back down the stairs did I realize we hadn't taken shelter this time around. "It's all good," he said.

"What now?" I asked.

"We go to work on the bomb fragments and other evidence from the scene and report back to your friend here." He tilted his head toward Patrick.

I wondered if my take on Walsh was accurate. Maybe he was just hard assed. Ruiz could be the same way sometimes, but I knew he was good at his job and he always had our backs. "Where does your boss fit into this?"

"Walsh? Nowhere, really. Unless we find something. Then he'll be there to take the credit."

I was warming up to Deputy Gonzales. He and Kevin loaded up the dogs and drove off.

Patrick went back to the cruiser across the street and got a big cardboard box out of the backseat.

"What's that?" I asked.

"Security," he said. Patrick had been assigned to the computer-crimes detail before he'd joined the homicide squad. We all tried to stay caught up on the latest technology, but his professional geek back-ground kept him well ahead of the rest of us. We went inside and he put the box down on the coffee table in my living room. The flaps weren't taped, but they'd been tucked into each other to keep the top of the box from opening. He pulled them apart and took out a shrink-wrapped package. It was a webcam. There were several more inside. He handed one to me.

"Open that," he said.

I tried to slit the plastic on the edge of the box with my fingernail while Patrick took out a folded sheet from a yellow legal pad. When he unfolded it, I saw it was a hand-drawn diagram of the floor plan of my apartment. It included the exterior as well, the front and back yards, side walkways, and detached garage. He studied it for a moment.

"I had to draw this from memory," he said. "I hope I got the angles right."

"You're going to set those up in here?"

"Yeah," he said, taking the first camera out of its package and fid-dling with it.

"I'm not sure I want to have my entire personal life on camera."

He didn't seem to be paying attention to me. "They won't be look-ing at you."

"What will they be looking at?"

He moved on to the next camera. "Doors and windows, mostly. They've got motion detectors, too."

As he worked, he lined them all up on the table in front of him. They were small, maybe three and a half or four inches tall and half as wide. I picked one up. It was heavier and more solid than I'd expected. A bulbous disk with a tiny dark eye mounted on a stubby shaft with a flat base on the bottom.

"Put that back," he said without looking at me.

When he was done, there were six of them lined up like toy soldiers.

Then he went through the boxes again and took out a power cord for each one. He placed one next to each camera, then referred to his diagram again.

"Okay," he said. "Your bedroom first." He stood, picked up a camera in each hand, then started down the hallway toward the back of the apartment. Halfway there, he called over his shoulder, "Bring the cords."

I did. My bedroom is in the corner of the building, with a window on each exterior wall. By the time I caught up with him, he already had one of the blinds raised and was positioning one of the cameras on the windowsill. He adjusted it, then held his empty hand out to me. I handed him a power cord. He plugged one end into the base and the other into the wall socket next to the dresser.

"We'll need to move the bed."

I helped him pull it away from the wall so he could squeeze in between the headboard and the window. He repeated the process he'd just gone through. When he finished, he said, "Laundry room next."

As he headed back up the hall toward the living room, I started to slide the bed back into place, but then realized he'd probably need to adjust the camera again. I thought about patting myself on the back for my foresight, but I knew that would just make my chronic pain flare up.

Patrick worked his way around the house. When he had all the webcams where he wanted them, he sat back down on the couch and opened his laptop. "What's your Wi-Fi password?" he asked.

"I don't know," I said.

He looked at me like a disappointed parent.

"It's in the spare bedroom." The people who had lived there before me had used the room as a nursery and had painted a mural of the sky transitioning from the deep shade of the night sky into the bright blue of morning, with a cow jumping over a smiling moon on one side and grinning sun decked out in shades on the other. If I did have to leave, I thought, I'd miss that most of all.

I took the sheet of paper onto which I'd copied the sixteen-digit mess of numerals and uppercase letters I'd copied off the back of the router into the living room and handed it to Patrick. The password-security lecture I'd expected didn't happen, though, and he just looked at it and typed. After he worked for a few minutes connecting each of the cameras to the network, he got up, computer in hand, and went from room to room adjusting the angle and placement of each camera as he watched the image it sent to his screen. When he was satisfied and I thought we were finally finished, he said, "Okay, now outside."

"More?" I asked.

He nodded matter of factly. "I don't want any blind spots."

The cameras outside were different. Self-contained and battery powered. They'd only record when their motion detectors were triggered. He put one ten feet up in the tree by the curb that faced the front of the duplex, and another under the eaves of the garage that faced the back.

We drank iced tea out of plastic bottles in the living room as he explained the whole setup to me. The inside units would record constantly. Because of storage-space limitations on the server they were wirelessly connected to, they'd be on a forty-eight-hour loop. We'd have to review them and manually save anything we thought we might want. He installed an app on my iPad and my phone that would let me monitor any one of the cameras in real time or access the recordings. I'd need to review everything from each camera anytime I came home, to be sure the bomber hadn't planted anything new. He showed me how to fast-forward through each feed.

"I have to do this before I come back here? All eight of them, every time?" I asked.

"It's the only way to be sure it's safe," he said. "I'll be watching, too. With both of us looking, we won't miss anything."

"What did you tell Ruiz?"

"Just that I was going to put up a couple of cameras. He thought it was a good idea."

"Eight is 'a couple'? Won't that eat up a lot of resources?"

"Yeah," he said. "But nobody will notice until next month at the earliest."

For the first time in hours, I thought I saw a bit of uncertainty in Patrick's face. While he'd been working, he was all confidence and assuredness. Give him something with wires and a Wi-Fi signal and he was unshakable. Now that the next step wasn't quite so clear, though, an unanswered question hung between us. *What next?*

I knew the surveillance setup was overkill. If it hadn't been my house, how many cameras would he have used? Three? Four? I thought about what I would do in his shoes. If someone came at him or Jen. Or even Ruiz or one of the other members of the homicide detail.

There wouldn't be enough webcams in the world.

• • •

Jen met Patrick and me for an early dinner at Lola's on Fourth Street. The restaurant was terrific, but I'd been in a long-term monogamous relationship with Enrique's, an older, more mature Mexican place. Lola's was young and sexy, but I always felt a pang of guilt when I ate there. Especially when I enjoyed it, as I usually did.

It was a few minutes before five o'clock, so we didn't have to wait to score a booth inside. Things got busy on Saturday nights. People would eat at one of the trendy restaurants along Retro Row, the strip of hipster heaven that was anchored on one end by Portfolio, one of Long Beach's oldest coffeehouses, and the other by the Art Theatre, an independent cinema that had been around for almost a century. I usually avoided the cool parts of town, but the food was good at Lola's and the movies were good at the Art, so I wasn't a stranger here. And I had to admit that since Julia and I had been together, I'd developed a higher tolerance for the buzzier parts of the city. I was even starting to like hanging out in the East Village.

I dug into the chips. The food there was always good, but they had a creamy green dipping sauce that was absolutely amazing. Salsa verde, they called it, but I preferred referring to it as green crack.

"I got the phone records for Denkins and Kobayashi and the search warrant for the upstairs studio," Jen said.

"Thanks," I said. "When can we execute the warrant?"

"Ruiz didn't authorize any more overtime for Denkins," she said.

"So we'll have to wait until Monday." I didn't want to delay any longer than we had to. If Kobayashi came home, he'd have a chance to clean up and get rid of any potential evidence. I picked up my phone and sent an e-mail to Harold Craig asking if his neighbor had returned.

The server came for our order. I went with the spicy carne asada and a beer. Jen and Patrick each chose one of the specials and iced tea.

Patrick hadn't heard about our case, so we gave him the rundown. "I don't think I ever saw a left-handed self-inflicted gunshot wound."

"I've seen two," I said. "Both while I was still in uniform. Both of those guys were actually lefties, though."

"And your guy, Denkins, he wasn't."

"No."

Patrick thought about it. "Think you would have caught it if whoever set it up put the gun in his right hand?"

I wanted to say yes, of course I would have. But I didn't. It wasn't true. The murder probably would have gone down as a suicide if I hadn't seen Denkins's handwriting on the tablets on his desk. I shook my head. "No."

"Good catch, then, I guess," he said.

We were silent for a moment and I knew they were asking themselves the same question I was. *How often do we miss them?* How many murders slip past us without us being any the wiser to the truth of the situation? None of us gave voice to our thoughts, though. I ate more chips and looked for the server. We needed more crack.

Harold replied to my e-mail. I hadn't expected an answer so soon. Kobayashi hadn't come back. I'm starting to worry about him, he wrote. So was I.

"What's next?" I asked Patrick.

"Headed back to the mechanic. Gonzales said they'd be wrapping up the scene soon, so I want to check in with him. And I need to talk to a few of the neighbors who the uniforms flagged on the initial canvass."

"Somebody see something?" Jen asked.

"Don't know," he said. "We think the bomb came in with the car. The security camera didn't catch anyone on the lot after closing. They do a lot of custom work after hours, so there's really no pattern in the evenings, and no way to know if anyone's there without checking. Because the explosion didn't happen until everybody was long gone, we think maybe he visited before setting the bomb off."

I tilted my beer bottle back and drained the last few drops. They didn't help. "So he doesn't want to kill anyone but me?"

"That's one theory," he said.

"What are the others?"

"I'll let you know when we come up with them."

"Maybe someone who works at the garage?" Jen said.

"We're checking all the employees out," Patrick said. "But at this point that seems unlikely. If it was someone with a grudge against somebody else at the shop, they could have done a lot more harm to the business by putting the bomb someplace else. Not in the car. That actually reduced the damage to the building."

I thought about it. "We need to figure out when they planted the bomb."

Patrick nodded. "I do, yeah."

He changed the pronoun to singular. I wondered if he did it on purpose. "The car was on the street across from the crime scene all night and most of the day," I said. "Before that, it was in Julia's parking garage for a couple of hours. The only other places it's been parked long enough for anyone to mess with it in the last week are my house and the station."

"Is there a camera in Julia's garage?" he asked.

"Yeah," I said.

He thumb-typed a note into his phone. "I'll check it. Gonzales said the bomber knows what he's doing. He wouldn't plant it any earlier than absolutely necessary, because there are too many things that can go wrong on a moving vehicle. No more than forty-eight hours, he said. Probably less than twenty-four."

"It's not going to be the station," I said. "So either at Julia's or on Belmont across from the Denkins scene."

"Yeah," he said.

I said, "I'm going back there tomorrow." I'd be off the clock, so the warrant would have to wait, but there were still a few things I wanted to take a look at. "Want me to knock on some doors and see if anyone noticed anything with my car?"

"No," Patrick said. "I got it."

We were close to finished with our food when Patrick got a text message. He read it and said, "That's Gonzales. Have to go meet him."

"Go ahead," Jen said. "I've got this."

As Patrick was leaving, he stopped at the door and looked at me over his shoulder. I couldn't really read his expression, but there was something in it that seemed pensive and worried.

Jen took a credit card out of her wallet. A free dinner was apparently one of the perks of being an attempted-murder victim. "I should have gotten something more expensive," I said.

After she'd taken care of the check, she said, "We need to talk."

"About what?" I asked.

There was a subtle change in her voice. She was using the calm-but-firm tone she adopted when she was going to tell me something she thought I wouldn't like. "Patrick's not the only one on the clock this weekend." She gave that a moment to sink in. "Ruiz doesn't want us to leave you alone for a while."

I wasn't sure how I felt about that. Part of me was glad. I had tried not to think too much about what I'd do after dinner, but hadn't been very successful. Would I be too rattled or pumped up with anxiety to get any work done? Or even to sleep? What would I be thinking about all night? Would I be able to focus on anything other than the bomber? On the other hand, I felt oddly obligated to resent being told I needed a babysitter. It occurred to me that I hadn't even considered going to Julia's as I'd planned. I knew, more instinctually than consciously, there was a chance I'd be putting her at risk. The same was true of Jen.

"I think he's wrong," I said.

"Of course you do." She did a respectable job of masking her inevitable exasperation with a good, thick layer of patience and understanding. "Mind if I ask why?"

"Because I don't want anybody else to get killed by a bomb meant for me."

She hadn't been expecting anything that sincere. "I understand that. It's maybe a good reason not to see Julia tonight. I get it."

"So why should I feel differently about putting you at risk?"

Jen looked at me as if I'd just asked a very stupid question. "Because I'm getting overtime."

• • •

Jen gave me the choice of where to stay that night—her house or mine. Normally I would have felt more comfortable in my own home. And I might have even then. But practicality weighed out. She had a guest room. If I chose my place, she would have to sleep on the couch. And it didn't even fold out.

She followed me to the duplex to pick up a change of clothes, and I showed her the process of checking the camera feeds. To fast-forward through all of them took almost three minutes. But that was only a few hours of recording. I wondered how cumbersome the process would be when I had to scan through twenty-four hours' worth of footage.

I wanted to work when we got to her house. And I did, but I didn't have access to either the paperwork from Denkins's apartment or his computer. So I went through my own notes again, as well as Jen's notes from her canvassing of the neighborhood. I wanted to get a better sense of who he was, because the more I knew about him, the more leads I'd be able to develop. After reviewing all the notes and case files I had on my MacBook, I realized there wasn't much else I could do.

Julia was waiting for a call from me and I was putting it off as long as I possibly could. I still had no idea what to tell her. That wasn't exactly true. I did know what to tell her, I just didn't know how.

I went out into Jen's backyard and sat at the teak table under the pergola. The landscaping had been impressive when she'd moved into the house, but it was even better now. Her father, Owen, was an avid hobbyist gardener, and he had seen a great array of possibilities of the kind that his own house had never afforded him. Since he'd recently retired from a thirty-year-long career at Toyota, he had an abundance of time and energy on his hands.

I didn't know the names of any of the plants, but there was a professional feel to the arrangements. A small patch of grass was sur-rounded by lush flowering bushes of several different varieties. There was a banana tree in one corner. One of those trees with the big white flowers that smell good was diagonal to it. Straight across from me, in the farthest corner, was an old oak with branches that projected out over the other plants. It seemed almost out of place among all the tropical greenery. Owen had wanted to remove it, both because of the aesthetics and because its roots were pushing up the cinder-block back wall and it was beginning to crack. Jen wouldn't let him. The whole yard felt secluded and peaceful.

At the other end of the yard, opposite the garden, were Jen's garage and the small guesthouse behind it. Her tenant was a young LBPD uniform named Lauren Terrones, who'd just completed her rookie year on the force. Jen told me she'd been working nights.

I was looking at the row of rosebushes along the back edge of the patio when Jen came out. She was wearing running shoes, shorts, and a tank top, with a workout towel slung over her shoulder and a bottle of water in her hand.

"Call Julia," she said and continued past me and into the side door of the garage. The light came on, and a few seconds later, I heard the motor on her treadmill hum to life. As the rhythmic thumping of her stride slowly gained speed, I picked my phone up off the table and thought about how I would tell Julia what I needed to tell her.

Forty minutes later I was still sitting there when Jen came back out of the garage, her dark hair matted to her forehead with sweat.

"What do I say?" I asked her.

CHAPTER FIVE

It was after nine when I finally sent Julia a text message.

I'm sorry, it said, Patrick caught a big case today and I've been backing him up. Haven't really been able to think about anything else.

The fact that it wasn't really even a lie made me feel even more cowardly than I already had.

That's okay, I understand. Of course she did. She always understood. Dinner tomorrow?

Yes. Definitely.

I hope you sleep well.

You too. I paused for a moment, then added, I miss you. I hit "Send" as quickly as I could. I didn't want to give myself enough time to think about that last sentence.

After what seemed like a very long time, she answered. I miss you too. Goodnight ☺

Jen was in the living room watching something on HGTV and drinking some kind of tea. "Did you talk to Julia?"

"Yeah," I said, knowing she could hear in the single, unenthusiastic syllable how disappointed I was in myself.

"You want something to drink?" I was grateful to her for changing the subject. "I could make another cup. Or maybe a beer?"

"I'm okay," I said, sitting on the couch next to her. I looked at the TV screen. "Which one is this?"

"The one you said you liked. *Fixer Upper.*"

"Oh, yeah," I said, recognizing the sandy-haired doofus who remodels houses with his much more grown-up and professional wife.

"How's your pain been today?" she asked.

Among the many things you learn when you suffer from chronic pain is how little anyone really wants to hear about it. They'll ask you, of course, how you're doing, but you quickly realize that, no matter how much you're hurting at the moment, the only socially acceptable response is "not too bad." But I knew with Jen I could always tell her the truth. And that's why she always made it a point to ask. Not because she didn't know. She was remarkably perceptive of the physical signs of my pain. One of the first things the doctors teach you when you're diagnosed is how to rate your discomfort on the pain scale, with one being "no pain" and ten being "the worst pain I can imagine." For a brief time, Jen and I played a kind of game in which she'd guess the number based on my behavior. The novelty quickly wore off when it became clear she got it right every time.

"Pretty bad," I said. "I was busy enough for most of the day to deal with it, but it's going to be a rough night."

"You take a Vicodin?"

I shook my head. According to my pain-management specialist, the new research was showing that opiates were not as effective for long-term treatment as doctors had previously believed. So I'd spent the last several months trying to wean myself off of them. I discovered that they weren't helping as much as I'd thought they were. But they were helping some. And when you hit eight or nine on the pain scale, even a slight help is better than none at all.

"No," I said. "Not yet. I'm figuring I'll need one tonight, though."

"Anything I can do to help?"

I shook my head.

We watched the TV for a while. Chip, the doofus, was gleefully sledgehammering a kitchen wall in his eternal quest for the magical open floor plan.

"There's something else I should mention," she said.

"What?" I asked.

"I actually spent a long time talking to Ruiz today." She took a sip of her tea. "He's worried about Patrick."

"About Patrick? He's not worried about me?"

"He's always worried about you." It was hard to imagine Ruiz expressing worry about anyone, least of all me.

"Why?"

"The captain was hesitant about letting someone on the squad investigate the bombing. He was worried it might be too close to home."

"Who did he want to work it? The Sheriff's Department?"

"That was discussed, yeah. But not even the captain wanted to cede jurisdiction to the county. They talked about a few other possibilities. Ultimately, though, the lieutenant talked him into the joint assignment with the bomb-squad guys and Patrick leading the investigation."

"So why is Ruiz worried? Patrick's got a great record. His closed-case rate is right up there with ours."

"He's not worried about his competence. He's worried about it blurring too many lines. About conflict of interest. About a cop investigating a crime against a friend."

I didn't bother adding that from the victim's point of view, that doesn't always seem like a bad thing. "The lieutenant's worried that Patrick won't be able to compartmentalize things effectively?"

"Well," Jen said. "He's more worried that you won't let him."

"Aha," I said. "So it is me Ruiz is really worried about." I grinned at her. She wouldn't smile back.

• • •

Jen went to bed around eleven. I thought about trying to sleep. Even though I was tired, I knew I wouldn't be able to quiet my mind enough to rest. I went through what I had on Denkins's case again, but I was just spinning my wheels. Without the files and his laptop, I'd done all I could.

I typed a text message to Julia, but didn't send it. If I had, it would have just resulted in a situation in which I'd have to come clean with her and tell her what was going on. That was a bridge I still wasn't ready to cross.

I wasn't the gym rat my partner was. Most of the exercise I got was from the stretching-and-strengthening routine prescribed for my pain by my physical therapist, or from the long walks I'd take several nights a week. Years ago, when my insomnia was much worse, I'd taken to walking my neighborhood late at night, sometimes for hours at a stretch. The quiet and the peacefulness made it seem almost like a different city, one that I shared with far fewer people than that place in the sun. Often, in those days, I thought I preferred the night, when it felt more appropriate to be solitary, to be quiet, to withdraw. But in the time since, I'd felt myself being pulled back into the daylight. By Jen, mostly. But also by Patrick, by Harlan, and, most recently, by Julia.

On another night, feeling as I was, I would have walked. I knew Jen wouldn't tolerate that, though, so I followed her example. After changing into the shorts and T-shirt I'd brought with me to sleep in, I went into her garage and turned on the treadmill. It was a good one. A top-end, gym-quality Star Trac model. I set the speed to three miles per hour and started walking. There were a dozen unplayed podcasts waiting on my phone. I saw the *WTF* with Keith Richards that Patrick had recommended, but I listened to *Wait Wait . . . Don't Tell Me!* instead, hoping it might elicit a few laughs.

Even though my back was to the corner opposite the door—the gunfighter's treadmill, I'd joked when I helped Jen move it into the garage—I still felt uncomfortable with earphones in both ears. The way they decreased my situational awareness was too distracting. So I tried one ear. Then I tried disconnecting them altogether and turning up the volume on the phone. That worked well enough once I knocked half a mile an hour off the treadmill's speed. Sure, I was going slow, but burning calories wasn't the goal. After a while, I found just the right balance of movement and focus to allow me to start letting go of the thoughts that had been racing through my mind. I knew, though, that as soon as I stopped, they'd return. So I didn't stop for a very long time.

The first podcast had ended and I was halfway through another when I heard something outside. My gun was on the weight bench three feet in front of the treadmill, and I was halfway to it when Lauren stuck her head in the open side door.

"Hey, Danny," she said. She must have seen the tense expression on my face. "Sorry. Didn't mean to startle you."

"Oh, no," I lied. "You didn't."

"I was surprised to see you. I expected Jen." She'd changed into her street clothes and carried her patrol-gear bag over her shoulder. "You crashing here tonight?" she said casually, as if finding me there was a completely normal experience.

Shit, I thought. *Everybody knows.*

"You heard?"

I was hoping she'd say "No" or "About what?" but she just nodded. "Kind of hard to keep an exploding car on the down low." She looked at me with genuine concern in her expression. "You okay?"

"Yeah, I'm fine. Just going to do five or six more hours on the treadmill, then I'll call it a night."

• • •

After my long, slow walk, I turned in. But half an hour was all I could manage in the guest-room bed before I got up again and carried my laptop out to the kitchen table. I skimmed through everything I had on Denkins one more time and didn't come up with anything new. Then I skimmed through all my old case files looking for potential bombers and didn't come up with anything new there, either. I decided to listen to the new Richard Thompson album I'd downloaded a few weeks earlier. I hadn't heard it yet, so I thought it might be enough to keep my mind engaged in something other than worrying about who was trying to kill me.

It was a good call. As soon as the first track came on and he started singing in his warm and familiar baritone, I felt myself being pulled into the music and, for a little while at least, forgetting.

I didn't remember going to bed, but when I woke to the familiar ache in my shoulder and neck, I realized I'd somehow managed a few hours of sleep. After getting dressed, I brushed my teeth and slicked my hair back with tap water from the bathroom sink.

Jen was in the kitchen eating oatmeal and drinking coffee. My laptop was on the table and the music was still playing.

"Did I leave that going all night?"

"Yeah," she said. "But it sounded good, so I left it playing." She gestured to a bowl and a cup on the counter.

I took them and joined her at the table. Oatmeal was never very appealing to me, but she'd added raisins and sprinkled cinnamon on top, and I had to admit that it tasted pretty good.

We sat and listened to Richard Thompson singing plaintively about a winding road.

• • •

Jen left me alone in the squad room with William Denkins's computer and the files I'd taken from his apartment. I checked in with Harold one more time. Still no sign of Kobe. At this point, I didn't expect him to return. Whoever he really was, he was still first on the list of potential suspects.

Over the next two hours, I was able to learn a great deal about Denkins. He was born in Reseda in 1963, went to high school in Lakewood, then to Cerritos community college and Cal State Fullerton. He graduated in 1984 and took a year off before going back for a master's degree in history. His MA was granted to him in 1987, as was a license for his marriage to Celeste Kelsky. Lucinda was born six months after the marriage, and the divorce came a little more than a year after that. Celeste married someone else in 1988, and she and her new husband were granted custody. Every other weekend, Lucinda stayed with her father. He taught history for eight years at a private high school. In 1999, when his parents died, his mother only eight months after his father, he inherited the apartment building on Belmont and another in Alamitos Heights. Both buildings had mortgages on them, but they were turning a small profit. Two years later he sold the property in the Heights and came very close to paying off the mortgage on the remaining building. He'd been investing in mutual funds for several years. There was a big dip in value and earnings when the recession hit, but even now his portfolio seemed to be worth close to a million dollars. The Belmont building had been appraised last year for $2.6 million. William Denkins had been a surprisingly wealthy man. The sole beneficiary of his will was his daughter, Lucinda.

Maybe Kobe had some competition at the top of the potential suspect list.

• • •

"Tell me more about your suspect," Patrick said. "What's his name, Kobayashi?"

"Why?" I asked.

"I've been all through your case files. Talked to a bunch of people. Checked with the ADAs on all of your pending court cases. Couldn't come up with a single solid lead on anyone who might have the experience, access to the hardware, or enough motivation to pull this off."

I thought about what he said. "You think maybe someone was hoping to stop me from discovering Denkins was murdered?"

He exhaled loudly through his pursed lips. "I know," he said. "Sounds like a long shot."

"Maybe not as long as it would have sounded a couple of hours ago." I told him what I'd discovered about Denkins.

"Shit," he said. "That's a lot of money."

The idea that the bomb might have been connected to my current investigation was an intriguing one. We tossed it around a bit. "So it would mean that whoever killed Denkins would have had to have known that they botched the fake suicide."

"Who could have known that?"

"Aside from everyone at the crime scene?"

"Yeah."

"We told the daughter and her husband the next morning that it may not have been suicide," I said. "Around eight or so."

"What about the upstairs neighbor guy?"

"He found out a couple of hours later."

Patrick considered that. "What time did Jen have your car towed?"

"I'm not sure. Two or three, maybe."

He scribbled a few notes on the yellow pad on the table in front of him. "So we're looking at, at most, an eight-hour window when someone could have gotten to your car."

"Unless something leaked earlier," I said.

"Eight hours doesn't seem like enough time." He tapped the end of his pen on the table. "Even if there was a leak. Let's call it fourteen hours. That's not much of a window. Maybe if somebody took a shot at you, tried to run you off the road, something like that, yeah, maybe."

"But?"

"A bomb?" he said. "I don't know. Somebody's got to realize they screwed up, come up with the completely mistaken idea that killing you will somehow magically turn a homicide investigation back into an open-and-shut case of suicide, build a bomb, plant it on your car in broad daylight, all in half a day?"

"Seems like a stretch," I said.

He tapped the pen some more, then seemed to come to some sort of conclusion. "Let me call Gonzales. People will do some crazy shit for three and a half million dollars."

By the time he got off the phone, Jen was back in the squad room. She'd been knocking on doors up and down Belmont Avenue asking if anyone had seen anything suspicious in the neighborhood on Friday, maybe something to do with a fifteen-year-old Camry.

"Get anything?" I asked her.

"Nothing solid," she said. "Everybody was at work all day. One retired man said he saw 'some Asian kid' walk down one side of the street and back up the other like he was looking for something he couldn't find. That's all I got."

"He think he could ID the guy?" I asked.

"Maybe," she said.

"I wonder if that could have been Kobayashi," I said.

Patrick rolled his ergonomic desk chair over to where we sitting.

"You catch that?" Jen asked.

"Most of it," he said. "Gonzales said our guy's a pro. Could have made the bomb in fifteen minutes if he already had the stuff on hand."

Maybe a bomb wasn't as outlandish an option for a spur-of-the-moment murder scheme as we had thought. "If all you have is a hammer," I said, "everything looks like a nail."

"So," Patrick said. "Tell me more about this Kobayashi kid. What's his first name?

"That is his first name." Even though I didn't think I needed to, I checked my note to make sure I got it right. "His last name's Maru."

"Kobayashi Maru?" he said incredulously. Then he just laughed.

"What?" I asked.

"You didn't even Google it, did you?"

I shook my head.

He was still giggling. "I've got to go. Look it up."

I texted Julia: `Dinner at Michaels in an hour or so? We need to talk.`

A few seconds later she replied. `Sure.`

"It's all set," I said to Jen.

Before she could answer, an alert sounded on my phone. One of Patrick's webcams had detected motion at my house. I could have checked it on the phone, but I wanted a larger picture, so I grabbed my iPad and opened the app, expecting to see a cat or a squirrel. So far they'd been my only visitors. But I sat up straight in my chair when the camera mounted in the tree by the sidewalk showed a man walking up onto my porch.

"Patrick," I shouted across the room. "We got somebody."

He and Jen rushed over to my desk and we huddled around the small screen watching the man doing something to my front door.

"What's he doing?" Jen asked.

"I can't tell." Patrick squinted and leaned in closer.

The man turned toward the camera and followed the walkway back to the sidewalk.

"What does he have in his hand?" I asked as he walked out of the frame.

Patrick reached over to the iPad and backed up the image a few seconds. Just before the man turned at the corner of my front lawn, Patrick froze the image.

He put his thumb and forefinger on the screen and spread them apart to zoom in on the image. The three of us simultaneously recognized what he was holding.

Doorknob hangers.

They smiled, not quite laughing, while I sat back in my seat and sighed.

"False alarm," Jen said, resting her hand on my shoulder.

"Look on the bright side," Patrick added. "Maybe you've finally got some good restaurant delivery in your neighborhood."

•   •   •

Michael's Pizzeria on the Promenade was only two blocks from Julia's house. It wasn't my favorite pizza in Long Beach, but the foodies liked it. Don't get me wrong, it wasn't bad, especially if you liked things like duck confit and fontina on your pizza, or if you weren't embarrassed to ask what the Italian words on the menu meant. I usually ordered the calzone. The crust and cheeses were excellent and it had some kind of meat in it that was kind of a little bit like pepperoni.

Jen wasn't comfortable leaving me alone at the restaurant. "Something might happen to Julia," she said, "and then I'd never be able to forgive myself." She found a seat next door on the patio of Beachwood BBQ that faced my seat on the Michael's patio fifteen yards away. Even from that distance I could clearly make out the words when she mouthed "Tell her" in exaggerated frustration.

I ordered the marinated-olive appetizer and wine Julia liked, and a few minutes later saw her walking toward me on the Promenade. Her hair was pulled back and she was wearing the faded-rose-colored dress

I'd complimented her on, the third time we went out together. She didn't seem to notice anyone on the other patio as she passed.

When the hostess greeted her at the gate, Julia pointed at me and smiled. I stood as she got close to the table and she gave me a quick kiss before sitting across from me.

"The appetizer's on the way," I said. "And wine. I think I got the right one."

"Danny," she said, her voice heavy and serious. "What's going on?"

I tried to pretend like I didn't know what she was talking about. "What do you—"

"Don't, okay?" She reached across the table and took my hand in hers. "You've hardly talked to me in two days and now your partner's sitting on the next patio over and pretending not to look at us. Just talk to me."

My eyes were locked on the water glass on the table in front of me. I should have told her about the bomb as soon as I found out. Instead, I'd kept it to myself, wanting to believe that if I pretended hard enough, I could make it go away. Or that it would turn out to be a false alarm or somehow easily resolved and I'd be able to just laugh it off. The truth was that if I acknowledged the reality of the situation to her, I'd have to acknowledge it myself, too. I was too embarrassed to look at her. But I forced myself. When I saw the concern in her eyes, I couldn't help myself. I did what she asked.

I talked.

I told her everything.

More than I probably should have. Every detail of the bombing and of Denkins's case came spilling out of me. I went on for what seemed like minutes, only pausing briefly when the waiter delivered the olives to our table. When I was finally done, I looked at her, hoping my fear and anxiety weren't etched into my face, and that she couldn't see the pain twisting up my shoulder and into my neck.

I didn't realize she was still holding my hand until she squeezed it harder.

"Jesus," she said, her eyes warm and tender. "I'm sorry."

"It's okay," I said.

"No, that's not what I mean." Her grip loosened and she looked away.

"What do you mean?" I asked.

She bit the corner of her lip. "I'm sorry that—" She stopped without finishing the sentence. "It's just that when you send a text saying 'We need to talk,' it—" She cut herself off again.

"What are you trying to say?"

"I thought you were breaking up with me."

• • •

"You never Googled the name?" Jen asked. I hadn't. By the time Patrick had stopped laughing and told me to look it up online, I was already running late to meet Julia, so I didn't get to it until after dinner. We were sitting at the table on her patio, the last vibrant-orange traces of the sunset fading in the sky.

"I had a lot on my mind." The embarrassment I felt at the oversight stung. But not as much as Patrick's laughter had. "The criminal-records check and the DMV both came back with no hits. I just didn't think of it."

"Show me the video," she said.

I spun my laptop around so she could see the screen and played the YouTube clip of the opening scene of *Star Trek II: The Wrath of Khan*. Less than a minute in, she leaned back as if she was trying get away from an unpleasant odor. "How long is this?"

"Three minutes and change."

"Never mind. Just tell me what it is again?"

"The Kobayashi Maru is a test scenario that Starfleet puts cadets through to see how they'll behave in a no-win situation. There's no possible outcome in which anyone can come out on top. Kirk's the only one who ever beat it."

"How do you beat a no-win situation?"

"That's the point of it. Kirk secretly reprogrammed the computer. He cheated."

She shook her head. "You're a nerd."

"Not according to Patrick."

• • •

"Raspberry Wheat." Harlan tipped the beer bottle back and took a sip. "I don't know how you drink this stuff. It's like something a frat boy would pour down his date hoping to get lucky." He'd shown up half an hour earlier claiming he'd had no idea I'd be there and that he'd just come to watch *The Bachelor* with Jen like they did every week.

"Don't drink it, then," I said. "More for me."

I could see a quip forming behind his eyes, but he let it go. "So tell me about this case," he said instead.

After I brought him up to speed on the Denkins investigation, he said, "That's not the one I was asking about."

"I know." I popped the top off another bottle.

We sat in silence for a while. He stopped pretending to not like the beer. Before he reached for another, he said, "Must have been early eighties. Reagan was still big news and I was only two or three years out of my county-jail rotation. I was riding solo. We never did that in those days, not in Wilmington after midnight. My partner, though, got a bad taco or something and started puking out the window. So I dropped him off at the substation and went back out."

He took another sip. Harlan wasn't one for nostalgia, but even though his eyes met mine, I was keenly aware that his gaze was focused more inward than out. "I was down close to the harbor, just a few blocks north of the water. All that industrial-port shit, shipping containers, train tracks, oil tanks, you know. Everything was quiet, nothing going on.

"Then I turned a corner and across the street, maybe a hundred fifty yards away, I saw two cars in an empty lot. A Cutlass and a tricked-out Impala, headlights on, pointed at each other, maybe twenty feet between them. Three or four bangers on each side, standing by the cars, hanging on the open doors. Two more, right in the middle, lit up, facing off."

He was quiet a moment. I said, "Drugs?"

"Maybe. Guns. Money. Never found out for sure. I called in for backup and instead of waiting like I should have, I hit the siren and lights and gunned it right toward them. They were in their cars and smoking the tires before I got halfway there. But one of the guys in the middle didn't make it back in time. He stumbled and fell. Still trying to get back to his feet when I skidded to a stop next to him and got out. Yelled at him to freeze. He didn't, of course. Managed to get up and take off, so I went after him. He was kind of fat and slow, so he wasn't hard to catch. Made it about thirty feet before I tackled him."

Harlan had a distant look in his eyes. I could almost feel him being pulled farther and farther back into the memory. "What happened?" I asked.

"You know those concrete parking-block things? The ones that catch your front tire so you don't go too far into the next space?"

I nodded.

"He went face-first into one of those. Fractured the frontal bone and the orbital socket, the whole side of his face. Messed him up pretty bad. They had to take out what was left of his eye."

That was the kind of thing cops dread. Most of us have similar stories of an occasion when things got away from us, when what should have been a routine incident suddenly turned into something much,

much worse. Still, I knew there was more to what Harlan was telling me. I wanted to speak, but I didn't want to interrupt him. There was a kind of anxious anticipation welling up in me. I both wanted and didn't want to know where his story was going.

"His name was Marcus Wilson. Twenty-three when he lost his eye, but already an up-and-comer with one of the harbor Crips sets. We didn't have anything to charge him with. He got out of the hospital a couple weeks later and went right back to work, eye patch and all."

Harlan opened another beer. I did, too.

"Cynthia was still little, wanted a puppy. We promised we'd get her one if she did her chores or was good in kindergarten or something. I can't remember what her end of the deal of was. But she came through, and so did we. Got her a golden retriever, practically a puppy. Had those huge feet, though, so we knew she'd get big. Even let Cindy name her. She called her 'Licksey.' You can probably guess why. I thought that was a bit on the nose, but Ellie wouldn't let me overrule her. So it stuck." He let himself smile at the memory, let himself relish it.

"A couple of months went by. I pretty much forgot about Wilson. Dog had to have been at least forty pounds by then. One day I'm out on patrol, and I get a call on the radio from dispatch telling me I need to go straight home. Right away."

"Oh shit," I said.

"Ellie'd gone grocery shopping. When she got home she found Licksey in the backyard in a puddle of blood, all cut up. Fucker who did it took her right eye. At least Cindy was at school. We got it all cleaned up before she came home. Had to run the hose for an hour until the red all washed away and soaked into the dirt. Told her the dog got out and was hit by a car."

He took a long pull from his bottle.

"The next morning when I got up and went outside, I saw somebody had taken their finger and written a message in the dust on the back window of my car. Said 'I got my eye on you.'"

"Jesus. What did you do?"

"Moved to Orange County."

"That end it?"

"I don't think Wilson ever found the new house," Harlan said. "But no, that didn't end it. Every couple of weeks, I'd get a letter at the station with no return address, or a phone message, or a piece of paper stuck under the windshield wiper of my cruiser. They all said the same thing—'I got my eye on you.' Slowed down after a while. A month or two would go by. Then three or four. Every now and again I'd run across some banger in Wilmington or Carson and out of the blue he'd say, 'Wilson got his eye on you, man.' I'd almost be able to forget about it, and then there it was again. 'I got my eye on you.' And every damn time I'd remember Licksey lying there dead in that puddle of blood."

"How long did that go on?"

"Until Wilson got shanked in the shower at San Quentin."

"When was that?"

"Nineteen ninety-eight."

What was that? Seventeen years? I tried to wrap my mind around it. "Why'd you tell me this?"

Looking at the empty bottle in his hand, he said, "Because we've all got targets on our backs." The corners of his mouth turned up into a sad, bemused smile. "Also, it's not as bad as you think it is to live in Costa Mesa."

After he left, I went inside and found Jen on the sofa reading a book. She looked up at me. "I hope you don't mind that I called Harlan. I thought he might cheer you up."

I decided to let my soft chuckle speak for itself and went to bed.

I didn't sleep.

Between them, Marty Locklin and Dave Zepeda had more than thirty years' experience working homicide. They were the old guard, the grizzled vets. Last week they'd been in North Division, investigating a complicated gang-related triple murder, so that morning in the squad room was the first time I'd seen them since the bomb went off.

"Heard you guys had your hands full," I said. "How'd it go?"

"You know," Marty said. "Thirty people at the murder scene, nobody saw anything."

"Twenty-eight of them were in the can," Dave said.

"What about the other two?" I asked.

"Screwing in the bedroom." Dave laughed. It sounded loud that early in the morning. It wasn't unusual for so many witnesses to claim they hadn't seen anything. The truth was that they had far more to fear from the gang members in their midst than they did from law enforcement. If I was in their position, I would have said I was taking a shit, too. Snitches don't get stitches. They get shot in the face.

"You guys get anything at all?"

"No," Marty said. "But you know how it works. Somebody else will try to cut himself a break on some other charge and we'll get the shooters that way."

"Or we won't," Dave said. It was easy to mistake Dave's attitude for indifference. I knew him well enough to know that he hadn't succumbed to the apathy that often comes when long-time detectives begin wistfully anticipating retirement. He was just a realist who understood that there was always some luck involved in closing any case. Marty and he had earned their pragmatism. They both liked to sell themselves as lazy, burned-out old farts, but I'd never seen either one of them slack on an investigation.

Neither of them said anything about the explosion or my car, so I didn't, either. They must have heard. I just figured they knew I'd be sick of talking about it by then.

"Oh, Ruiz said to tell you not to go anyplace," Marty said. It seemed like an afterthought.

I hadn't seen him in his office when I came in. "He's here already?"

"Yeah." Dave leaned back and slurped his coffee. "Had to go upstairs and talk to the brass about something."

I opened my laptop and started reviewing my e-mail.

"Crap," Dave said. It sounded like he was talking to himself.

"What's wrong?" Marty asked.

"I'm out of staples. You have any?"

While I looked back down at my computer screen, I could hear Marty making desk noises. "No," he said. "I don't think so."

Not waiting for Dave to ask, I pulled open the top drawer on my desk and looked inside. It only took a fraction of a second for me to recognize the gray, claylike block with a burner cell phone wired to its top.

I yelled "Bomb!" and tried to stand and back away from my desk.

But my thigh hooked itself under the arm of my chair and I wound up lifting it off the floor, stumbling backward, and falling sideways on top of the backrest and rolling onto the linoleum. As I struggled to untangle myself and get away from the desk as fast as I could, I heard Dave and Marty cackling behind me.

With the realization of what they'd done, the fear began to dissipate, but a simmering humiliation flowed into its wake. Before I could draw my weapon and shoot them both, Ruiz returned.

"Get up off the floor and come into my office," he said as he walked past me without looking down.

I got to my feet, righted my chair and slid it back toward the desk, and followed him.

"Close the door and sit down," he said. "How's it going?"

"Not bad," I said. "You?"

"All right." He nodded unironically. "Here's the thing. I'm going to pull you off the Denkins case."

"Why? Jen and I are making progress. We've got a warrant to execute this morning."

"I know," he said. "Patrick thinks there might be a connection to the bomb."

"But that's a long shot. The window of opportunity—"

"I talked to Walsh. He said the bomber knows what he's doing. If he had the supplies on hand, he could have rigged it in half an hour. It's a feasible theory."

That was the same thing Gonzales had said to Patrick. I remembered what he'd told me about Walsh taking credit after they'd swept my apartment, and I filed it away.

"Feasible's a long way from solid," I said. "Why would they use a bomb? That doesn't make any sense."

"Still," Ruiz said, "if there's even a possibility they're connected, you can't be anywhere near the investigation."

I knew he was right. He usually was. But I wasn't convinced there was anything to the theory. "Look," I said. "At this point, there's nothing even close to solid. It's just speculation. Don't take me off Denkins yet. If Patrick comes up with anything that backs up the connection, I'll let it go. But until then, let me keep working it."

He looked at me. His elbows were on his desk, forearms forming a triangle, fingers interlocked at its top point, and as his eyes narrowed over his hands, I realized he hadn't really intended to take me off the case. At least not yet.

"Okay," he said. "But if Patrick comes up with a solid connection, I'm going to have to hand it off."

He'd given me a small win, something to make me feel a sense of relief. But why?

"Things going all right with Jen? Staying at her place?"

"So far it's okay. Why didn't you tell me she'd be babysitting me?"

"Because we both know how you would have responded if I did." He was right. I would have argued with him and resisted all the way. Jen had never even discussed it with me until it was already happening. She knew how to work me better than anyone.

"She talked to you about letting Patrick do his job, right?"

"Yeah."

"You've got to stay out of his way. It's his case. I know you don't like it, but you're the victim here. When's the last time you invited a victim to help investigate their own case?"

I wanted him to think I was letting that sink in, so I didn't answer.

"Stand back, Danny. If you don't, they'll pull us off the case altogether. I had to fight the captain to begin with. You trust Patrick, right?"

"Of course," I said. I couldn't help but admire Ruiz's technique. He'd pulled three agreements in a row out of me and sapped me of my instinctual need to challenge his authority.

"Good," he said. "What was that with Marty and Dave out there?"

"They put a fake bomb in my desk drawer."

He nodded. I couldn't read his expression.

"Assholes," I said.

He nodded again. "It was a long weekend for them. They were up in Glendale all day yesterday."

"Why?" I asked.

"Because somebody had to liaise with the ATF, try to track the source of the land mine that was in your bomb."

I wasn't sure what bothered me more. The fact that now I couldn't stay pissed off at Dave and Marty or the fact that my boss had just used "liaise" as a verb. "So," I said, "am I the only one in the squad who wasn't on the clock all weekend?"

Ruiz nodded. "Victims don't get overtime."

● ● ●

Harold Craig opened his door a few inches and peeked out at us as Jen and I climbed the stairs. I nodded at him as we passed. He'd replied to an e-mail I sent early that morning. Kobe still hadn't returned home.

Bill Denkins had conveniently labeled his master keys, so it was easy to find the one we needed. With Jen and Ethan, the crime-scene technician, behind me, I opened the door to Kobe's studio apartment.

I'm not sure what I expected to see, but there wasn't much. The studio was small, with a kitchen to the right of the door and a living/sleeping area to the left. In the back corner, behind a well-worn futon on a low pine frame, was the door to the bathroom. There was hardly any furniture. A small flat-screen TV on a flimsy stand, with a video-game console beneath it, a makeshift milk-crate nightstand, and a pale-green upholstered chair, small and worn, in front of the window.

It wasn't clean, really, just empty. Kobe had left little behind. In the kitchen, there were only two cups, a bowl, a handful of mismatched utensils, a few paper plates, and an almost-used-up roll of paper towels. The refrigerator held a Styrofoam take-out container full of pad thai and a quart of milk that, according to its expiration date, was still good for two days. The only other food was a box of cherry Pop-Tarts with one package gone.

"How long had he lived here?" Jen asked.

"A year and a half," I said.

The closet was close to empty as well. A hoodie, a pair of jeans bunched up in the corner on the floor, and a mismatched pair of socks. In the bathroom were a toothbrush, a nearly empty tube of Colgate, and a container of Tums. One lonely and threadbare towel hung over the shower curtain rod.

"Not quite the cornucopia of evidence we were hoping for," Jen said.

"So the question is, did he take a lot with him, or is this just how he lived?"

We'd been careful about what we touched. "Ethan?" I said.

He was young. Every new crime-scene technician I worked with seemed younger than the last.

"Yes?" he said.

"Think you can find us some fingerprints and DNA?"

He smiled pleasantly. "I don't think that should be a problem at all."

We went outside and let him work.

From the landing, I saw a man with a garden sprayer on the other side of the concrete-block wall that ran in front of Denkins's door and the next apartment building, the one that faced out on Second Street.

I pointed him out to Jen. He was tall and lean and wore olive-colored pants and a beige work shirt with the sleeves rolled up. Aviator glasses and a floppy boonie hat protected his head from the sun. "Think that might be the manager?"

"Maybe," she said.

I went halfway down the steps and spoke to him over the top of the wall. "Excuse me, sir?"

He stopped spraying, put the tank down, and turned. "Yes?" he said.

Midfifties, I guessed, hard and stiff, the kind of man who wouldn't take kindly to kids on his lawn. I held up my badge. "I need to ask you a few questions."

He exhaled heavily. "Come around the back," he said. "I'm not going to shout over this wall." His voice was thick with irritation, but he hadn't shouted yet.

I went through the back gate and around the garages and met him. He hadn't moved.

"What do you want?"

"My name is Danny Beckett," I said, extending my hand.

He looked down at it, but his arms remained at his sides. "You're the one left the business card on my door."

Jen had actually left the card, but I didn't see any reason to go into the details of the canvass. "Yes."

"It fell down in between the screen and the decorative grating on the front. Had to fish it out with a coat hanger." His posture was straight and stiff. I could imagine him playing the asshole drill sergeant in a war movie. A Vietnam War movie.

"I'm sorry about that," I said.

"I tried to get it out with my hand, but that was going to stretch the screen out and ruin it." His scowl was so pronounced that I almost laughed. It was clear I needed to find a balance between strength and deference for him to take me seriously.

"Sir, do you know what happened to William Denkins?"

He nodded. "They say he killed himself." There was no doubt about the contempt he felt for whoever "they" were.

"You don't think so?"

"Bill was soft, sure. But he wasn't a pussy. He didn't kill himself."

"You're right about that," I said.

The lenses in his sunglasses masked it, but I could still see a sense of smug satisfaction in his expression.

"I knew it," he said so softly that I thought the words were more for himself than for me. "You know who did it?"

"Not yet," I said. "Were you close to him?"

"He was a friend, yeah."

"You're the manager here?"

"For twenty-two years."

"What's your name?"

73

"Acker. Kurt Acker."

"How well did you know Bill?"

"Well enough."

I let the silence hang. Most people get uncomfortable when there's a dead spot in conversation with a cop. This is one of the most useful tools in a detective's repertoire. Acker was stubborn, though. He lasted almost thirty seconds before he spoke.

"He didn't know what the hell he was doing when he took over that building. I watched him. Fuckup after fuckup. He was too proud to ask for help."

"But you helped him anyway?"

"He hired an incompetent painter. I held my tongue as long as I could. But they barely prepped anything at all, and what they did was shoddy as hell. Somebody had to say something."

"That was nice of you."

"Nice? What's wrong with you?" He sucked his teeth and I half expected him to spit at my feet. "What do you think would have happened to rental rates in this building when the paint job on that one started flaking and peeling and looking shitty six months after it was done? People won't pay top dollar to live next to a dump."

"What did he do after you told him?"

"Asked my advice. Set him up with a solid guy. You need any painting done?"

"No, I rent, so my landlord handles that. I'm lucky. He's a good guy. Knows what he's doing."

"A good guy. That's important. Those goddamned management companies? They don't care. Do shoddy work, rip off their tenants. It's not just some business. People live here."

I picked up the thread. "It's their home," I said.

"See, Bill knew that. Right from the beginning. I never had to teach him that." His jaw clenched, as if he was biting down on something, trying to hold it back. He exhaled through his nose and checked his watch. Then he bent over, picked up the sprayer, and started around the corner.

"Mr. Acker?" I said.

He looked over his shoulder and said, "Come on, then, I ain't got all morning."

His building wasn't as old or as charming as Bill's, but it was clean and seemed well maintained. His one-bedroom was furnished in a utilitarian fashion, and I had no doubt there was a place for everything and everything was damn well in it. In the nook off of his kitchen, we sat at a new-looking Formica-topped table that was probably older than me. He poured two cups of black coffee and handed one to me. If there were any cream and sugar in the house, he must have been saving it for the pussies. I pretended to like the coffee.

He told me about Bill. How much Acker had helped him in those first years. How they'd become friends, even though Bill was too nice for his own good, letting himself be taken advantage of all the time. "By tenants, mostly," he said. "But a few years ago, when Lucy married that jerk-off, then by him. Bill had loaned him money to start a restaurant." Acker didn't know exactly how much, but he thought low six figures. "It was one of those gastropubs or something. First, it was supposed to be downtown, but that didn't work out, so then he set sights on Retro Row. Struck out with that one too, though, and wound up in Bixby Knolls. Found a place he liked, some vacant shop, and started renovating. It was almost all ready to go, had the furniture in, all the decorations up, appliances in the kitchen, staff hired. Then something went south. I never knew what. They delayed the opening. Bill sunk even more into it. They finally got it up and running and the damn place folded after two months."

We talked for a few more minutes. He offered more coffee and I declined. When it was clear Acker didn't have anything else of value, I thanked him and excused myself.

• • •

Upstairs in Kobe's studio, Jen said, "You and Old Hickory must have really hit it off."

"Got some more background on Denkins," I said.

"Anything useful?"

"Maybe. How'd you do up here?"

Ethan came out of the bathroom. "Found a ton of prints," he said. "And I think we've got some solid DNA samples, too." He looked pleased.

Jen led me into the kitchen. "We also found this." She opened a small manila envelope and tipped it onto the tiled countertop. A yellow three-by-three Post-it note slid out. There were two perpendicular crease marks in the paper. It looked like it had been folded into a tiny square. "It was tucked into the coin pocket of those jeans in the closet."

I flipped it over with my fingernail and saw three names—S. Wise, C. Shepard, and B. Darklighter—written in tiny, neat handwriting. Each was followed by a different phone number.

"Those names mean anything to you?" she asked, putting the flap of the envelope down on the tile like a dustpan and sliding the note back inside.

"No. But I'll bet they mean something to Kobe."

• • •

"Take a right up here," I said to Jen on the way back to the station.

"Why?" She checked the rearview mirror.

There was an Accord that had been behind us for the last mile and a half.

"The white Honda?" she asked.

"Yeah," I said. "It's been two cars back since we turned onto Broadway."

She cast a doubtful glance at me, but didn't say anything else until she'd made the turn.

I watched over my shoulder. The Accord didn't follow. I kept looking on the off chance it might have been a two-car tail. No one else turned behind us.

"Around the block?" she asked.

I nodded.

She looped around onto Vista, then took Euclid back to Broadway. "What was his name again? The guy from the building next door?"

"Kurt Acker."

"Get anything from him?"

I told Jen the story and she asked, "So when was that? The loan Denkins gave to the son-in-law?"

"Two years ago, I think. There was a record of the loan in the files, but nothing specific about the restaurant."

We stopped at a red light and she looked at me. "When are you planning to re-interview the daughter?"

"I don't know yet. Looks like there's a lot more I need to find out before I do."

•   •   •

I wasn't anxious to repeat my Kobayashi Maru mistake, but Patrick came into the squad room before I had a chance to Google the names from the Post-it. I called him over to my desk. "Any of these names mean anything to you?"

"What names?"

"S. Wise?"

He shook his head. "Nope."

"How about C. Shepard?"

"Not that one, either. They all have initials?" he asked. "What are these? Where are they from?"

"A note we found in Kobe's apartment. Just have one more."

"Shoot."

"B. Darklighter?"

A broad grin spread across his face. "These guys really are nerds, aren't they?"

"Why?" I asked. "Where's the last one from?"

"*Star Wars*. The 'B' stands for Biggs."

"Biggs Darklighter? I don't remember that name from *Star Wars*. Who is he?"

"Barely shows up in *Episode IV*. He's Luke's friend from Tatooine. Supposedly there was a whole subplot, but it wound up getting cut."

"And that's just bouncing around in your head?"

"What were those other two names again?"

"C. Shepard?"

"Wait. Mass Effect? Commander Shepard?"

"Are you asking me? That's a video game, right?"

"What was the first one again? S. Wise?"

Something clicked. "Wait," I said. "*Lord of the Rings*?"

He nodded. "Samwise Gamgee."

I thought about it. There had to be some significance to the selection of names. If Kobayashi Maru was an alias, it stood to reason that these were, too.

Patrick wrote the full names down on a notepad. Then, underneath each one, he wrote them with just the first initial, as they had been on the Post-it note. He studied them intently.

"See something?" I asked.

"They're inconsistent," he said.

"What do you mean?"

"Samwise is one word, just his first name. Why break it up into two? And it looks like they used the initials so the names wouldn't be too obvious. S. Wise and C. Shepard seem really generic, right? So with those two, you wouldn't even get the reference. If Kobe's name was on here, too? K. Maru, even that one would fit. But Darklighter's a dead giveaway. Without that one, I wouldn't have seen the pattern."

As I thought about it, I had something of an epiphany. Because Patrick owned a couple of fedoras and had once used the word "artisanal" in conversation without the requisite tone of mockery, for years we'd been teasing him about being a hipster, when, in fact, we should have been giving him shit that whole time for being a nerd.

• • •

Fortunately, Bill Denkins had saved passwords on his laptop, so when I opened his browser history and clicked on Facebook, they autofilled and logged me in. His feed was filled with dozens of condolences. I read each one but nothing in particular stood out. They were standard you're-in-our-prayers kinds of things. He was in people's thoughts, and quite a few mentioned his daughter, Lucinda, but many didn't. There were a few links to articles about depression and suicide prevention. Only a few people knew that he'd been murdered, and my conversation with Kurt Acker, the manager of the adjacent building, suggested that his death had been rumored to be a suicide. I wondered how many of the messages were from current or former tenants. I would read them all again later and check out those who'd left them, but I'd had a different purpose for logging in then—I wanted to see what I could learn about Bill's daughter and her husband.

Lucinda didn't post much herself. Mostly Instagram photos that looked like they were automatically shared on Facebook. There didn't seem to be any pattern to them, other than that she was fond of flowers and trees and unusual buildings. She had a good eye, too. While the subjects were fairly common, there was always something interesting about them. Aside from the pics, though, most of her wall was taken up with the standard cute pictures and funny videos and share-if-you-agree memes.

Joseph Polson, on the other hand, was a lot more active. He apparently never ate a meal he didn't photograph or read an article he didn't share. Lots of reviews of things—restaurants and movies and TV and music. He was also big on the Onion and ClickHole, and was experiencing a good deal of anticipatory anxiety over the new season of *The Walking Dead*. I had to scroll back a long way to find what I was really looking for—the restaurant he'd opened at the end of last year.

It had been called Winter. The place looked like a thousand others I'd seen online and in person, all communal tables and brushed-aluminum chairs and rough-finished wood. There didn't really seem to be any theme or anything, other than a heavy this-looks-really-right-now-doesn't-it vibe that, at least in the images he put on his feed, didn't seem to be doing its job very well. I searched for it on Yelp and found only a few reviews. Three or four raves that seemed like they were probably written by friends or family, and a dozen more by underwhelmed customers. The consensus was that the service was slow and spotty and the food ranged from mediocre to adequate. Most gave it two or three stars. One commenter wrote, "The road to dinner hell is paved with good intentions." I started feeling bad for Joe. Winter had, either appropriately or ironically, closed in March.

I was keeping track of what I was reading on a yellow pad, making notes about what I knew about Lucinda and Joe. How much support had Bill given them beyond the loan? How much did she make? How hard had Winter's failure impacted their finances? How much money, in addition to the loan from Bill, had been sunk into the restaurant, and where had it come from? They all led up to one central question—could any of this have given Joe a strong-enough motive to kill his father-in-law?

• • •

No one was in the squad room in the early afternoon when I decided it was time for lunch. Before I'd met Julia, and before someone was trying to kill me, I spent a lot of time alone. Having a meal or going to the movies by myself had never been a big deal to me. I never thought too much about it. A certain degree of introversion has always felt right to me, and, honestly, I liked it that way. It suited me. It was comfortable. But in the last few days I'd had pretty much constant company, as per Ruiz's dictate. There had been so much on my mind with both cases that I hadn't really had a chance to be bothered by the lack of time to myself. The lieutenant had been smart. I was used to spending a lot of time with Jen. When one of us caught a case, it wasn't at all unusual to spend most of our waking hours together for days at a stretch. If he had assigned the babysitting duty to anyone else, even Patrick or Marty or Dave, I'd be bristling and looking for escape opportunities every chance I got.

I decided to eat at The Potholder Too, the second location of one of Long Beach's most popular breakfast mainstays. It was only a block away from the station, and an omelet for lunch always seemed like a good idea to me. The more I thought about it, the hungrier I got. And the better I felt about having the chance to be by myself for a while.

The walk was a short one. Out the back into the parking lot, around the building, right on Broadway, and just down the block. Door to door in less than five minutes. How many times had I done it? Fifty? Seventy-five?

As soon as I got outside and felt the sun on my face, the pang in my stomach that I'd attributed to my hunger grew deeper. My sense of situational awareness intensified as I scanned the lot. I watched the uniforms and the suits coming and going. Most of the faces were familiar. I scrutinized the ones that weren't, assessing potential threats, one by one.

I'd dealt with threats to my life many times. I had no idea why, but now for some reason I was feeling a kind of vulnerability I never had before.

"Hey, Danny," a voice said to my right.

I turned too quickly.

"You okay?" It was Stan Burke, a patrol vet who I'd known for years. He'd been one of my field-training officers when I was a rookie.

"I'm sorry, what?" I said.

"You all right?"

"Yeah, yeah," I said. "I'm fine."

He didn't look like he believed me. "I heard about what happened. Hell of a thing."

I nodded. "That it is." I noticed I was breathing. "Just heading out for lunch."

"Where you going?"

"Potholder."

"Want some company?" he asked.

To my embarrassment, I did.

"I thought there would be more blood." Lucinda sounded far away when she called. We'd released the crime scene so she could begin to sort through her father's things.

"Sometimes there's not that much," I said, remembering her father's slumped-over body. A few drops had found their way onto the sofa. I wondered if she'd looked closely enough to see them.

"I'm calling because of the funeral," she said.

"How can I help?"

"I was wondering about his computer and his phone?"

"What about them?" I asked. We'd be able to get them back to her eventually, but it would likely not be for quite a while.

"The contact lists? He knew a lot of people, a lot of tenants, I don't know who they all are."

"We need to hang on to his things for now, but I can get you copies of the lists."

"Thank you," she said. "That would be a big help." There was a tired sadness in her voice. She seemed to be genuinely grieving, but I couldn't help but question whether figuring out who to invite to the service was the only reason she wanted his devices. They also held a lot of other information about his finances and would be useful to her if she'd been involved in his death and was trying to stay ahead of our investigation. I was betting she didn't know how much information we'd taken from both his hard and electronic files. The more she was in the dark in regard to that, the better off we were.

"He also had an address book. I'll copy that for you too, okay?"

"Brown leather with his initials on the cover?"

"That's the one."

She tried to say something, but her voice broke into a sob. While she cried I listened. I like to think I'm a good judge of people's tears. It comes with the job. Even over the phone, hers struck me as genuine.

When she was able to compose herself enough to speak, she said, "I gave that to him for his fiftieth birthday. He loved it."

"I'm sure he did," I said. "It's a really beautiful piece of craftsmanship." I thought about the book. It was nice, but I couldn't imagine I'd call it beautiful under other circumstances.

"Thank you," she said.

I told her I'd drop the copies off as soon as I could and ended the call.

It was far too early to draw any conclusions, but I began to wonder how close she was to her husband.

• • •

"Jesus," Dave said across the squad room. He and Marty were huddled behind Patrick's desk, staring over his shoulders at something on the screen of his iPad.

"What are you guys looking at?"

Dave glanced at Patrick, who nodded.

"You should come over here," Dave said.

"What is it?"

"It was your car," Marty said.

They made room for me behind Patrick. Before I got a good look at the image on the screen, Patrick started side-scrolling through photographs. "You should start with this one," he said.

I looked down at the screen and saw a straight-on side view of my Camry. The front and rear ends were both relatively intact, but the same couldn't be said for the middle. Where the driver's door should have been was a gaping hole. It looked like a giant shark had opened its jaws wide and taken a huge bite. The driver's seat was completely gone, as were the steering wheel, much of the dashboard, and a significant portion of the roof. What remained was a jagged mess of metal and plastic, upholstery and fabric, all twisted and blackened by the explosion. Part of the passenger's seat was pressed against the door on the other side, and all the windows had blown out. What remained of the roof bulged upward like the top of a botulism-tainted can.

It suddenly became difficult to think of anything other than what would have happened if I'd been inside when the bomb exploded. There wouldn't have been much of me left. My shoulder and arm tightened and I leaned into the pain.

"You would have been even deader than we thought," Dave said.

Marty clapped me on the back. "Bet no one's ever been so grateful for a bad spark plug."

"ATF confirmed that it was a South African land mine." Patrick checked his notes. "A Mini MS-803. It's like a smaller version of the claymore."

I was still looking at the photograph. "That's the small one?"

Patrick nodded. "The feds thinks we might get lucky with the source. They found another one of the same model, undetonated, a few weeks ago."

"Where'd they find it?"

"Some Serbo-Croatian crew in the valley," he said. "We're running them down now. Looking for possible Long Beach connections."

"Keep me in the loop, okay?" I'd worked several cases involving eastern European gangs in the last few years, but none with any known connections that fit.

"I will," he said. Then he added, "As much as I can."

Back at my desk, I found a voice mail from Ethan. "Only one set of prints from the Kobayashi Maru apartment," he said. "But no matches to anything in the databases. Maybe we'll get a hit on the DNA."

Maybe, I thought. And maybe Kobe would turn out to be one of those Asian Serbians we always hear so much about.

● ● ●

"Somehow it never occurred to me that I'd have to get a new car," I told Julia on the phone. After a pit stop at home to pick up fresh clothes, I was settling in for another evening at Jen's house. The days were getting shorter, but dusk was still hanging in the air.

"What do you think you'll get?"

"I don't want a new car," I said. "I want my Camry."

"It was pretty old. Didn't you say it had a lot of miles on it?"

"Two hundred fifty-seven thousand."

"Danny, I don't know much about cars, but I know that's a lot. You even said you didn't think it would last much longer."

"I know. It's just that I thought it would go from natural causes."

I thought I heard her stifling a laugh. "What are natural causes for a car?"

"I don't know. A cracked engine block? Transmission cancer?"

She went ahead and laughed out loud.

"I know how it sounds," I said. "One of my first homicide cases was a ninety-three-year-old lady. Grandmother, great-grandmother, big family, everybody loved her. A stray bullet from a drive-by went through the living-room window right into her chest. I could never shake that. To live so long and then die just like that. It didn't feel right."

"Would it have been better if she had to suffer for months with some debilitating illness?"

"No," I said.

"Is that what you'd want?"

When I realized we weren't really talking about my car anymore, I said, "You like your Subaru, right?"

• • •

I used to listen to the BBC Overnight broadcast on KPPC, one of the local public-radio stations, when I couldn't sleep. There was something I found relaxing about the British voices reporting stories that were vaguely interesting. It had just the right balance. If my insomnia was particularly bad, I could focus and pay attention, and that would distract me from the thoughts running incessantly through my head. If it was a calmer night, though, I could let my attention drift and the voices became a kind of white noise that was just strong enough to hold the silence at bay and lull me into a kind of sleepless relaxation. I'd often find myself struggling to maintain that state at two a.m., when the programming transitioned from the BBC to *Morning Edition*. The American voices were never quite as calming.

More recently, I'd taken to listening to podcasts. I got sucked in quickly and before I knew it had subscribed to more than a dozen. *Mystery Show* had become a particular favorite. It was kind of a parody of our cultural obsession with the mystery genre, undertaking a new and admittedly minor investigation with each episode. How did a book written by an author friend of the host, Starlee Kine, wind up being photographed in the hands of Britney Spears? Could she find the owner of an unusual belt buckle that had been at the bottom of a friend's junk drawer for years? How tall was Jake Gyllenhaal, really? What struck me about *Mystery Show* was the way Kine would follow the threads and loose ends that inevitably arose as she looked for clues and doggedly pursued lead after lead to the people whose stories, while not directly connected to the main narrative, imbued the case with genuine humanity. Julia and Harlan had both come into my life the same way.

But that night I'd tried listening for a while and found myself unable to summon the small degree of focus and concentration needed to pay attention. I'd keep zoning out and realizing I'd missed thirty seconds or a minute or more. I'd hit the little counterclockwise-circular-arrow icon to back up again and again until I found something I remembered. The fourth time I went all the way back to the Stamps.com pitch, I decided to give up.

It was long past midnight. If I'd been home I would have gotten dressed and gone out for a walk. Of course, I knew walking around Long Beach alone in the middle of the night, even in a neighborhood as nice as Jen's, wasn't the wisest of moves, but in terms of self-destructive cop behavior, it ranked pretty low on the scale.

I kept thinking about that afternoon in the parking lot. Something so simple, walking a block up the street to the Potholder, something I'd done so many times before. But I froze. Or at least I would have if Stan hadn't come along. What would I have done if he hadn't showed up when he did? Would I have a taken a few deep breaths, gotten a hold of myself, and strolled off to lunch? Or would the anxiety have gripped me so tightly that I wouldn't have been able to overcome it? What would I have done? Could I have even made it back up to the squad room, or would I have humiliated myself by losing my shit right there in front of everybody?

I'd been in dangerous and life-threatening situations before without being rattled at all. When I'd been in uniform, I'd faced bigger and more tangible dangers on practically a weekly basis. Where was this fear coming from? It was true that I'd never had to deal with so direct and sustained a threat as the one the bombing represented, but how could I be afraid of walking alone to lunch?

The photos of my car were working their way into my mental feedback loop, too. There was no way I would have survived if I'd been in the car. What would it have been like? It's standard procedure for homicide detectives to tell victims' families that their loved ones had died instantly. That's one of the many lies that we're not only allowed, but often encouraged, to tell. And it's a good lie. It brings comfort. No one wants to know that their loved one was in excruciating pain and very likely aware that they were dying for seconds or even minutes before they expired. My death from the explosion probably would really have been instantaneous. That didn't make it any less disturbing.

I sat up in the guest bed and wondered how pissed off Jen would be if I went out for a walk. After a few minutes, I realized that she wouldn't be pissed off at all if she didn't know. But it didn't matter, anyway. I knew I had to walk and I had to do it by myself. Not only because my nighttime walks were so ingrained in my routine, but because, after my near–anxiety attack, I needed to prove to myself that the afternoon incident had been a one-off experience, an aberration, and not something that I was going to let affect me any more than it already had.

The weather app on my phone told me it was still seventy-three degrees outside, so I pulled on a pair of shorts and my walking shoes. My shoulder holster went on over the t-shirt and under a short-sleeved plaid button-up. It wouldn't conceal well through the thin fabric, but it was late enough that I didn't really care. I wasn't likely to run into anyone, anyway.

The plan was to keep it short. Maybe half an hour, forty minutes. I went out the back door and around the side to the gate. It felt good to be outside in the fresh air. There was a light breeze, but the night was still warm. I put in one earbud, set the volume low, and played *The River*, just loud enough for me to recognize each song and follow along in my head.

Walking down the driveway, I looked over my shoulder one more time. The light in Jen's room was still off and the coast was clear.

As soon as I turned left onto the sidewalk, I felt the tension that had been building inside me since Saturday begin to lighten. The pain in my shoulder and neck eased. I'd been carrying more weight than I realized, and the small sense of freedom that came from venturing out into the night on my own surprised me.

I was careful, though, not to let my guard down. As relieved as I was to find my earlier anxiety dissipating, I refused to let it go entirely. In fact, as I turned right onto Argonne, just as Springsteen was finding his way into "Jackson Cage," I turned the music off and stowed the headphones in my pocket.

I had the streets to myself. No one was out and I'd only seen one car. The quiet stillness was relaxing. I heard crickets chirping, the leaves moving in the light breeze, and the distant, rhythmic hum of traffic blocks away rising and falling as I walked.

The calmness of the night made me feel awake and alert. And ready. If anyone came at me now, I thought, I'd be prepared. Part of me almost wished they would so we could finish things and I could get on with my life.

As I approached the small traffic roundabout at Vista I sensed something behind me. There was no need for subtlety. If anyone was back there I wanted to see them and for them to see me. As I turned, I caught some motion in my peripheral vision, but it was only a gray cat that stopped in its tracks as soon as I saw it. When I looked it in the eye, it crossed the street and kept walking.

My pulse had quickened, but I was reassured that my vigilance was at its peak.

I continued down Argonne and took another right on Broadway. The street was busier. A car would pass every minute or two, and I saw another pedestrian on the south side of the street. He seemed completely oblivious to me, his face lit by the glowing screen of his smartphone. I watched him over my shoulder as he passed and continued on.

It had been a little over fifteen minutes since I'd left Jen's, so I turned north on Prospect to loop back home. The round-trip would be half an hour or so. A short walk, but a good one. It felt like I had actually put some tangible emotional distance between the present moment and the anxiety I had experienced earlier in the day. And the walk provided the added benefit of clearing away much of the fog that had been clouding my mind, and I felt optimistic about finally being able to sleep. After I turned the last corner back onto Colorado, I walked the last quarter of a mile and crossed the street toward Jen's house on the other side.

Just as I stepped up onto the curb, I felt something hard and sharp strike the back of my head. I spun around and my right hand found the grip of my Glock hanging in its shoulder holster.

Jen was standing on the asphalt in the center of the illuminated circle shining down from the streetlight. She cocked her arm and threw another rock. Hard. It caught me square in the chest.

"Ow," I said as the rock bounced to the grass at my feet.

She walked by me without saying a word or making eye contact.

I didn't get much sleep after all.

• • •

"Even that damn cat could have offed you last night," Jen said, glancing in the rearview mirror. She'd spent most of the morning ragging me and critiquing my lax situational awareness. "I wasn't even trying to hide anymore by the time you got to Broadway and you still didn't know I was there."

"That's the third time you've told me that," I said.

"You're not as badass as you think you are."

I didn't think I was badass at all. I never had, really. But for years, since Megan had died, I'd thought I didn't really have anything to lose. There was a kind of freedom to be found in that. It wasn't bravery or courage, really, just the lack of fear. That might not have been good for me as a person, but it was good for me as a cop. Now, as the wheels of self-justification kept turning in my head and I thought about loss and freedom, the lyrics to "Me and Bobby McGee" popped into my mind and I gave up on my attempted rationalization and imagined I was listening to Kris Kristofferson instead of my irate partner.

Jen parked across the street from Lucinda Denkins's house. We weren't sure if she would be home. She'd told me on the phone that she would be taking some time off from her job in the human resources department of the Long Beach Unified School District.

No one answered the knock on the door, so we walked over and looked up the driveway at the detached garage in back of the house. I had Bill Denkins's address book in a manila envelope tucked under my arm. We'd made photocopies of every page and the book had been processed for evidence, but we didn't find anything of potential use. I wanted to see how she'd react when I returned it to her. She'd indicated a personal attachment to it when we'd spoken on the phone, and I thought I might be able to get a stronger read on her. At that point, her grief had seemed honest and genuine. But I'd need a lot more than my instincts to clear her of suspicion. The more I could find out before I interrogated her, the better off the investigation would be.

"She's not here," Joe told us. He was wearing cargo shorts and a dirty T-shirt and he looked tired. There were half a dozen large cardboard boxes, filled mostly with books, scattered around him on the concrete floor. It looked as though he'd been digging through them. "We ran out of food," he said. "I told her I'd go to the store, but she said she wanted to go. She needed to get out of the house."

"How's she doing?" Jen asked.

"Not very good," he answered. "She's trying to keep it together, but it's hard. Her dad was a good guy."

Jen nodded. "It takes time."

"She wanted me to find some book out here that her dad gave her. Poetry. But she didn't know the name or who wrote it."

While Jen talked to him, I looked around the garage. I didn't want him to notice me, but I did want to get a sense of the two of them, of their life. There were shelves along the back wall and a washer and dryer on the right. Things were neat, but not obsessively so. The trash cans were in one corner, the blue recycle bin's lid held up a few inches by a garbage bag filled with empty water bottles and aluminum cans. Behind them were a bunch of gardening tools, shovels, rakes, and the like. Two bikes were leaning next to each other on their kickstands in the opposite corner. The one thing that stood out was a large framed poster leaning against a stack of boxes in the back. It had a black background with simple white block lettering that announced "WINTER IS COMING." I knew it must have been a leftover from his failed restaurant. I recognized the catchphrase. Had he been trying to get a marketing bump from *Game of Thrones*?

"You still need to talk to us again, right?" Joe asked.

"Yeah," I said. "For the formal interview. We'll let you know when. The more we can put together beforehand, though, the quicker and easier it will be for you guys. We know how hard it is right now, and we want to make it as simple and straightforward as we can."

"Thanks," he said. "We appreciate it." He tried to smile, but it didn't quite work. There were a few gray hairs in the soul patch under his lip that I hadn't noticed before.

"Good luck finding the book," I said.

Jen and I walked back down the driveway. I still had the unopened envelope tucked under my arm.

In the car on the way back to the station, Jen said, "What do you think about Joe?"

"I'm not sure how to read him," I said. "On the one hand, he seems to have the strongest motive, with the loan Bill made him for the restaurant. He flushed six figures down the toilet. And we still don't know where the rest of the money came from. Was he into somebody else for it? Who? How much?" I drifted off into speculation.

When it was clear to her that I'd lost the thread, Jen said, "What about the other hand?"

She glanced away from the street ahead long enough to see the puzzled expression on my face. "You started that out with 'On the one hand' but you never got to the other hand."

"Oh, yeah. Does he seem like he's got enough spine to fake a suicide?"

She thought about it. "Not really, no."

"But."

"Desperation can really straighten up your posture."

I'd sent Jen links to the Facebook and Yelp pages for Joe's failed restaurant. I asked if she'd had a chance to look at them.

"Is it just me," she said, "or is 'Winter' a really stupid name?"

"I thought the same thing."

"Looked like the name was the least of its problems, though." She checked the rearview mirror. I wondered if she was looking at the Honda two cars back in the other lane that had turned the corner behind us onto Seventh Street.

"Right? Why would Bill invest in something like that? Seems like he had pretty good business sense."

"Maybe he was investing in Joe," she said.

"That sounds like a worse bet than the restaurant."

"Yeah, but maybe he did it for Lucinda."

That made more sense to me. From the limited amount I knew about Bill, that seemed like a more credible theory.

"What about his ex?" she asked.

"Lucinda's mother? She's on my list to interview. Lives up in Pasadena, though, so I was waiting until it looked like we had half a day to spare."

"You ready to talk to her?" Jen asked. "We go right now, we can probably beat the rush-hour traffic coming back."

I considered it. My notes were in my jacket pocket, and I could access most of the files on my iPad while Jen drove. "Let's do it."

• • •

Celeste Gordon was waiting for us when we arrived. Normally, we like to drop in on potential witnesses unannounced. Often the surprise allows us to catch them off guard and they will reveal information that might not have been so forthcoming if they'd had time to prepare for our arrival. But we didn't relish the idea of spending most of the after-noon on the freeway only to knock on an unanswered door. So we had called ahead and she had agreed to meet us at her home.

We had followed the Waze app's directions on my phone, even though I was hesitant about taking the 110 through downtown LA, but the nav system was taking us around an accident on the more logical route that would have taken us up the Long Beach Freeway. We still hit some congestion, but we made the trip in an hour and fifteen minutes.

The exclusive neighborhood was tucked in between Cal Tech and the Huntington Library and Gardens, not far from the dividing line between Pasadena and its wealthier neighbor, San Marino. The houses were on big lots, set back from the street with privacy hedges or finely wrought fences crawling with ivy. Gordon lived in an expansive single-level ranch with a circular driveway and enough lush greenery to make it appear as though the California drought was considerate enough not to cross the San Marino city line.

The front door opened as Jen pulled the cruiser up to the porch, and Celeste Gordon stepped outside to greet us. We introduced our-selves and she led us inside.

She looked younger than I'd expected. At fifty-one, she was less than two years younger than Bill had been, but she could have easily passed for forty. She looked like she was dressed for a tennis match, in a short skirt and a sleeveless top that showed off her trim and athletic figure. If she'd had plastic surgery, it was good enough not to show.

The house was even more impressive on the inside. It had been fully remodeled into what looked a photo spread for *Architectural Digest*, artfully mixing rustic and contemporary styles. She led us to a large dining table that I had no doubt had been hand-built from reclaimed wood.

"Can I get you something?" she asked. "Coffee? I have some fresh iced tea?"

"A glass of tea would be nice," I said, returning her friendly smile. Usually, I turn down beverage offers. But I wanted to get a better sense of her before we started talking.

She looked at Jen. "Detective Tanaka?"

"Nothing for me," Jen said. "Thank you."

She went into the kitchen, opened a glass-paneled cupboard over the counter, and took a moment to select a proper glass, then took a pitcher out of the enormous stainless-steel refrigerator. As she poured, she said, "Sugar?"

"Do you happen to have any Splenda?" I asked.

"Of course," she said. She came back to the table with the glass, two yellow packets of sweetener, and a tiny spoon to stir it with.

I poured one packet into the drink. The glass was thick, intentionally indelicate, with an uneven wave to the outside surface, carefully crafted to simulate a rough-hewn artisanal effect. It went well with the table. It made me think of that line from Springsteen's song "Better Days," about a rich man in a poor man's shirt.

"Thank you," I said, clinking the ice cubes around with the little spoon.

"No problem." Celeste smiled pleasantly.

"We're very sorry for your loss," Jen said.

"We hadn't been close, Bill and I, for a long time," Celeste said. "But still, it's much more difficult than I would have imagined."

"I understand," Jen said. "When was the last time you saw him?"

"That would have been Lucy's anniversary party. In April."

Four months, I noted.

"Where was that?" Jen asked.

"Here," Celeste said. "They were having a rough time with the restaurant, so Larry and I wanted to do something nice for them."

"Was that before or after it closed?"

"Just after."

"How were they doing?"

"Oh, Joe was practically distraught." Celeste looked down at her hands. They were clasped together on the table. "I'd never seen him so down about anything."

Jen said, "How about Lucinda?"

"Lucy was taking it better than he was. She'd had her doubts about it all along. We all did, really. Larry had even tried to talk him out of it."

"What about Bill?" Jen asked.

"He didn't think it was a good idea, either."

I thought about speaking, but decided to let Jen keep at it. Celeste seemed to be warming to her.

"Did you know about the loan Bill made to Joe?"

"Yes."

"Why would he do that if he didn't think it was a good investment?"

"Because he could never say no to Lucy." Celeste sighed. "I asked him if he really thought it was a good idea to give Joe that much money. He said he didn't know, but he wanted to do it anyway."

Jen thought for a moment. "Did he say why?"

"No, but I think I understand. Bill always had a soft spot for Joe. I think he saw a bit of himself in him."

"In what way?"

"Bill wanted to be a history professor. He loved teaching. But all he could ever find were part-time jobs. He applied for hundreds of openings, literally hundreds, but he could just never land a full-time appointment. 'If someone would just give me a chance,' he'd say. Then he inherited the properties from his folks, and he just gave up. I think he wanted to give Joe a chance. It didn't really matter to him that Joe wasn't ready. There was an opportunity with some other investors and Lucy asked him to help, and he just couldn't say no."

I wanted to ask what she knew about the other investors she mentioned, but I didn't want to derail Jen's line of questioning, so I made a note and let her move on.

"Was Bill close to Joe?" Jen asked.

"I think so." There was a distant sadness in Celeste's eyes as she spoke. "He always wanted more kids, but it never really worked out for him."

Jen studied her and I could see her thinking, evaluating how far she could push without alienating Celeste. When she spoke, there was softness in her voice. "What happened with you and Bill? Why did you split up?"

Celeste looked out the French doors to the dark-bottomed swimming pool and the lush greenery surrounding it. "Bill was a very kind man, a sweet man. And he loved me very much."

Jen let her sit in silence and stare at the sunlight glinting off the surface of the pool.

"As much as I wanted to," Celeste said, "I could never love him the way he loved me. He saw a future for us that I never did. Lucy wasn't planned. I knew he'd be such a good father and he wanted it so badly that I thought I had to try."

Someone, I thought, had given him a chance.

"It took a long time, but he learned to live with our split. We were a good team when it came to Lucy. Larry and I were granted full custody and he just had visitation rights initially, but that didn't last long. He was so good with her that we changed it to joint custody before she started school."

"How is Lucy doing now?" Jen asked.

"She's having a very hard time with it. They were still very close."

We talked to her for a while longer. Celeste didn't know much about Bill's financial situation and seemed to be convinced that he was not nearly as well off as he actually was. I looked down at the melting ice cubes in the bottom of my glass, and at the expansive kitchen, and the leather sectional, and the warm white walls, and I thought I understood something about Celeste. Even with her genuine love for her daughter and her wistful affection for her ex-husband and her perceptive awareness of her family's shared history, she was still a person who couldn't seem to understand that someone might have money and not spend it.

• • •

"Patrick still hasn't texted me back," I said as Jen's cell phone chirped with a new text message. "That's not him, is it?"

We were passing USC. Waze had taken us back the way we came. The Long Beach Freeway was still jammed.

"No. It's my mom. She wants to be sure you're coming to the anniversary party."

"Of course I am," I said. "Tell her I said hi."

After a moment, she said, "What did you text Patrick about?"

"I asked him for an update. Wanted to see if he came up with anything new."

"Danny," she said.

The tone in her voice made me turn toward her to be sure my partner hadn't been replaced by a middle-school teacher. She didn't need to say anything else. I knew I was pressing Patrick too hard. But I couldn't let it go. It wasn't that I didn't trust him, I did. And I fully understood why I needed to be kept as far from his investigation as possible. My involvement could potentially taint the case if it came to trial. Ruiz was already bending the rules as far as he could. The fact that he hadn't removed me from the squad and assigned me to a desk someplace until the whole case played out was all the evidence I needed of that. But, like most people, I sincerely believed that the rules should be different for me.

• • •

"You never answered my text," I said to Patrick back in the squad room.

"Sorry about that," he said, without looking up from his computer. "Nothing new to report. We're still working the same leads. I'll let you know when there's something to tell you."

I went back to my desk. What I was hoping to get from him, I didn't really know. It made me think about all the times I'd blown off conversations with the family members of victims, and worse, with the victims themselves, before I transferred to Homicide. I wanted to believe that I'd never made them feel excluded, that I'd always made time for them, that I'd listened. But had I? How often had I hurried off the phone or hustled them out of the office because I had something else to do?

When I was five, my father, an LA County sheriff's deputy, was killed on a routine domestic-disturbance call. I was far too young to understand what was going on, but in those hazy and distant memories of the time following his death, I seem to remember lots of cops at our house for weeks and months afterward. It seemed that there was always a deputy or two there, checking on us, trying to help, offering comfort. Often I have difficulty sorting out real memories of my father from the stories his friends and colleagues told after his death. Did I actually remember him singing "Danny Boy" at the barbecue in the backyard, or had I just heard the story so many times that it had rooted itself deeply enough in my imagination that I could no longer distinguish it from reality?

It wasn't until years later, when I was in the academy myself, that my mother told me to be careful, that she was worried I didn't really know what I was getting myself into. I reminded her of that period after

Dad's death, when I'd felt so protected and cared for by all the deputies who were looking after us. "Oh, no, Danny," she had said. "Don't you know most of them were just trying to fuck me?"

I've always felt like being a homicide detective was a kind of calling for me. During my marriage, I'd put the job first and it had damaged our relationship, perhaps irreparably. Megan's death might have been the only thing that spared us from divorce.

But I wasn't the only good cop on the homicide squad. Patrick's drive and commitment were respectable. The cop part of my brain knew that and understood it. But the civilian part, the human part, the friend part, was having trouble. Of course I wanted to be a part of the investigation of the attempt on my life, but I understood the reality of the situation. It was that I was learning a lesson I should have learned long ago—what it feels like to be a victim.

Jen found me moping at my desk at the end of the workday. She asked me what I wanted to do that night and when I told her I didn't really care, she said she had an idea. When we got back to her house, Julia was waiting with pizza from Domenico's. Jen told us to have a good night and that she'd be back late. So we settled in with some ground pepperoni and Amazon Prime Video.

A few hours later, we were still sitting on Jen's couch. We'd just finished watching the first season of *Downton Abbey* and I was digging through the popcorn dregs in the bottom of the big bowl in her lap looking for a few more edible bits.

"What did you think?" Julia asked me.

"Could have used more car chases and explosions."

Her phone rang on the coffee table in front of us. She picked it up and I could see that the display read "Unknown." She silenced it and put the phone down and picked up the conversation where we'd left off. "Well, World War One is coming up."

"I guess that's something. How about you? What did you think?"

"I liked it," she said.

"You don't think it whitewashed the aristocracy a little too much?"

She made a sour face at me. "That what you think?"

"Maybe."

"You know that's kind of what the whole thing is about, right? The fall of the British upper classes."

"How do you know? You said you weren't watching it without me."

"I didn't. But I read that somewhere and thought it sounded good."

I smiled. "What do you like about it?"

"The grandeur. The romance. The tragedy I know is coming."

Surprisingly, I agreed with her, but I wouldn't give her the satisfaction of telling her that. Not when I was having so much fun teasing her about it.

"And I like Bates," she said.

"The stoically noble valet? Why?"

"He reminds me of you."

"What?" I said, surprised. "Why? Just because he was injured and I was, too? It's not like I limp or anything."

"It's not the injury so much as it is how you've dealt with pain. How you still deal with it."

"What do you mean?"

"That which does not kill us makes us stronger. Sometimes that's true."

"Not always."

"No, not always. But sometimes."

I put my arm around her and as she leaned her head on my shoulder, the tea-tree scent of her shampoo made me feel far away from home. But for years, home had been a dark and lonely place for me. I wanted so much to believe her, to see in myself the things she was seeing in me. That's what I should have told her. "Funny," I said instead, "I didn't figure you for a *Conan* fan."

"What are you talking about?"

"That's the quote at the beginning of *Conan the Barbarian*, the Schwarzenegger movie."

She looked at me with a playful warmth in her eyes.

"What?"

"You're really cute when you pretend to be stupid."

She kissed me then, so I shut up.

● ● ●

Julia didn't stay the night, but I still managed to get some sleep. In the morning I showered and found Jen in the kitchen, oatmeal and coffee waiting for me.

"Thanks for last night," I said.

"You guys have a good time?"

"Yeah, actually, we did."

I sat down at the kitchen table and checked my e-mail. There was a short note from Patrick. **Sorry about yesterday. Maybe we should have let someone else take the case.** He included a link to a podcast I hadn't heard before. I clicked on it.

I Was There Too with Matt Gourley. It was a series of interviews with people who'd played small parts in famous movies, like the lady with the baby carriage from *The Untouchables*, one of the colonial marines from *Aliens*, and the insurance guy Bill Murray runs into over and over again in *Groundhog Day*.

The e-mail seemed like an honest apology, but the podcast just seemed like an insult that reminded me I was sidelined on the bombing. A bit player in the investigation of my own attempted murder.

Jen said, "What did you just read?"

I looked at her.

"A minute ago you were all smiling and happy," Jen said. "Now you might as well have cartoon steam shooting out of your ears. What is it?"

"Nothing. Just got a reminder of where I really stand."

● ● ●

The next morning, I was at my desk in the squad room when Dave Zepeda called and told me they found a body in a Dumpster in the alley behind a donut shop on Atlantic. Three small-caliber bullet wounds in the back of his head. A man had been hoping the shop had thrown away some old pastries like they did sometimes and flipped up the lid and saw him. The man called it in to 911 but didn't wait for the responders.

"Anyway," Dave said, "Nathan says you probably want to come out here."

"Who's Nathan?"

"The Forensics kid. Said he helped you search the apartment of that Asian guy you're looking for."

"You mean Ethan?"

"Is that his name? I thought it was Nathan."

"What did Ethan say?"

"He had somebody take over the scene so he could rush the prints on our John Doe here. He says they match your guy."

"Did the ME take the body yet?"

"Nope," he said. "They're waiting on you."

I found Jen coming out of the women's restroom.

"You busy?" I asked.

"No. What's up?"

"Dave caught a new case. Kobe's dead."

By the time we got there, the ME was getting impatient. There really wasn't a good reason to hold up the scene to wait for me. It wasn't my case, it was Dave's. But he knew I'd want to see it. In Homicide, we get a little bit of indulgence if we've proved we can close cases, and he had closed a lot of cases. Also, he'd run out of fucks to give years ago.

"How long is this going to take?" the ME said. He was a tall, twitchy guy, whose name, if I was remembering correctly, was Jerry.

Dave looked up into his face and spoke in a friendly chirp. "You got someplace else to be? If you'd like, I can call your boss and have him send someone else out. Want me to do that?"

Maybe-Jerry shook his head.

"I'll let you walk it," Dave said to me.

"Thanks," I said.

The donut shop shared a small parking lot with the neighborhood grocery store. The lot and the alley that ran behind it had been cordoned off with yellow crime-scene tape. There were a dozen or so evidence markers scattered around on the cracked asphalt. I didn't look closely at any of them. The Dumpster was actually behind the market rather than the donut shop, and that put it farther away from the street. Still, it wasn't a very private place to dump a body. The donut shop was on the corner of Atlantic and Pacific Coast Highway, and PCH had a steady flow of traffic all night long. Why use the Dumpster when they could follow the alley halfway up the block and have complete privacy?

The lid was propped open. I leaned over and was hit by the familiar smell that longtime cops still sometimes call "eau de Dumpster." Inside, I saw the body prone on top of mounds of garbage. The head was turned slightly so I could see the edge of his face and the outside corner of one open eye. I moved around to the end of the Dumpster to get a better look at the back of his head. His short black hair was matted with dried blood. He wore shorts and a hoodie and looked even younger than I had expected. There was what appeared to be an unopened loaf of bread next to his right hip. I wondered if the guy who discovered the body had seen it.

I found Dave and Jen just outside the crime-scene tape. He was eating a chocolate-frosted buttermilk donut. She wasn't eating anything at all.

"Any good?" I asked him.

"No, not really." He finished it with one huge bite. After he managed to swallow the whole mouthful, he said, "So what do you think?"

"Dumpster's pretty close to PCH," I said. "Why not just drive up the alley where there wouldn't be a chance of anyone seeing anything?"

"Good question."

"When do they empty the Dumpster?"

"Truck came this morning while the uniforms were still blocking off the scene," he said. "They sent it away."

"So whoever dumped the body knew the collection schedule."

"That's my bet."

Maybe-Jerry came over. His mood hadn't improved. "You guys finished now?"

"Yep," Dave said, layering his words with smug satisfaction. "What's your hurry, anyway? I've never seen anybody so anxious to climb into a Dumpster before."

• • •

I found Ethan loading his equipment into the LBPD Crime Scene van.

"Thanks," I said to him.

"No problem."

"You didn't need to break protocol, though." I told him that because I didn't want to encourage him to approach established procedure lightly, but the truth was that I was glad he had. If he hadn't, Kobe's body might have slipped past us. And I needed to see him. To witness his murder scene. He'd been so central to Bill's case that even though I knew next to nothing about him, his loss was still palpable. He might have been able to lead us to whoever had killed Bill. It was possible he still could, depending on what his killer had left behind.

Ethan's eyes widened with sudden worry. "I didn't mean to, it's just we had all the photos already and Jerry was ready to hop in there and start moving things around anyway, so I told Detective Zepeda that I thought it might be the guy you were looking for and he said to go ahead and do it."

"It's okay," I said.

"I just did the thumb and forefinger. Hardly moved anything at all."

"Stop worrying. Thank you. If you had waited, it would have been another day or two before anyone even made the connection."

He looked relieved.

"It was the right call. You gave us a head start that could make a real difference. Good work. I owe you one."

When his relief transformed into outright happiness, I figured I'd gone too far.

• • •

"This changes things," Jen said as we drove on PCH toward downtown. "Can you imagine Lucinda or Joe putting three slugs in the back of Kobe's head and dropping him in a Dumpster?"

"No," I said. "Not really."

"It's no coincidence they disposed of the body when and where they did," she said. "If the guy who called it in hadn't been looking for the breakfast Dumpster-diver special, the body would have made it all the way to the landfill before anyone found it. Could have been days or even weeks before anyone could trace it back here. They might have even gotten away with it."

Everything she said was true.

"Maybe Kobe wasn't running because of Bill," I said. "Maybe he was into something else and just bolted when he saw the cops showing up."

"That's possible," she said. "But it's a long shot."

As had become my habit, I lowered the passenger's visor and checked the traffic behind us. I saw a white Accord that could have been the same one I'd seen before. If it really was a tail, they'd chosen a good vehicle. The Accord is one of the most popular cars in California, and white is the most popular color.

"You see that Accord behind us?" I said.

Jen checked her mirror. "Yes. We're seeing a lot of white Accords these days."

"I know, but humor me, okay?"

She turned right off of PCH onto a small side street called Henderson. To our surprise, the white Accord followed.

"Now what?" Jen asked.

"Pull over."

She did, and the Accord drove past us. I eyeballed the driver. He looked midtwenties, possibly Latino, wearing a white long-sleeved oxford.

Jen said, "Six Tom Victor Zebra Two Four Four."

I wrote the plate number down and said, "Follow him."

She pulled away from the curb and fell in behind him. He continued north on Henderson. We were in Wrigley, a neighborhood that ran along the east side of the Los Angeles River all the way north to the 405. For the last ten years, everyone had been expecting it to be the next big gentrification hot spot, but the rich people never showed up.

I called in the plate number. It belonged to a white Accord, but the owner was a fifty-seven-year-old woman named Dolores Webber who lived in Irvine.

Jen said, "Why is somebody driving her car randomly around Long Beach?"

"Maybe he stole the plates from another white Accord."

"I don't like this." She checked the rearview mirror. "He could be trying to lead us into something."

"Like an ambush?" If my car hadn't exploded a few days earlier, I would have found that funny. I looked over my shoulder. There was no one behind us.

"I'll call in for backup." I did, and then called Patrick.

When he answered, I told him what was happening.

"What does Jen think?"

"She's worried."

He thought about it for a few seconds. "I'm in the car and heading back to the station, but I'm twenty minutes away. Stay with him unless something looks really wrong. Try to keep the backup out of sight and see where he leads you."

We followed him through the residential neighborhood all the way up Henderson until it ended at Burnett. He turned right and then took the first left on Eucalyptus to continue north. There hadn't been anything suspicious about his behavior, other than not exceeding the speed limit, since we'd started following him. Five minutes earlier, I was ready for a gunfight. Now, though, I was beginning to second-guess my suspicions.

A patrol unit notified us that it was traveling parallel to us on Magnolia and asked for instructions. I told them to keep heading north and wait for word from us.

The Accord crossed Willow, but we got stopped by cross traffic. It was hard to tell, but it looked like he might be slowing down so we wouldn't lose him. He could only go straight for a few more blocks.

When he got to Thirty-Third, he turned left and pulled to the curb in front of a big new building I hadn't seen before. It looked like an office building, with big red letters reading "PBBC." As we got closer, I could read the smaller black letters next to the large ones. They said "Pacific Baptist Bible College."

The driver got out of the car and looked around, as if he was unfamiliar with the area. He had a nine-by-twelve clasp envelope and some loose papers in his hands.

Jen shot me a look that I didn't quite know how to read and got out.

"Excuse me," she said to the young man. She held up her badge and said, "Hi, we noticed you driving slowly through the neighborhood and wondered if everything was okay."

He looked surprised and maybe frightened. "Yes, it's okay. I was on my way to drop off my application and I got a little lost, is all. I don't know Long Beach very well."

Jen introduced herself and asked his name.

"José," he said.

"Who is Dolores Webber?" she asked.

That threw him, but he answered quickly. "She's my aunt." He realized how we made the connection and added, "Oh, she loaned me her car. It was going to take two hours each way from Santa Ana on the train and the bus."

Jen looked at me. I shook my head.

"I'm sorry I was going so slow." He shuffled through the papers in his hands and held out a Google Maps printout for us to see. "I was trying to read this while I was driving. We don't have GPS. I should have pulled over. Am I going to get a ticket?"

"No, no ticket," Jen said.

José looked as if the weight of the world had been lifted off his shoulders. "Thank you so much. I'm sorry. I'll be more careful."

"You're welcome. Good luck with your application."

"God bless you," he said.

We headed back to the car.

"Excuse me?" José said behind us. "You don't happen to know where Admissions is, do you?"

I called Patrick and told him what happened. He seemed disappointed. Sure, it would have sucked if we'd been led into an ambush, but it probably would have cracked the case.

Another false alarm. Everything was setting me on edge. I was jumping at shadows and seeing danger everywhere. I had to get a handle on things, or my growing paranoia would make me useless.

We weren't far from Bixby Knolls, so I suggested Jongewaard's Bake-n-Broil for lunch. They have a good chicken potpie. I knew from experience that it would probably be enough to smother my feelings.

• • •

When we got back to the station, Jen had to go to court and left me in the squad room to go over with Dave the notes I had on Kobe. He wasn't back yet, so I went through them again myself to make sure there was nothing I could add or elaborate on. There wasn't much there, only a few pages that consisted primarily of Harold Craig's statement.

My phone chirped with a text message from Julia. Thank you ☺

I wasn't sure what she was thanking me for. You're welcome, I replied. For what?

The flowers. They're beautiful.

Flowers, I thought. I hadn't sent any flowers. Halfway through composing my reply, Dave came in the squad room and I put my phone down.

I intercepted him and asked if they'd found anything else at the scene.

"No wallet, no watch, no keys," he said.

"He wear a watch?" I asked. Watches were old school. Most people, especially if they're under thirty, check the time on their phones these days.

"There was a little bit of a tan line on his wrist. So either a watch, or some kind of bracelet. Looks like they took everything. Make it look like a robbery, or harder to ID him. Or both."

"No phone?"

"That's the interesting thing. He had a phone." Dave had something he wanted to tell me, but he also wanted to make me fish for it.

"Why didn't they take it?" I asked.

"Because they didn't search him good enough. It was tucked in his underwear. Right up against his nutsack."

"Why would he do that?"

"That's the big question," Dave said. "I'm thinking he had another one. Probably an iPhone. They found that, didn't think they needed to keep looking."

"What about the one in his underwear?"

"It's just a cheap basic model. Probably a burner."

"You check it to see if there was anything on it?" I asked.

He nodded. "No texts, no voice mail, no call history. Probably deleted them, if they were ever there at all."

"What was there?"

"A contact list."

I opened the folder and showed him the names we'd found on the Post-it in Kobe's apartment. "Any of these look familiar?"

He pulled his reading glasses out of his pocket and put them on. Then he leaned over and read from my notes. "Yep, those are all there. And K. Maru."

"That's Kobe," I said. "Are there more in the phone?"

"Just one," he said. "Winters. That mean anything to you?"

● ● ●

"So," Ruiz said, "you think the cell-phone contact connects the son-in-law to Dave's victim, the upstairs neighbor?"

Dave and I were sitting in the chairs facing the desk. Jen was standing behind us.

"Yes, I do." We'd gone over everything in detail with him.

"And you think the others on this list of aliases might be in danger, too?"

"They could be. Maybe Kobe was killed because of his proximity to Bill Denkins. Maybe it was because he saw something someone didn't want him to see that night—it's possible."

"But?" Ruiz said.

"It seems like too much of a coincidence."

"How do you know 'Winters' isn't just another alias and not connected to the restaurant at all?"

"It doesn't fit with the others. It's not an obvious reference to a character in pop-culture fantasy like the others are."

"But you said you thought it was connected to *Game of Thrones*."

"I do think that, but it's a different kind of connection."

We'd started losing him as soon as we mentioned *Star Wars* and *Lord of the Rings*. His eyes glazed over with Mass Effect and I hadn't been able to unglaze them. If Patrick were there, he might have been able to do a better job translating nerd into English. I was struggling.

"Honestly," Ruiz said, exhaling through his nose and spreading his hands palm up over his desk. "I'm not sure why you're telling me this right now."

We hadn't actually tried to articulate everything for each other, and we should have before we attempted to explain it to Ruiz, but it wasn't that important that he understood the specifics of the popular-culture references in the aliases. What we were really looking for was strategy. We found ourselves in a position in which it seemed like we needed to prioritize one murder over the other. If we brought Joe in for questioning about Kobe before we'd made a solid case against him for the murder of his father-in-law, we might undermine our ability to make that case. On the other hand, the longer we looked at Joe, the less likely we'd be able to find Kobe's killers and the greater risk there was to the people using the other aliases on the list.

I slowed down, more for myself than for Ruiz, and explained it as carefully as I could.

"Damn," he said. "I'm inclined to say 'a bird in the hand' and all that. You've got two-thirds of a solid case against the son-in-law. The smart money says pursue that first, but there might be three more people at risk." He raised his hand to his face and scratched at his chin. After a few moments of contemplation, he said, "Don't prioritize. Not yet. Keep working them both and don't let either one sink the other."

"How do we do that?" I asked without a trace of snark or irony in my voice.

"I don't know," he said. "I figure out the strategy. The tactics are on you."

• • •

Two hours later we had a game plan. Dave had written one warrant request to gather metadata on the cell numbers in the contact list from Kobe's phone, and another to monitor any activity on them moving forward. We decided to hold off on interrogating Joe, but I made arrangements for Lucy to come into the station for an interview the following morning. I'd be fishing, but I'd have to plan the questions very carefully in order to gain as much information as possible without alerting her to our suspicions about her husband.

I was at my desk, working on the line of questioning I planned to use, when Patrick came over with his iPad wanting me to look at some photos.

"What are they?" I asked.

"Faces. Just tell me if any of them look familiar."

He showed them to me one at a time. A mix of Caucasians and African American males who ranged in age from early twenties to mid-forties. Some were mug shots, some were taken on the street, some looked like they'd been pulled from social media. As he scrolled through them, I took my time with each one and studied the features of the face, searching my memory for hints of recognition. Out of fourteen pictures, only one looked vaguely familiar. One of the black men. He had a scar running up the left side of his nose.

"Where do you recognize him from?"

"A case, I think. Maybe a year and a half, two years ago? I couldn't tell you his name."

"You remember which one?"

"Jen was the primary. It was an Insane Crips thing, somebody popped one of them outside the Target up on Cherry. I remember this guy because of the scar and because he was willing to talk to me."

"Was he involved?"

"No," I said. "Just a witness. He gave us a description of the get-away car."

"Anything come of it?"

"No. Case got closed because an ADA on another murder got somebody a better plea deal in exchange for information."

He nodded and flipped the cover of the iPad closed. "Okay," he said. "Thanks."

"Who are the other guys?"

"Three of the white guys are connected to that Serb crew I mentioned. They move a lot of weapons. The others are guys they've done business with."

"You're trying to link them to me?"

Patrick stood halfway up and looked at the lieutenant's office. I knew Ruiz wasn't there. "Yeah," he said. "The mine in your car was manufactured in the same lot as the one the ATF guys already found. It's a good bet they were smuggled in together. We've got to tiptoe around all this, though, because they're putting together a federal case to take the whole operation down."

"They stonewalling you?"

"No," he said. "But we know there's a lot of information there that might be useful, and they won't jeopardize what they've got in the works."

"Not even for an attempted murder on a cop?"

He shook his head. "They lost an undercover guy in the lead-up to the original raid. As far as they're concerned, that trumps everything."

I could understand that. But it left Patrick stumbling around in the dark. And it left me someplace I still didn't want to think about.

The question I didn't want to ask wouldn't go away, so I let it out. "You find anything that might be a link to the Denkins case?"

"No, but Kobe's murder might change that."

"That's what I was thinking. Three shots in the back of the head."

Patrick was on the same page. Bill Denkins's murder was a botched fake suicide. Kobe's looked like a professional hit. People who put the gun in a right-handed man's left hand before they pull the trigger for him aren't the same kind of people who use .22-caliber pistols for executions and know when the trash truck is going to empty the Dumpster.

But the killings had to be related. It was far too much of a coincidence for them not to be. If we were looking at different killers, how were they connected?

"You've been checking the cameras?" Patrick asked.

"Yes. Every time I go home and then a few extra times a day. There are a lot more cats in my neighborhood than I realized."

He laughed. "You watch last night yet?"

I hadn't but he clearly had.

"You've got a possum in your backyard, too."

• • •

The incident with José on the way to the Bible college seemed to have lightened the weight of the paranoia that I'd felt building for the last few days. I took a break and went downstairs and walked out through the back entrance to the station. Outside, the sun was shining bright and I felt none of the anxiety that had frozen me before. I took a good look around. Uniforms and suits. Marked and unmarked units pulling in or pulling out. Everything looked as it should. I scanned the edges of the lot and walked toward the gate on Magnolia. On the sidewalk, I paused long enough to take a quick glance in each direction, looking for anything out of the ordinary. Surveying each pedestrian and passing car, I assured myself there was no imminent risk. Turning right, I walked up to Broadway and did a clockwise loop around the block, paying close attention to spot any potential threats. It was clear all the way around.

When I made it back to the rear entrance, I felt even more foolish about the day before. Whoever had put the bomb in my car was still out there. There was no question about that. I don't know if it was the incident that morning purging the paranoia from my psyche, or time diluting the urgency I'd felt, but it was a relief. I didn't feel safe, and I wouldn't until Patrick closed his case, but I felt alert and better able to function than I had in days.

At my desk I went back to my interview notes for Lucinda Denkins. I reread the list of questions to which I'd hoped I'd find answers, even if I couldn't ask them directly.

Why didn't she take Joe's last name?

After the loans from her father and the bank, what was the source of the extra funds for Winter?

How close were Joe and her father?

Why did Joe think he had what it takes to be a restaurateur?

How did he take the failure?

How much debt had he incurred?

How solid was their relationship?

Who would her father drink with in his apartment?

Did she know Kobe? Harold? The other tenants? Kurt Acker?

What other debt were she and Joe carrying?

Was he a good husband?

Had he ever been unfaithful?

I could have gone on and on, but I stopped when Jen texted me. Going to be later than I thought—meeting with ADA. Probably be here until 6.

Waiting didn't sound appealing. How about if I just go home? It didn't seem strange to me that I meant her home. Apparently, it didn't seem strange to her, either.

No, wait for me.

It'll be ok. I'll check out a fresh car and go straight there.

She didn't answer immediately, but I watched the little ellipsis on the screen that told me she was composing a reply. It was taking her so long, I expected it to be lengthy. To list her objections and tell me why I needed to stay put and wait. When it finally came, though, it wasn't.

`Be careful,` it said.

Before I could reply, another message came through.

`Text me when you get there.`

I told her I would, packed the notes I'd been working on into my messenger bag, and headed downstairs to the garage.

• • •

The first thing I wanted to do when I got to Jen's house was to take a hot shower. The pain in my arm and neck had been building up all afternoon. One of the surest ways of easing my pain was adrenaline, and I'd had a minor rush when I thought we were being followed by the white Accord. When the adrenaline fades, though, the pain comes rushing back in to fill the void.

Then I remembered Jen's low-flow showerhead. Everybody in drought-stricken Southern California was mandated to use them. My problem with them was that the anemic pressure they produced was ineffective in providing the deep heat my aching muscles needed for relief. Because I am a selfish person with no regard for the greater good, I have an illegally modified showerhead that blasts enough hot water to poach a small cow.

I needed a change of clothes, too. And my banjo. I'd been trying to spare Jen the annoyance of listening to my inept practice sessions, but I'd been lax even before I'd started staying at her place, and I could feel the difference in my left hand and wrist. Just as my physical therapist had suggested, the playing, bad as it was, did help reduce the numbness and tingling and increase the dexterity and sensation in my hand.

When I got home, I sat in the unmarked cruiser in front of my duplex and fast-forwarded through the surveillance video. Everything was clear, so I got out and went inside, locking the door behind me.

While I waited for the shower to heat up, I tossed some clean clothes in my duffel bag and draped a fresh suit on its hanger over one of the chair backs in the dining room.

The water was as hot as I could make it without scalding myself. The pressure drove the heat deep into the muscles of my neck and shoulder. I stayed in until the water heater ran low and the temperature began to drop. After toweling off and going back into the bedroom to put on jeans and a T-shirt, I headed to the living room to pack up my banjo.

I thought I heard the floor creak as I passed the kitchen, but before I could turn toward the sound, an arm clenched around my neck and choked me into unconsciousness.

CHAPTER TEN

The pain came first.

A squeezing, grasping, wrenching tightness between my temples, behind my eyes. I wanted to reach up, to touch it, but my hands wouldn't move.

What happened? Where was I?

I was lying down in the dark. My head throbbed. I couldn't focus.

The shower. I'd been in the shower. But I wasn't in the shower now. Dry. Dressed. On my side, hands behind my back, hard to move.

The spinning in my head slowed and I slowly began to realize where I was. Something was covering my head. A bag or a pillowcase? My hands were bound with handcuffs. Were they mine? I tried to move my legs. Something was holding them together.

Where was I?

Breathe, I reminded myself. *Just breathe.*

Pay attention. Listen. Be quiet.

I heard road noise. I felt movement. I realized I was in a car. No, not a car. The space wasn't tight enough. A truck or a van. My feet were toward the front, my head to the rear.

Was I alone? No one said anything. Maybe there was just the driver.

Think, Danny, think.

Of course I didn't have my gun. I couldn't reach the front pocket of my pants, so I rolled on my hip. No phone, either.

There was nothing I could do.

Keep breathing, I told myself. *Listen.*

The van wasn't moving very fast. It stopped and turned, then resumed a straight course. We were on surface streets.

Where were we? I paid close attention to noises from outside, listening for something that might provide a clue to our location, but I couldn't pinpoint anything. There was only the noise of the van, the engine, the tires on the pavement.

There were more stops and turns. I'd lost track of how many.

What was that smell? Fabric softener? It must have been a pillowcase on my head.

Did anyone know where I was? Would Jen be looking for me yet?

I had no idea how long I'd been unconscious. I remembered getting out of the shower, drying myself off, and getting dressed. Heading back to the front room.

The kitchen. There was a noise in the kitchen. An arm around my neck.

If I'd only been choked out, I wouldn't have stayed unconscious long enough for him to bind me and wrestle me outside into the van. Did he do something else? Had I been drugged?

I felt dull and groggy and nauseous. He must have given me something.

How long had I been out? It could have been hours.

We could be anywhere by now.

Just breathe, I told myself. *Don't let the panic in.*

I focused on my abdomen and started counting each exhalation. When I got to ten, I would start over at one.

If they wanted me dead, they would have killed me by now.

Inhale, exhale. One.

Maybe Patrick has seen the video.

Inhale, exhale. Two.

Was that the sound of a train?

Inhale, exhale. Three.

Jen's going to be so fucking pissed off at me.

Inhale, exhale. Four.

I was a good cop.

Inhale, exhale. Five.

How long have we been moving?

Inhale, exhale. Six.

I'm going to throw up.

Inhale, exhale. Seven.

My head hurts.

Inhale, exhale. Eight.

Fuckfuckfuckfuckfuck—

Inhale, exhale. Nine.

I'm sorry.

Inhale, exhale. Ten.

I started over.

• • •

When the van finally stopped, I heard the sound of the driver's door slam shut and waited. A few seconds later, the side door slid open and I realized I could see some light and shadow through the pillowcase.

It was dark and quiet outside. I could hear some kind of industrial noise in the distance, a faraway metallic drone. A shadow moved into the open frame of the doorway.

"I know you're awake," he said.

He lifted my feet off the floor and started dragging me out. I realized in a second or two my shoulders and head would clear the floor of the van and slam down to the ground. I tried to tuck my chin. My shoulder took most of the impact, but the back of my head still bounced off the pavement. The pain throbbed in my skull. I couldn't remember if it had stopped while we were driving.

The man pulled me a few feet farther away from the open door. From the ground, his shadow appeared huge and looming.

He kicked me once in the gut. Not as hard as he could have.

"Stay away from her," he said. His voice was softer than I expected, younger.

"What?" I said.

He said it again. "Stay away from her." Louder. More emphatic.

I nodded and realized he might not have been able to see it because of the pillowcase. "Okay," I said without understanding. Stay away from who?

He kicked me again, harder, and left me gasping. When I could get enough air into my lungs, I said, "I'll stay away."

His shadow rocked back and forth, as if he was agitated, unsure of himself. "I'm not going to warn you again."

"I'll stay away," I said.

"Next time I'll kill you." He paused. "But I'll kill everybody you care about first. That's how you'll know I'm coming."

"I swear," I said, hearing the fear and desperation in my own voice. "I'll stay away."

His shadow shifted and I knew he was going to kick me again. He went for my head, but he lost his balance and stumbled and his foot glanced off the crown of my skull.

He grunted and reset himself for another try and I turned my face away. That time he connected solidly with the side of my head and everything went dark.

That Nina Simone song Julia had been playing. What was it called? The French one. Shit. Did she even say? I don't think so. Have to figure it out, add it to the playlist. She'd like that, I think.

The eggs smell so good. The butter, the cheese. I can almost taste them.

Megan used to cook scrambled eggs. When I made detective and didn't have to work on the weekends. Scrambled eggs on sourdough toast. Why did I give her so much shit about liking Coldplay? I put "'Til Kingdom Come" on the funeral list for her. That was her favorite song. And "Fix You." I watched that documentary about the chorus of senior citizens who sang popular songs. Old people singing the Ramones. Ha. She would have loved it. Then that one old guy with the oxygen tube in his nose sang "Fix You" and I wept because she died thinking I couldn't stand her favorite songs.

We danced to "If I Should Fall Behind" at our wedding. That song was the anchor. So much Springsteen. Crazy Janey. The ragamuffin gunner. Wild Billy. Mary and the Magic Rat. The dogs on Main Street. That stranger passing through who put up a sign.

Jesus. I was almost the chicken man. Still could be.

Still could be.

"Forever Young."

Buckley's "Hallelujah" because it wasn't everybody's ringtone yet. "Somewhere Over the Rainbow/What a Wonderful World" by Bruddah Iz—same reason. Are they still on there? Cut them.

"Tears in Heaven." The antidepressants took a long time to start working.

"Spirit in the Sky" or "(Don't Fear) The Reaper." Which is funnier?

"Night Comes On."

"The Weight."

"The Boy in the Bubble."

That Deb Talan song you like so much. For sure that one.

The cast is still on my arm from the last surgery when you come to visit. I get up to answer the door without closing the file and you see it on my laptop. *You're early, partner,* I say. "Don't Think Twice, It's All Right" is still playing.

What's this? you ask.

Bob Dylan.

Not the song. This. You point to the screen.

A playlist.

Songs For My Funeral?

Yeah.

What the fuck?

Something to do, I say, embarrassed, trying to play it off. *No big deal. Just killing time.*

Suicidal ideation. The therapist kept asking me about it. *Have you wished you were dead or wished you could go to sleep and not wake up? Have you actually had any thoughts of killing yourself? Have you been thinking about how you might kill yourself? Have you had these thoughts and had some intention of acting on them? Have you started to work out or worked out the details of how to kill yourself and do you have any intention of carrying out this plan? Have you done anything, started to do anything, or prepared to do anything to end your life?*

No?

You say, *You're still seeing the therapist, right?*

Twice a week, I say. But I think, *If you don't count last week. Or this week.*

You're really worried. You're trying not to let it show. You aren't doing a very good job.

It's just a list of songs, I say.

I don't think it is.

I'm not thinking about killing myself.

What are you thinking about?

Dying.

You don't say anything. How long has it been then? Three years? Almost four?

You saw me through Megan's death. You stopped the bleeding, saved my hand, saved my life.

Now you look so sad.

Do you smell eggs?

"Hold On." The old one, Tom Waits. Not Alabama Shakes. That one is good but it's a different song. The wrong song. Not born yet. Maybe Neko Case, though. "Hold On, Hold On."

You keep asking me questions like the therapist.

I lied to her. I tell you the truth.

You listen. You understand.

No, I say, *I'm not okay.* I pause for a long time, then say, *But I will be.*

Because you believe it, I start to believe it, too.

This is a lot of songs, you say.

Haven't you ever been to an Irish funeral?

You're Irish all of a sudden?

My grandfather was Irish.

I thought it was your great-grandfather.

Same thing.

No, it's not.

Did you read the whole list?

I didn't get past the part where you included every song Springsteen ever wrote.

Look at the end there.

You know we're just going to get a bagpiper and play "Wind Beneath My Wings," right?

But then you do look. When you gave me the CD, I asked which song was your favorite. *They're all my favorites,* you said. I know, I said, but which one? *"Ashes on Your Eyes."*

It's the last song on the list.

I'll make some eggs, I think, but I don't because there isn't any sourdough.

CHAPTER TWELVE

NE ME QUITTE PAS

William Denkins's entire case file was spread out before me on the dining-room table. I didn't know what time it was, but it was late. I'd been working alone for hours. Everything was there. All the reports, the crime-scene photos, the personal records, the warrant requests, the witness statements, the yellow pads filled with notes. The stacks of pages—more than a hundred of them by that point in the investigation—were arranged in staggered piles that covered every inch of the surface. My eyes moved from one pile to the next and back again.

Then I saw it. Once it clicked, it seemed so obvious I couldn't believe I hadn't seen it sooner. I began riffling through the pages, pulling one here and one there, rearranging them. Everything fell into place. *Of course, of course.* I felt the adrenaline as one piece of the puzzle after another fit together.

The answers were there. And I could see them as clearly as I'd ever seen anything before.

I knew.

I knew.

"Danny?"

My eyes opened and I was staring up at a fluorescent-light fixture recessed in the ceiling.

"Danny?" she said.

Someone was holding my hand.

"Jen?" I said, turning my head to look into her face.

"No," she said. "It's me."

I looked at her. There was concern in her green eyes and she looked tired. Her brown hair was pulled back, but a few strands hung down along the side of her face. Somehow I knew she'd been there a long time. We'd been there a long time. She squeezed my hand and I squeezed hers too. I knew her. There was a connection I could feel deep in my abdomen. She had a name. I knew it. I wanted to say it. But it hung just out of reach.

"You're in the hospital," she said. "You have a head injury."

I tried to sit up, to get out of bed. There was something attached to my arm. I looked at it. She leaned forward and gently pushed me back down. I felt the pillow against the back of my head.

"But I know who did it," I said.

"That's good," she said, reaching across my body and fishing for a heavy gray cord. There was a handle with a button on the end. I recognized it. That was how you called for help.

She pushed the button with her thumb. "They wanted me to let them know when you woke up."

I nodded.

"I know who did it."

"Who?" she said.

When I tried to tell her, though, the certainty I'd felt only a few moments before had vanished, leaving nothing in its place. Only an emptiness that felt unimaginably vast and desolate. It was only when she wiped the tears from my eyes that I realized I was crying.

• • •

Two hours later, most of the confusion had passed and I was able to recall what had happened. Most of it. A doctor had come in and given me a neurological exam. I had a concussion and several bruised ribs. He was concerned about the potential for a subdural hematoma. They'd need to watch me for a while.

The first thing Jen said when she came in was, "Dumb shit." She was angry. That's how I knew I probably wasn't going to die. Julia told me Jen had been there most of the night, only leaving to join Patrick when the doctor told her the CT scan didn't show any signs of major damage or intracranial bleeding.

"How's he doing?" Jen asked Julia.

Julia told her everything the doctor had said, then smiled at me and said, "I'm going to run down to the cafeteria, okay?"

I nodded.

"What were you thinking?" Jen asked.

There was no good answer, so I pretended it was a rhetorical question.

I started to tell her what I remembered.

"Save it for Patrick," she said. "He'll be here soon."

We sat in silence. I tried to read her. She was angry. With me, of course, but also with herself. I knew she would hold herself responsible for what had happened to me, even though it was completely my fault.

"I'm sorry," I said.

"You should be. I told you to go straight to my place."

"He could have got me there, too."

"No, he couldn't. Lauren was off yesterday. Home. I called her and asked her to keep an eye out for you. Otherwise I never would have said okay to you going alone."

"I don't know. She's still a rook—"

"Shut up. She would have had your back. And she's not a rookie anymore." She wasn't just upset. She was angry. I hadn't seen her like this often. She was very good at keeping things in check.

"Look, Jen, I'm really—"

"Stop, just fucking stop." She looked out the window and I could see that she was thinking through something. After a long silence, she looked like she came to a decision and turned back to face me again.

"You need to grow up. There are people who care about you. Do you have any idea what you put us through last night?"

When she saw my blank stare, she told me.

• • •

Jen's testimony the previous day should have been straightforward and relatively quick. The case was an attempted murder-suicide, but after shooting his ex-wife, the man had second thoughts. Jen had been surprised it even went to trial. The evidence against him was so overwhelming, she had expected a plea deal. But the defense attorney was stringing things out so much, she was worried she'd have to come back the next day. The judge curtailed him, though, so they were able to wrap things up by the end of the day.

When she read the text message asking about going straight to her house, she checked with Lauren to make sure she was home and, against her better judgment, gave the go-ahead.

Then she phoned in a take-out order from Enrique's. Carne asada, chicken enchiladas, and tacos. She sent a group text saying she'd be bringing dinner. The only reply came from Lauren.

By the time she got home, she'd started to worry. She checked in with Julia to see if she had heard anything, then called Patrick, who was alone in the squad room.

"Is Danny still there?"

"I think he left a little while ago, but I'll check around," Patrick told her. "Make sure he's not somewhere else in the station."

"Thanks," she said. "I'm going to go check his place."

She got back in her RAV4, drove for five long minutes, and parked on Roycroft. The cruiser from the motor pool was there and the back door was unlocked.

"Danny?" she called when she went inside. Some papers had fallen off the table, and a dining chair had been pushed back away from the table.

Were these signs of a struggle?

Yes, she realized, they were. It hit her in the stomach first, and as she felt it rising into her chest, she swallowed hard to push the apprehension back down.

She called Patrick back. Told him what she'd found.

"I'm on the way," he said. "I'll bring a crew and tell the lieutenant." He didn't need to tell her he'd put out a BOLO, too.

Jen tried the phone again. Instinctively, she put her hand on the grip of her Glock and spun around when she heard the ringing in the bathroom. She went in and found the phone. Someone had been in the shower recently. The walls and sliding glass were still peppered with drops of water, and the towel hanging over the top rail was wet.

She saw the iPad on the table, thought about potential trace evidence, and decided that the video was more important. She'd never seen the icon for the app that linked to the surveillance cameras, so she started opening anything that looked unfamiliar. On the fourth try, she found the right one. It wasn't hard to figure things out. The feeds from the two cameras covering the front of the duplex were clear, except for me pulling up to the curb, checking the same iPad she was holding, and then getting out and heading inside, so she switched to the one pointing out my bedroom window at the backyard.

She kept moving and she saw him. It was clear he knew about the camera because he wore the hood of his sweatshirt pulled up over his head and he turned away from the lens as he jogged across the lawn.

She switched to the garage-mounted camera and watched him from behind as he peeked in the bedroom window and then went around the side of the building. When he'd seen what he was looking for, he came back and went to the back porch.

He crouched down and began working on the doorknob. He was too far away for her to see much detail, but even still she knew he was working at picking the lock. It took him a minute and a half for the first lock, which she assumed to be the doorknob, and almost two for the other, the deadbolt. And then he disappeared inside.

She watched the time signature as she fast-forwarded. Five minutes sped by in accelerated time and she knew he was waiting for the shower to stop. She checked her watch. The footage she was watching had been recorded fifty-three minutes earlier.

They could be anywhere now, she thought.

Then she saw it. The man in the hoodie dragging an unconscious body across the porch, one hand in each armpit, as my feet clunked down the three stairs to the concrete below. He pulled his awkward load across the lawn and disappeared.

She looked up from the screen as flashing red lights lit up the living-room picture window that faced out onto Roycroft.

Then Patrick was knocking on the front door with two uniforms behind him.

Before he could say anything, Jen said, "Somebody grabbed him. One guy. Dragged him out through the backyard and into the alley."

"How did Danny look?"

She didn't answer. No matter what she feared, it was standard procedure to assume a kidnapping victim was alive until there is definitive proof otherwise.

"Don't worry, we'll get him." Patrick got back on his phone and called Ruiz to tell him they had confirmation of a kidnapping.

Jen played back the video for him. The kidnapper looked like he was a bit under six feet tall, weight 170 or so. Athletic build. Patrick slowed the playback and froze on a frame of the kidnapper midway across the backyard, just as he was moving toward the edge of the camera's field of vision.

"He knows where the camera is," Patrick said. "He's making sure we don't get a good shot of his face."

Jen looked again at the table and chair. At the papers on the floor.

"I think Danny was coming from the bedroom or the bathroom. He was in the shower. Walks up the hallway. The hoodie's waiting for him."

"Where?"

Jen looked around again. "The kitchen. It's the only place for a good ambush." She showed him. The arched opening was the size of a standard door and there was two feet of empty wall to the side. It would give an attacker a good place to hide. Unlike the opening from the hallway into the dining room, which was larger and had a bookshelf next to the jamb that wouldn't provide much concealment.

She had Patrick walk past the kitchen door and she grabbed him from behind in slow motion. It was clear to both of them that the likely trajectory of my body would be into the table in the same direction as its displacement. The chair and the papers supported the theory.

Jen called the crime-scene tech over. "Get pictures of everything. Bathroom, bedroom, hallway, kitchen. And get everything here." She swept her hand to indicate the dining table and the area around it.

She went into the bathroom and found the phone on the counter. There was a call from an unknown number that synced up with the time on the video when the kidnapper was on the back porch. He'd been making sure his target was really in the shower.

"Why would he shower here?" Patrick asked. "Why not just wait until he got to your place?"

"Because I have a low-flow shower," Jen said. She remembered the day last year when she'd stood in my bathroom and used a pocketknife to remove the flow limiter in the new showerhead the landlord had just installed. As she explained it to Patrick, she felt a twinge of guilt rising in her chest. Why hadn't she just switched one of hers out for this one? She knew how much it helped the pain. She knew it would be days at least before the threat was neutralized. If she had, she thought, she might have prevented this. She pushed the thought out of her head. Replaced it with anger. At the kidnapper. At me.

Patrick's phone rang. It was Ruiz. He was on the way.

Jen went outside and huddled with several patrol officers. She told them to start knocking on doors and asking if anyone had seen an unusual vehicle in the alley within the last few hours.

They stood on the lawn and waited. For the techs inside. For Ruiz. For the patrol officers to report back. For anyone who could give them something, anything, that would tell them what to do next.

Jen's phone rang. It was one of the uniforms on the next street over. Someone had seen something.

She hurried around the corner and found the officer four houses down from the corner. If it didn't line up with the duplex on Roycroft, it was very close.

The woman who lived there was older, late sixties or early seventies. Jen guessed she was retired. The uniform introduced her as Mrs. Rosenfeld.

"Can you tell me what you saw?" Jen asked.

"Yes, I was just taking my trash out. We keep the bin in the alley. And there was a white van parked on the other side."

"Show me," Jen said.

Mrs. Rosenfeld led her around the side of the house and across an immaculately maintained yard to the back gate. The old woman unlatched it and pushed it open. "Right there," she said, pointing ten yards up the alley at the back of my garage.

"Do you know what kind of van it was?" Jen asked.

"White, like the gardeners use."

Jen's gardener used an old Ford Ranger. "You're sure it was a van? Not a pickup?"

"Young lady, I might be old, but I know the difference between a van and a pickup truck."

"I'm sorry, ma'am. Do you happen to know what kind of van it was?"

"It's harder to tell the newer ones apart."

"How new was it?" Jen asked.

"Oh, not brand new. A few years old. Five, maybe? It was dirty, but it didn't look too bad."

"Did it have windows on the sides?"

"No," Mrs. Rosenfeld said. "It looked like a work truck. Like Edgar used to drive."

"Edgar?"

"My husband. He was an electrician. Died in '05."

"I'm sorry to hear that. Was the truck as old as Edgar's?"

"It's been fifteen years since he had his truck. Did I say it looked fifteen years old?"

"No, ma'am, you didn't."

"It was newer than that. I could still tell the difference between the Fords and the Chevys in those days."

"Is there anything else you can remember about the van, Mrs. Rosenfeld? Any marks or dents? Any writing? The license number?"

"No, it was just plain white. I didn't have my glasses on so I couldn't see the license plate."

"And it was still parked there then when you went back into the yard?"

"Yes. I was only out long enough to dump the trash. Honestly, I didn't pay that much attention. We get trucks and things back there quite a bit, with the service people and the gardeners and everyone."

Jen thanked her for her help. She told the uniform to keep knocking and hurried back to find Patrick so he could add the late-model white van to the BOLO.

She found Ruiz first, though, and told him what she'd learned. He called in the update himself.

"What was he doing here by himself?" he asked.

"He wasn't supposed to be here. He was supposed to go straight to my house."

"Why was he in a position to make that call himself?"

"I don't know," she said, biting down on her anger. "Because he's a grown-ass man?" She stormed off, her right hand clenched into a fist, looking for something to hit.

• • •

An hour and a half later they had knocked on every door on the block. They didn't find anyone else who had seen the white van. The techs had found some trace evidence that might be useful down the line if they ever had a suspect, but nothing of any immediate usefulness.

Patrol units had pulled over a dozen white vans. None of the stops yielded anything other than angry drivers.

Jen made the call she'd been dreading. Julia answered immediately, and Jen knew she'd been waiting for a call since she'd talked to her earlier.

"Danny's been abducted," Jen said.

After a long silence, Julia said, "What does that mean?"

Jen told her what had happened since they'd last spoke.

"Oh god." Her voice was quiet.

Jen felt the panic. She knew. She was feeling the same thing.

"What should I do?" Julia asked.

"There's really nothing you can do except wait. I'm heading back to the station. It will be easier to monitor things there." She thought about Julia, alone, staring helplessly at the cell phone, waiting for news. Already worried she was making a mistake, she added, "Do you want to meet me there, or should I pick you up?"

When Julia got into the RAV4, Jen could see she had been crying. "Why was he alone?" Julia asked.

"I was late getting out of court. He didn't want to wait for me. He was supposed to go straight to my house."

Jen stared out the windshield as she drove. She couldn't look at Julia. She was afraid to see the accusation in her eyes. "It was my fault."

"What?" Julia said.

"I should have stopped him, made him wait for me."

"Stop it," Julia said.

"Stop what?"

"Blaming yourself." There was a firmness in her voice that Jen hadn't heard before. "It's not your fault."

Jen didn't reply.

"It's not anybody's fault except the man who abducted Danny."

Even though she didn't want to hear it, Jen listened.

"Danny made a mistake. He shouldn't have done what he did. But it wasn't his fault, either. He was in pain. So he took a shower in his own house. How could that possibly make it his fault that he was abducted?"

Before she'd transferred to Homicide, Jen had worked in Sex Crimes. By the time she'd been on the squad three months, she'd lost track of the number of times she'd had to school someone about victim blaming. *She was blaming me for my own kidnapping.*

Still, though, if I had just done what she'd told me to, if she had made me listen to her, I would have been sitting on her couch right now with Julia watching Downton Abbey.

Jen checked in with the watch commander as soon they were inside the station. There was no news. Ruiz was back, too. She wondered if she should apologize for her crack at the scene.

Shit, she thought, as the realization that she had just thought of *my* home as a crime scene swept over her. She was depersonalizing. "Stop," she whispered.

"What?" Julia said.

"I'm just trying to keep a handle on this," she said.

"Me too." Julia reached out and touched Jen's arm. "Me too."

• • •

Jen listened to Patrick on the phone. "I feel like I should be out there." He was still at the duplex in case any of the crime-scene techs pulled off a miracle with a new piece of evidence everyone had missed.

"I know," Jen replied. "Keep me updated, okay?"

Patrick said, "Check it again anyway" to someone there, then spoke to her again. "I will."

She was in the squad room with Julia, just outside of Ruiz's office. He was talking to someone on the landline and had another call going on the speaker of his cell phone.

Jen knew there was nothing she could do but wait. The entire department was on high alert. The SWAT Hostage Rescue Team was standing by, ready to roll, and every available patrol unit was scouring the city looking for the van. *She should have stayed at my place. There wouldn't be any more for her to do there, but she'd be closer to things.* Well, she thought, she might not actually be closer, but she'd feel closer. But when she spoke to Julia and heard the fear in her voice, Jen knew she couldn't leave her alone. As impotent and powerless as she felt, she was keenly aware of how much worse it would be for Julia.

Jen looked at her. She was sitting in a chair outside the lieutenant's office, wearing a navy-blue sweatshirt and black workout pants, her hair pulled back into a ponytail. Julia held her phone in her lap with both hands and looked down at it, as if waiting for it to ring.

"Can I get you anything?" Jen asked.

"No, I'm fine."

None of us are fine, Jen thought. "How about a coffee? I'm going to get one for myself."

"Okay."

Jen went into the break room. There was half a pot on the machine. It had probably been there for hours. She poured two cups and realized she didn't know how Julia liked it, so she grabbed a handful of sugar packets and little plastic creamer containers and put them in her jacket pocket.

She found Julia where she'd left her, sat down next to her, and handed her a cup.

"I brought some cream and sugar if you need it."

"No, this is okay."

They sat there sipping bad coffee for what seemed like hours.

When Julia finally finished her coffee, she looked into the empty cup and said, "It's a good thing he has you."

Jen thought about that. She knew it was true. "He's been different the last few months, since you guys have been together."

Julia looked at her but didn't say anything.

"Since his injury, since Megan, he hasn't really had anything but the job. But he's different. Reminds me of how he used to be when we first partnered up. Before everything weighed him down."

"Thank you," Julia said.

Jen nodded.

• • •

When she heard Ruiz shout in the office, she couldn't tell if it was good news or bad. She stood and turned to look. He waved her inside. Julia followed.

"They found him. He's alive and on the way to Memorial."

Jen rushed Julia downstairs and drove to the hospital. Ruiz followed in his own car.

Patrick was already there when they arrived. He told them I'd been found in the parking lot of a vacant warehouse near the harbor. That I was unconscious after suffering multiple blows to the head. A concussion was likely, and they were doing a CT scan to evaluate further possible damage.

• • •

I wanted to apologize to Jen again, but I held my tongue. She was exhausted. I could see it in her face, around her eyes, in the slump of her shoulders.

"What were you doing this morning?" I asked. "Julia told me you and Patrick left when the results from the scan came back."

"A patrol unit found the van abandoned in a parking structure by the aquarium."

"How do you know it's the same one?"

"It was stolen, but the owner hadn't realized it yet. Collected hairs and fibers in the back that we're ninety percent sure will match you."

"Did you get the guy on video at my house?"

"Only well enough for a rough physical description. He knew the cameras were there. Hid his face."

"Patrick's still working on the van?"

"Yeah."

"Why'd you leave?"

"Somebody had to take your statement. We rock-paper-scissored it."

"You won?"

She shook her head. "Patrick did."

"He said 'Stay away from her,'" Jen repeated.

"Yeah, several times," I said.

"And you had already made arrangements with Lucinda for the interview?"

"Yes. For this afternoon." I was still in the hospital bed. The back had been raised so I was almost sitting up. I looked around for a clock and didn't see one. "What time is it?"

Jen checked her wrist. "Ten thirty."

"I've got to call her," I said. "Reschedule."

"No, you don't. Ruiz wants me to take it."

I didn't say anything.

"You've got a concussion. It will be at least a few days before you can get back to work. You think we should let it sit that long?"

"No." I knew Jen would handle the interview at least as well as I would have. It wasn't that. The idea of being sidelined in the investigation was what frustrated me. I'd worked up a solid sense of momentum and I didn't want to let it go, concussion or not. "I need to get you my notes. Think I came up with a pretty solid plan."

"They're on your dining table, right?"

I nodded.

"Run it down for me," she said.

I told her what I'd planned about going after Lucy at an angle. I gave her the list of questions about Bill that I'd come up with to act as smoke screen for the few direct questions I'd ask about Joe. So with a bit of luck and some perceptive and delicate questioning, we'd get what we needed without tipping her off—and, by extension, Joe.

"That's a solid plan," Jen said when I finished explaining it to her. "How much does last night change things?"

I thought about it. My attacker knew about the interview and didn't want it to happen. He made that clear when he told me to stay away from her. As far as I knew, the only person outside of the squad who was aware it was happening today was Lucinda herself. Joe had known I needed to talk to her, and she likely told him when we'd scheduled it for.

"Could it have been Joe who attacked you last night?"

The pillowcase over my head had made any solid ID impossible. And the fact that I was on the ground the whole time made it difficult to estimate even the attacker's height and build. "I think I would have recognized Joe's voice. And I can't swear to it, but the guy last night seemed bigger than him."

"Still, though, we've got to think the attacker is connected to either Joe or Lucy, right?"

"That seems like all we've got to go on."

We sat there awhile. The silence was uncomfortable. She wanted me to think she was just angry. But there was more to it. The anger was there, but my stupid carelessness had hurt her, too. I knew how worried she had been, how afraid. And I knew I'd caused her that pain.

"I am sorry," I said.

"What's new?" There was neither anger nor sadness in her voice. Only a dull emptiness that made my chest hurt.

"There was some good news," I said.

"What?"

"If he had really wanted to kill me, I'd be dead."

She leaned toward me, put her hand on the edge of the bed, gave me a sad smile, and said, "That is good news, Danny. It really is."

She reached into her jacket pocket and pulled out a handful of sugar packets and coffee creamers. Then she got up, dropped them in the wastebasket, and left.

* * *

"Jen's gone?" Julia said when she came back from the cafeteria.

I told her what we talked about, then apologized to her, too.

She held my hand and smiled at me much less ambiguously than Jen had. She looked tired. There were circles under her eyes.

"Why don't you go home and get some rest?" I said.

"You sure? I don't mind staying."

"No, it's okay. I should probably try to rest, too."

She took my phone out of her bag. "Jen gave this to me last night. Asked me to hang on to it for you."

"Did they check it?"

"She said there weren't any fingerprints or anything. Is that what you mean?"

I nodded and took it.

After she left, and there wasn't anything or anyone to focus my attention on, I realized how bad my head, and my whole body, really, were aching. I needed something to distract me, so I downloaded the first few episodes of the podcast Patrick had recommended to me, *I Was There Too*. At that point, I didn't really care if the recommendation had been meant sincerely or as a dig. I just wanted something to listen to.

The first thing I noticed was the theme song. It had a synthy, poppy sound to it, and as soon as I heard it, I knew I would be stuck with an earworm for a while. But the lyrics were what really clicked and lodged themselves in my brain.

Napalm smells best in the evening
It's not worth believing what you've heard.
Soylent Green's really just a Triscuit
Not a people-biscuit, take my word.
It's been said you can't handle the truth.
But that ain't so.
How do I know?
I was there too.

Listening to the song four times in a row didn't help.

The first episode had an actor and comedian named Paul F. Tompkins, who I only knew because he provided the voice of Mr. Peanutbutter on the Netflix show *BoJack Horseman*. He talked to the host, a guy named Matt Gourley, about a small part he had in *There Will Be Blood*. It was funny. Even more than the humor, though, I liked the way they were taking something familiar and looking at it from a different perspective. Each story was different, it reminded me, depending on who was telling it. I kept thinking about that line from Eliot's "The Love Song of J. Alfred Prufrock," where Prufrock observes that he is not Prince Hamlet, but merely an attendant lord, there to swell a scene or two. David Copperfield wondering whether he would be the hero of his own life came to mind, too. I double majored in English and criminal justice. I couldn't help it.

I was trying to choose the next episode when a doctor came in.

"Mr. Beckett?" he said. I didn't bother asking him to call me "Detective."

He wasn't the same doctor I had seen earlier. At least, I didn't think he was the same one. My memory of the hour or two after I woke up was a bit hazy. "Did I see you this morning?" I asked.

"No, that was the neurologist. I'm on call today. How are you feeling?"

"Okay. My head hurts. Have a little ringing in my ears."

He looked at my eyes and had me follow the glow of a small flashlight with them. Then he asked me a few general "what day is it" kinds of questions. Next he gave me a series of words and told me to remember them. He asked a few more general questions, then told me to repeat the series of words.

"Door, shoe, yellow, chair, window," I said, feeling pretty good about my response. He didn't seem to have any opinion about it at all. "When can I go home?"

"We'll probably want to keep you one more night. I'll order another CT scan to make sure the swelling has gone down."

"What swelling?"

"Nothing too serious. We just want to be cautious."

"Did I get some of those words wrong?"

"Let's not worry about that, okay?"

"Okay," I said, worrying.

• • •

After three more episodes of *I Was There Too* I noticed the battery in my phone was down to 20 percent. I wondered if Jen had finished the interview with Lucy. So I sent her a text message asking about it. She didn't respond, so I assumed it was still going. Julia got a text from me, too, asking her to bring her phone charger when she came back to the hospital.

Without my phone to keep me occupied, all I had was the TV and its limited afternoon choices. I found the news on a local Los Angeles channel. There was weather, celebrity gossip, crime, and an occasional story about someone giving something back or paying something forward. At the end of the hour, I found another station where different faces said the same things.

There was still no word from Jen, but Julia said she'd be back soon with the charger.

I wanted to turn the TV off. The problem, though, was that I didn't want to be alone with my thoughts.

It had been stupid to go to my apartment by myself. Even stupider to get in the shower. If I hadn't done that, the man in the hoodie probably wouldn't have been able to get the drop on me. And because of me, the entire department had been on alert all night. How much had that cost the department? But it wasn't just the money. Every patrol car that took an extra detour or pulled over a white van because of me could have been someplace else doing something else. How many times last night had someone gotten away with something they otherwise might not have? How many crimes had been committed that could have been prevented if the uniforms were where they were supposed to be, doing what they were supposed to do? I didn't want to think about it. How many people were hurt last night because of me?

I'd never know how many strangers felt the impact of my stupidity. But, shit, I knew about Julia and Jen and Patrick and Ruiz. Probably Dave and Marty, too. Even Harlan. I let a lot of people down. And I felt like shit because of it.

And because I had a concussion.

The guy on the TV said it was going to be hot.

• • •

A nurse came to check on me. They wanted me to get up and walk a bit. There was some discomfort in my side as I sat up, but it was nothing compared to the pain I felt when I planted my feet on the floor and stood up. My head throbbed and a sharp pain stabbed at my neck. The room spun. A dull soreness ran down the entire right side of my body and I didn't want to move, because moving made everything worse. But the nurse encouraged me. She was right. The more I moved, the looser I felt and the better my balance became. The headache remained constant.

The nurse just wanted me to walk to the end of the hall and back, maybe forty feet each way. When I got to the end, though, I saw a uniformed cop in the lounge area at the entrance to the wing where my room was located. It was only then I realized that the only way in or out was past the cop. Ruiz had a guard on me. His voice echoed in my head, saying, "Victims don't get overtime."

The cop was a guy I had known for years named Hank Mears. We weren't close, but he had always seemed like a good guy. People liked him. Not only had the lieutenant seen to it that someone was there to provide security, it looked like he'd made sure it was someone I knew. Hank waved and nodded when he saw me walk by, but he didn't move toward me. He was giving me privacy. But was it out of courtesy or disdain?

My phone was still in the room. When I got back, the battery was at 8 percent. Still no reply from Jen. I sent her another message, even though I knew it would probably just make her angrier. The interview had to have been concluded by now and the least she could do was tell me what had happened. *No,* I thought, *the least she could do is just what she is doing—nothing.*

• • •

Julia was getting ready to head home for the night when Harlan came in. They hadn't yet met, but they'd heard about each other. I introduced them.

"How's he doing?" Harlan asked her.

"They say he'll probably be able to go home in the morning."

Harlan grunted. "Hope they have somebody to babysit him, keep him out of trouble."

Julia smiled pleasantly at him. "I'm sure they've got that under control."

"I saw the uniform out in the lobby. He's there for Danny, right?"

She nodded. "Why don't I let you two visit?" she said. She picked up her bag, gave me a kiss, then started for the door. "It was a pleasure to finally meet you, Harlan."

"Likewise," he replied, smiling more warmly at her than he ever had at me. When she was gone, he looked me in the eye and said seriously, "Boy, you were right. She really is way out of your league."

He sat down, and we talked about banjo music and the weather and a dozen other inconsequential things.

It was almost eight when Jen finally texted me back. The inter-view went well. I'll fill you in tomorrow.

I told Harlan what had happened with Jen the night before and that day, told him how upset she had seemed. He said, "Can you blame her? Honestly, I'm surprised she's being as cordial as she is."

"Cordial?" I asked. "You think this is cordial?"

"Danny," he said. "We both know you're a good cop. I'm not saying that just to make you feel good. I couldn't give a rat's ass about your self-esteem. Every cop I've ever met thinks they're better at the job than anybody else. So what? It doesn't make you special. Most cops are good at their jobs. Sure, a lot of them are assholes and douchebags, but they still try to do their job right, and usually they do. You close a lot of cases. Good for you. So does everybody else on your squad. Being a good cop isn't that big of a deal."

"Why are you telling me this?"

"Because if you're not careful you're going to fuck it all up."

• • •

The next morning, it still took two hours after they told me my CT scan looked good for them to release me. I was so intent on getting out of the hospital, I hadn't thought about what would come next. I sent a group text to Patrick and Jen. They're letting me go. What should I do?

My clothes were in a plastic bag in the closet. The T-shirt was dirty from the asphalt of the parking lot and there was still a piece of duct tape stuck to one of the legs of my jeans. I pulled a latex glove from the dispenser on the wall next to the hand sanitizer. After slipping my hand into it, I carefully pulled the tape off and dropped it into the now-empty plastic bag. Any trace evidence would probably be useless because of cross-contamination, but I saved it just the same. They should have taken all my clothes, anyway. I wondered why they hadn't. Did Patrick drop the ball?

"Hey, Danny," someone said from the doorway.

I looked up from tying my shoes to see Lauren Terrones. She was in uniform and, I assumed, on duty.

"Hi, Lauren."

She could tell I was surprised to see her. "I took over for Mears out in the lobby. Jen just called me and said you were ready to go."

I didn't know whether to be upset that Jen didn't seem to be talking to me, or grateful that she had apparently arranged for someone I knew to pick me up. "Do you know where I'm supposed to go?"

"Jen said to take you home to get cleaned up, then back to the station to see Lieutenant Ruiz." I always had to remind myself she had less than two years on the job. She'd gone to college and law school before joining the LBPD with the first new class of recruits we'd had since the beginning of the recession. Being older and more experienced than her fellow rookies had served her well. She'd excelled at the academy and had glowing reports from her field-training officers.

"I hope you didn't get in trouble or anything," I said.

"Why?" she asked.

"Because you must have pissed somebody off to get stuck with babysitting duty."

She looked puzzled. "Babysitting? I don't know what you mean. Ruiz said Jen recommended me for this. I was happy to help."

"You heard what happened the other day, right? Nobody's very pleased with me right now."

"Where did you get that idea? Everybody's just glad you're okay."

"Maybe not everybody."

"Stop it," she said firmly, surprising me.

"That's a lot of attitude for a rookie."

"I'm not a rookie anymore."

"I stand corrected."

"And Jen told me not to put up with any of your shit."

The lecture I'd been expecting from Ruiz since I had left the hospital never came. Instead, he sat me down in his office with his hand on my shoulder and said, "Jesus, I'm glad you're back. You had us worried." He stepped around behind his desk and sat down. There was a rare smile on his face. "How's your head?"

"Not too bad," I said. The constant headache had become so normal at that point, I barely paid attention to it anymore. It's surprising how quickly you can become used to pain once you have some experience with it.

"Good," he said. "Traumatic brain injury is serious business."

That was the first time anyone had mentioned TBI to me, even though it had been worming its way around my imagination since I woke up in the hospital. I had Googled it, but was hoping my self-diagnosis had been off base. It wasn't. My grade-three concussion qualified.

"I seem to be doing okay," I said, hoping it was true.

He said "Good" again and I could tell he was preparing himself to say something he didn't want to say. I was pretty sure I knew what it was going to be.

"Yesterday, I officially took you off the Denkins case and made Jen the primary."

"I understand," I said.

He sighed and seemed relieved that I didn't argue with him. "I'm sorry I had to do it. But there's clearly a link between the bombing and the suicide investigation."

I still didn't want to acknowledge it, but my attacker warning me off of the interview with Lucinda couldn't have meant anything else. But I also knew that until the case was closed—or, failing that, until it cooled down considerably—I'd still be considered a target. What I was unsure of was what that meant.

"We've got two choices," Ruiz said. "You can use some vacation time, but only if you want to get out of town for a while. We don't have the manpower to keep someone with you 24-7 if you're just going to be hanging out at home."

Maybe Julia would want to take a week and go away someplace. We hadn't taken a trip together yet. It might be good for us. The thought left as quickly as it had come. It would be hard enough for me not to be working the Denkins case, but to walk away completely? I couldn't do it. At least if I was here I'd be able to follow Jen's progress, maybe keep a toe in the water.

I didn't really need to ask about the other choice, but I did. "And the alternative?"

"Administrative duty, keep you at your desk for a while. Besides, that's all the doctor has cleared you for at this point. That's what you'd be doing anyway."

"Okay," I said.

He nodded. I imagined he thought things were going much more smoothly than he had anticipated. "How do you feel about Officer Terrones?"

"She's good. Jen's right. I like her. Why?"

"I've gotten her temporarily reassigned from patrol. She'll be backing you up whenever you're not in the station. It'll work out well with you staying at Jen's house."

"You think I should still be there?"

"Yes," he said. "Don't you?"

I did, but I couldn't bring myself to believe Jen would agree. She wouldn't even return my texts. But that's not what I told Ruiz. "If he was keeping close-enough tabs on me to know when I got in the shower, I'm sure he knows I'm staying at Jen's house. I'm worried about putting her and Lauren at risk."

"I don't know," he said, chewing on the idea. "You had a bag over your head, but did you get an impression of the guy? Think he was a heavy hitter? He the kind of guy who'll drive by with a car full of bangers and AK-47s?"

"I couldn't tell, not really. He didn't sound street, or foreign. But he apparently has access to South African antipersonnel mines."

"He does," Ruiz said. "But if he's that serious, why didn't he just kill you when he had the chance?" He let that sink in, then added, "If he doesn't want one dead cop on his hands, it doesn't seem very likely he'd want three."

"Still."

"Danny, somebody's got to watch your back for a while. They're up for it. They want to do it."

I wondered if he'd talked to Jen recently. "All right," I said.

We talked for a few more minutes about my other open cases and how I'd prioritize things now that the Denkins case was out of my hands.

"One last thing," he said. "Patrick and Jen will need to consult with you, but give them the space they need. You're going to want to keep your fingers in the pie, but don't. Let them work."

. . .

There's always more work to do. When a new case comes in, it jumps immediately to the front of the line. Often, there's little actual investigative work required. It's perfectly clear who killed whom, and it's just a matter of documenting the incident and passing everything up the line to the prosecutors. Other times, it will take a few days or weeks of sorting through the evidence until we reach the conclusion that was more or less forgone the moment the body of the victim was discovered. There are others still, fortunately a small minority, that don't offer answers to our questions of who and why. We run out of leads, or don't have any to begin with. We follow the stream of evidence until it runs dry. Every homicide detective has a backlog of these cases, waiting for either that new bit of information that will bring them back to life or the lack of it that will eventually consign them to the open/unsolved files.

I was sitting at my desk sorting through my open cases and prioritizing them, making lists of things to review and follow up on, looking for new questions to ask or new threads to pull, when Patrick and Jen came into the squad room. He said something I couldn't quite hear and she laughed.

"Hey, guys," I said, raising my hand in a halfhearted wave.

"Danny," Patrick said. "How are you doing?"

They came over to my desk, Patrick more enthusiastically than Jen.

"Not too bad," I said. "Still have a headache."

Nobody said anything, and I wondered if the silence felt as awkward to them as it did to me. To break it, I said, "I talked to Ruiz. I'll be riding the desk for a while. I made copies of all my notes and files for you. The murder book's on your desk, Jen." It took every bit of willpower I could muster not to ask them about the investigation. They must have had something new. How did Jen's interview with Lucinda Denkins go? Did they get anything from the van? What about Joe? Had they talked to Dave about Kobe's case? Was there any progress on identifying S. Wise and C. Shepard? I kept my questions to myself, shoved them down into that deep empty pit where I keep my emotions. "Let me know if you need anything, okay?"

Patrick said, "Thanks, we will."

"I've been listening to *I Was There Too*," I said. "Napalm smells best in the evening."

He laughed. "Have you gotten to the one with Stephen Tobolowsky yet?"

"That's my favorite so far. *Groundhog Day* and *Deadwood*. Doesn't get better than that."

"We're getting takeout for lunch," he said. "Anything sound good?"

I smiled as pleasantly as I could. "Whatever you guys are getting is great."

Patrick went back to his desk. Jen remained where she stood, leaning against a file cabinet, arms crossed in front of her chest. She stared at me, frowning, her expression impossible to read. "How long until you follow up with the doctor about your head injury?"

•   •   •

While I was trying to decide whether to eat the second half of the pastrami sandwich or save it for later, Jen sent me an e-mail. The body of the message was blank, but the subject line said "Interview" and there were two attachments. The first was a written report, the second an audio file. I opened both files, put my earbuds in, and read while I listened. Cross-referencing between the words and Jen's description was the next-best thing to being there.

•   •   •

Jen had met Lucinda downstairs and brought her back up to the squad room. Marty was the only one there. Jen's phone rang, and she looked at the display and said, "Could you excuse me for a minute? I really need to take this." She answered the call and asked whoever was on the other end to hold on. "Marty?"

"Yeah?" he said.

"Could you do me a favor and get Ms. Denkins set up for her interview?"

"Sure," he said with a smile. "No problem."

Jen stepped out into the hallway and ended the call while Marty led Lucinda into the small interview room and sat her down at the table pushed up against the wall. The carpet and the walls were the same dull gray. The table and two chairs were gray as well, just a few shades lighter. The walls were bare, and the light fixture recessed into the ceiling flooded the room with a harsh fluorescence.

"Can I get you anything?" he asked her. "Coffee, water?"

"No," she said. "I'm okay."

He closed the door and joined Jen back in the squad room. "How long are you going to make her wait?"

"Not long," she said.

Seven minutes later, Jen opened the door and found Lucinda waiting patiently. "I'm so sorry to keep you waiting," she said.

Lucinda looked up at her and said, "Oh, that's okay."

Jen sensed she was a bit apprehensive, but didn't detect any traces of anxiety or fear. "I'm not sure why Marty left you in here," she said. "I wanted him to show you into the conference room. Why don't we go in there? It will be more comfortable."

"All right," Lucinda said. She picked up her purse and stood to join Jen, who led her out and down the hallway to the conference room.

It wasn't anything special, just a big rectangular table with eight chairs around it. But the table was wood and the chairs had fabric on the seats and backs, and there was a poster of the Long Beach skyline on one wall and a window on the other. And there was a clock. It was just like thousands of other conference rooms. It was only after someone had spent a while in the claustrophobic cell of the interrogation room that the conference room seemed warm and inviting.

That was the effect Jen was counting on. "What would you like to drink? Coffee? Water?"

"Just water would be okay."

Jen went to the break room next door and came back with two bottles of Aquafina.

"Here you go," she said, sitting down next to Lucinda. She put her phone on the table beside a notepad. "I just need to record this," she said, reaching over and touching the screen.

She started with small talk, asking Lucinda how she was holding up, about work, whether she'd been able to get into her father's apartment without any trouble. She went on for a few minutes, until it seemed more like a conversation than an interview. Subtly, Jen led her to more discussion of her father. Lucinda didn't seem to notice the transition.

"How is Joe doing?" Jen asked.

"I don't know. He seems like, in some ways he's taking it even harder than me."

Jen let the opportunity for a direct question about Joe pass, and instead went at it obliquely. "Your dad liked Joe, didn't he?"

"Yes," Lucinda said. Her voice was weighted with sadness. "He worried about him businesswise, but he really cared about him."

"That's why your father invested in the restaurant?"

"Yes, he was really hoping that would work out." A hint of optimism slipped into her tone, as if the failing of Winter was still something that could be forestalled, but it disappeared just as quickly as she continued. "We all were, of course."

"But it didn't?"

"No, it didn't."

"How did your dad feel about that? Did he take it personally?"

"He was disappointed, but I don't think so. I even went to him and asked if he could help a little more. I knew he'd already given Joe a lot, but I thought maybe if he could just see him through a couple more months until the business picked up, that might be all we needed."

Jen waited before asking the next question, to give Lucinda a chance to continue. She did.

"There was another investor who pulled out at the last minute," Lucinda said. "After the last minute, really. Right when the opening was happening. Joe thought it was too late to postpone again, that it would cost more than going through with the plan."

"This other investor," Jen said, sounding as if the question were an afterthought, "is he someone your dad knew?"

"No. Goran was someone Joe worked with before. At one of the restaurants where he was assistant manager down in Laguna. I think Goran was the co-owner or something."

Jen hadn't written anything on the notepad. While Lucinda hadn't seemed to notice the gradual transition into the formal part of the interview, she was surely aware of it now. Unless Jen wrote constantly, Lucinda might take notice of the specifics she was discussing when the notes were taken and be able to discern what information Jen seemed to find most interesting.

"Did you know him? Goran?" Jen asked.

"I met him once, years ago, when Joe worked for him, but I hadn't seen him since then."

"How did your dad take it when the business failed?"

"He was okay. He felt bad, of course, but he was actually really supportive. I never told Joe, but he helped us with mortgage payments a few times afterwards."

"It didn't seem to hurt him financially, your dad?"

"No, I don't think so. He wasn't rich or anything, but he always told me to never invest anything you can't afford to lose. So I don't think he ever did."

"Are you going to be okay with the house payments now?"

"I hope so. We're supposed to meet with Dad's lawyer about his will. I keep putting it off. But I think we'll be all right."

"Good. I'm glad to hear that," Jen said warmly. "It sounds like your dad gave you guys a lot of support."

"He did. But not just money. It wasn't like that. That wasn't even the most important part. He was always there for us, you know?" Her voice cracked on the last few words of her sentence. She'd been fine with the financial stuff. This was more abstract. Now, she was dealing more palpably with the loss.

"Do you need a minute?" Jen asked.

"No, I'm okay."

"I talked to a lot of the tenants in your dad's building. They liked him. A few of them said he was the best landlord they ever had."

"Yeah," Lucinda said. "He was like that."

"Do you know any of them?"

"Not well. I've met Harold a few times. He lives in one of the studios? A few others, but just to nod or say hi to."

"Did you know Kobe?"

"No, I don't think so." She thought about it. "Kobe, like the basketball player?"

"Yes," Jen said. "He was renting the other studio."

"Oh, he was the young Asian guy, right?"

"Yes, that's him."

"I've seen him once or twice. Why? Do you think he had something to do with my dad's death?"

"We don't know. But we do need to talk to him. He hasn't been home lately."

Jen kept talking to Lucinda, but she'd gotten most of what she wanted. Her goal with the close was to fade out the same way she'd faded in. A few minutes later, she said, "Thank you very much for coming in, Lucinda. It's really been a big help."

"I wanted to. I want to help," she said, sounding almost sad about the interview coming to an end. The dynamic wasn't unusual. When someone felt like they could contribute to the murder investigation of a loved one, an interview often gave them a way to feel useful, as if they were making a difference, and sometimes they were sorry to let go of that feeling. Unless they were guilty or holding something back. Then they usually felt so glad to be done they couldn't hide their relief.

• • •

When I took the earbuds out and closed the files, I knew Jen had aced the interview. Honestly, she did much better than I likely would have.

I also came away convinced that Lucinda didn't have anything to do with her father's death. That gave me some comfort, until I remembered I was off the case and what I thought didn't really matter at all anymore.

The stack of files and the notes I'd made about them before were waiting for me, but I tried to ignore them while I logged on to Motortrend.com and started shopping for a new car.

• • •

I've never really cared that much about cars. Megan helped me choose the Camry and I hadn't really considered another car since then. For most people, a new car is a big deal, a major change. Maybe even a fresh start. *This is a big deal,* I told myself, *it matters.* I decided to treat it like what mattered most to me—an investigation. By the time Lauren came to pick me up at five thirty, I'd pretty much narrowed it down to three choices.

One, just get another Camry. It was the easy choice, even if it was lazy. My old Camry had served me well, if not very excitingly. Aside from a single flat tire and a one-time-only dead battery, I'd never had a problem with it. I just got in and started it up, and it took me anyplace I wanted to go for well over a decade. Also, Jen's dad had spent his entire career working for Toyota and I wasn't sure I could face him at the anniversary party if I bought another brand. Still, I also wasn't sure loyalty to the model and a desire to avoid a bit of social awkwardness were enough to overcome my desire to try something new and different.

Two, opt for the equivalent model from Honda, which every car writer and their mother said was the far superior choice. It had been on *Car and Driver's* ten-best list for like a hundred years. But that equivalent was the Accord, and I was fairly certain that all the white Accords I had imagined were following me in the last week had caused me to develop a conditioned stress response to the model. I might be okay with it, though, if I never looked at it over my shoulder or in a mirror.

Three, the Subaru Legacy. It wasn't quite as popular with the auto-magazine staffers as the Honda, but the customer-loyalty numbers were through the roof. And while it didn't impress the *Road & Track* crowd very much, the *Consumer Reports* guys were keen enough on it to make it their midsized sedan "Top Pick." I was also pretty sure it came with granola and a kayak, both of which would probably be good for me. And Julia had a Subaru. Hers was a Forester, though, and I've never been much of an SUV guy. But I couldn't buy the same model as her anyway because that would just be weird.

When I explained the situation to Lauren in the car on the way home and asked what she thought I should do, she looked at me like I'd just asked for advice about which knitting needles would be best to use to make some booties for my grandbabies. "I don't know," she said. "But I'm glad there won't be another Camaro in the parking garage."

• • •

When we got back to Jen's house, I was surprised to see a Sheriff's Department Yukon parked in front. There was a K-9 insignia on the side.

Lauren went first up the driveway, calling out "Hello, anyone here?" loudly enough for anyone in the backyard to hear. As I followed her up the driveway, my foot slipped off the edge of the concrete and I nearly stumbled onto the lawn.

Around the corner came Steven Gonzales, the bomb-squad deputy who'd swept my duplex for explosives last week, with a dog at his heel. God, had it really only been a week?

"Beckett?" he said, spotting me behind Lauren. "Heard you might show up while I was here."

Patrick must have told him. And asked him to check the house, too. I introduced him to Lauren. He held her hand too long and said, "Call me Steve."

She waited for him to let go while looking directly at the scar on his face. "What happened?" she asked.

"Iraq," he said, releasing her hand.

"It sure left a mark," she said.

"That's not the only one."

"What's that?" she asked, pointing at some ink on his bicep that extended below the cuff of his short-sleeved uniform shirt. I wondered if the LASD still had their no-visible-tattoos policy.

Gonzales said, "That's my Explosive Ordinance Disposal badge."

"The scars weren't enough of a reminder?" she asked, touching the tattoo. "Are those wings?"

"It's a wreath," he said. I think I saw him flexing a bit.

I gave them a few seconds in case either one of them wanted to engage in any more flirtatious banter. Neither did, so I said, "Is the house going to explode?"

Gonzales looked down at the dog as if to confirm his assessment and said, "I don't think so, but if you'll let us inside, we'll make sure."

He and the dog walked through the house, then the garage and Lauren's place in back. After he'd cleared them all, I walked out to the SUV at the curb with him. "I'll let Glenn know everything's secure," he said, opening the back door and letting the dog in.

"Thanks," I said.

"Can I ask you something?"

"Sure." I knew what he was going to ask.

"What's the deal with Terrones?" At least he pronounced her name right, all three syllables. He even got the Spanish inflection that I could never manage to.

"She's a good cop."

He nodded. "You think she might want to—"

"I'll ask her," I said.

"Thanks, man."

He drove away and I went back inside and found Lauren in the kitchen. "I thought you had a girlfriend," I said.

"I do."

"Gonzales wanted me to give you his number. You want it?"

"Not really," she said, surveying the open refrigerator in front of her. "But why don't you text it to me so you won't have to lie when he asks."

• • •

Julia came over again. Honestly, I was embarrassed that we had to keep seeing each other at Jen's house. I suggested we hold off for the night, but she wouldn't hear of it. It felt like being in high school again—sitting on someone else's couch with a girl and hoping not to get caught. At least I'd convinced Lauren that we'd be okay with her out back in her own place. She'd told me that it didn't feel right hanging out at home while she was technically on the clock. Especially after Jen had texted her saying she'd be home late and that Lauren should keep an eye on me. Eventually I'd worn her down and convinced her to give Julia and me some privacy.

When I complained to Julia about feeling awkward, she said, "I think you're overreacting."

"I don't think I am." We were sitting on the couch again, but hadn't turned the TV on.

"How's your head feeling?"

"Still have a headache."

"Any other symptoms? Have you felt dizzy at all or nauseous? Confused or sluggish?"

"No, I feel okay except for the headache. The doctor said I should expect that for a few days."

"When do you go back to see him?"

"Not until the end of the week, unless I have a problem. Why?"

"You seem more irritable than usual."

"They took my case away. I'm on desk duty for, shit, I don't even know how long. So yeah, I'm irritable."

"Are you angry at me?"

"No," I said, surprised. "Does it sound like I am?"

"A little bit."

"I'm sorry."

"It's okay." She slid closer to me and lifted my arm up so I'd put it around her, and she put her head on my shoulder. "Let's watch season two. See how Mr. Bates and Anna are doing."

I fumbled around with the two remotes until I got the show to start streaming on the big flat-screen across the room.

But even as the opening credits rolled, I couldn't stop thinking about the fact that irritability and behavior changes were two of the things the neurologist told me to be on the lookout for.

• • •

It was after ten when Jen came home. Julia had already gone, and I was in the kitchen looking for something stronger than cabernet and not finding anything. I heard voices outside and looked out the window to see her conferring with Lauren just inside the gate on the side of the house, their faces illuminated from below by the pathway lighting along the edge of the driveway.

Jen came inside and said, "Lauren says things are under control."

"Yeah, it's been quiet. Julia just went home a little while ago."

"Sorry I missed her. She holding up okay?"

"Pretty well, I think."

She studied my eyes while we talked.

"You nailed the interview with Lucinda," I said.

She reached to the wall behind the sink and flipped a light switch. A recessed fixture in the ceiling directly over our heads lit up. Holding her extended index finger in front of my face, she said, "Watch." I stared at her fingertip as she moved it back and forth horizontally across my field of vision. When she was satisfied, she flipped the light off.

I stopped myself from making a joke about standing on one foot, or doing a walk-and-turn. A joke about field sobriety tests wouldn't help me.

"What were you and Patrick working on?"

"Cross-referencing cell-phone records." She opened the refrigerator and took out a plastic container of premixed greens.

"You hungry?" she asked, dumping salad in a bowl and adding diced chicken and shredded cheese.

"No, I ate."

She tossed some sunflower seeds and vinaigrette into the salad with a fork and sat down at the table to eat. "I used your notes."

"What?" I said.

She forked some lettuce and chicken into her mouth and chewed before she spoke. "For the interview with Lucinda."

"I wondered."

"It was a good prep."

"Thanks."

Another bite.

Then another.

I wanted to apologize again. To tell her how sorry I was and ask for her forgiveness. But she seemed to be going out of her way to let me know that she wasn't interested in talking, so I didn't. "I guess I'll turn in," I said.

She looked up from her salad and gave what someone who didn't know her as well as I did might mistake for a smile. "Good night."

After I brushed my teeth and went into the bedroom, I could see that there was a light breeze outside, just strong enough to make the shadows from the tree in the yard dance on the translucent window shade. I turned my head on the pillow while I listened to P.J. Soles from *Halloween* talk about getting killed by Michael Myers.

CHAPTER FIFTEEN

WHITHER MUST I WANDER

I was at my desk when Harold Craig called me.

"How are you doing, Harold?" I asked.

"All right, I guess." He didn't sound all right, but I couldn't remember him ever sounding that way.

"What can I help you with?"

"Well, last night I heard someone outside knocking on Kobe's door, so I peeked out the window and saw that it was a young lady."

"Can you describe her?"

"Yes. She was young, Kobe's age. Thin, with blonde hair."

"Did you notice anything else about her?"

"Well, I was nervous," he said. "But I opened the door."

I waited for him to continue, but he didn't. "Did you talk to her?"

"Yes. She said she needed to talk to Kobe."

"What did you say?"

"I told her that he hadn't been home for several days."

"How did she take that?"

"Well, she'd already looked worried, but when I said that, she said 'oh' very quietly, and she got very anxious." He paused for a few seconds. "I can tell when someone's anxious," he said. "I can see the signs."

I know you can, Harold, I know. "What happened then?"

"She started to go, but I stopped her. Asked her to wait. Then I went back inside and wrote your phone number down, so I could give her the card you left me."

"And she took it?"

"Yes. I told her she should call you, that you could help. That you were kind."

"Did you tell her that Kobe was dead?"

"No. She was so upset that I thought it might be too much for her."

"That was a good call, Harold. What happened next?"

"Nothing. She just went downstairs, took her bike from where she'd left it leaning up against the wall, and went out the back gate into the alley."

"She had a bike?"

"Yes."

"Thank you very much, Harold. This is going to help us out a lot. You did the right thing."

"I did?"

"Absolutely."

"Good. I'm glad to hear that."

I was just about to end the call when I heard his voice again.

"Detective Beckett?"

"Yes?"

"I was wondering, if it's not too much trouble, could I get another one of your cards? I gave the one I had to the young lady."

"Sure, Harold. It's no trouble at all."

As soon as I disconnected, I called Patrick.

"That happened last night?" he said.

"Yes."

"You think she'll call?"

"I hope so. Could be the break we need." As soon as the words were out of my mouth, I realized I'd used "we" instead of "you."

Patrick didn't catch it, or just decided to let it go. "You'll call me if you hear from her?"

"The second it happens," I said.

"Good," he said. "This is good." He seemed to be talking to himself as much as he was to me.

I ended the call, put my phone down in the middle of my desk, and stared at it, willing it to ring.

· · ·

The phone didn't ring. Well, it did, but not with the call we were hoping for from the mysterious young woman. It had only taken a few days of not being able to leave my desk to turn me into a clock watcher. When Lauren came to pick me up, I already had my messenger bag packed and ready to go and had been watching the second hand on the old clock on the wall, above the window to Ruiz's office, for two minutes.

I asked her to stop at Gelson's, even though it was out of our way, to pick up something to grill, fresh vegetables for a salad, and a good bottle of wine.

At Jen's house, I lit the barbecue and turned the heat low to warm it up. I wasn't much for cooking, but I knew my way around a grill well enough. Once it was going, I went into the kitchen, got out a big steel bowl, tossed some baby spinach in with the bagged salad, and added some cherry tomatoes and sunflower seeds on top.

Jen didn't let me know when she was on the way. I hadn't expected her to. But when she sent a text message to Lauren, I turned up the heat and put the chicken and beef skewers I'd bought on the grill and went back inside to finish the salad.

"What are you doing?" Lauren asked.

"Making dinner."

She raised her eyebrows and said, "You okay?"

"Why does everybody keep asking me that?"

"Because you had a major concussion a couple of days ago and you're acting weird."

"Making dinner isn't weird."

"It is for you."

I stopped what I was doing and looked her in the eye. "I'm okay."

"You think if you make a nice dinner one time, everything's going to go back to normal and Jen's going to forgive you?"

The timer on my phone started chiming. It was time to turn the skewers. I picked it up and silenced it.

She sighed and said, "It's not about her forgiving you. She's still blaming herself for letting it happen."

"That's stupid."

"Then you should understand it."

"You know you're on the clock, right?" I meant it to sound light and funny, but it came out bitter and hard and I felt like an asshole.

"My apologies, sir. I best get back to work, then."

She went outside and I expected her to head to her place, but she didn't. After pacing to the far end of the yard and back again, she took up position with her back against one of the support posts for the pergola and gazed out past the gate and down the driveway. It was a solid sentry post.

Her eye never wavered when I went outside to turn the skewers.

• • •

Jen and I ate mostly in silence. She gave me a truncated progress report of the day's work that didn't tell me anything I didn't already know.

"Thanks," she said when she finished the last piece of chicken on her plate. "That was good."

"You're welcome," I said. "It's the least I could do after you've put me up for so long."

She drank the last of the wine in her glass. I reached for the bottle to pour her some more, but she stopped me by raising her hand a few inches off the table and showing me her palm. "I'm good."

"It wasn't your fault," I said.

"Don't even start."

"I feel like shit," I said, looking down at the paper napkin I'd balled up in my fist. "What can I do?"

"Nothing." The bland evenness of her voice cut me deeper than any shout or cry could have. She looked me in the eye and I could see her recognize the pain I was feeling. "Be patient, all right? It'll get better."

She picked up her plate and mine, took them inside, and put them in the sink. In the years we'd been partners, we'd had many disagreements and I'd frustrated her in more ways than I could even come close to remembering, but I'd never felt this kind of distance before. I'd never felt her pulling away the way she seemed to be doing.

All I could think was, *But what if it doesn't?*

. . .

It was lunchtime the next day when the call came. Jen had another afternoon in court and Patrick was in the valley conferring again with the ATF. Everybody else was out of the squad room, either working or eating.

My phone was on the desk, but the woman Harold had given my card to still hadn't called, and I figured the window of time was closing. She'd had my number for more than a day and a half. If she was going to call, I thought, she probably already would have.

Still, though, when the phone started vibrating on the desk and the screen lit up with a number I didn't recognize, I felt a welcome tingle of anticipation in my stomach.

"Detective Beckett," I said.

"Uh, hello?" Her voice was quiet, barely above a whisper.

"Hi, what can I do for you?"

"I think I need some help?" She was afraid of something. I couldn't be sure if it was me or something else.

"Is this Kobe's friend?"

"Kobe?" she said uncertainly. "Oh, you mean Ryan?"

I wrote the name down, even though I knew I wouldn't forget it. "Yes, Ryan. Tell me how I can help you."

"There's someone following me. A man."

"Where are you? Are you in danger right now?"

"No," she whispered. "Not right this minute. I'm in the bathroom at Viento y Agua. It's a coffee—"

"I know it. The man who's following you. Is he in the shop or outside?"

"In the shop."

"Do you think he knows you're aware of him?"

"I don't think so."

"What's your name?" I asked.

"Kayla."

"Kayla, I'm Danny. Stay in the bathroom for now. I need to make another call to get you some help. Don't hang up. I'm going to be right here listening. You just say my name if you need me, okay?"

"Yes."

I switched her call to the speaker and put the cell down on my desk. She needed help immediately, but I didn't want to spook her tail. I called the watch commander and quickly explained the situation. She'd send a patrol unit to Viento, but it would remain out of sight unless needed.

"Kayla? You okay?"

"Yes."

"Can you describe the man to me?"

"Uh, he's kind of average-looking."

"Young? Old?"

"Thirties, maybe?"

"What's he wearing?

"Shorts, I think, with a light-blue shirt. The sleeves are rolled up."

"Is he white?"

"I think so, but dark hair, kind of tan. He looks like the kind of guy you see coming to coffee shops to work."

"That's good. Hang on for a minute. I need to make another call."

"All right."

I put the cell back down on the desk and picked up the landline.

Jen was in court, but I tried her anyway. The call went straight to her voice mail. I didn't want to take the time to leave a message, so I disconnected. Patrick was at least an hour away, probably longer with the traffic. I didn't have a car and it would take too long to check one out of the motor pool.

Lauren answered on the second ring.

"Where are you?" I asked.

"Home. Why?" She could hear the urgency in my voice.

"How fast can you get to Viento y Agua?"

"Ten minutes."

She was already in her car by the time I finished explaining.

I hung up and called the watch commander and told her I needed a ride and I'd be there in two minutes. She was still talking when I put the phone down, picked up my cell and earbuds, and headed downstairs.

● ● ●

There was a patrol officer waiting for me and we rolled out Code Three. I kept Kayla talking on the phone, but it was hard to hear her over the siren. I killed it when we turned left on the red at Junipero and cut up to Fourth Street.

A white bubble popped up on the screen of my phone. It was a text from Lauren. `I'm here. Outside. Next door at yoga place.`

`Stay put. Almost there.`

"Kayla? How's it going?"

"I'm still in the—shit, someone's knocking!"

"It's okay," I said. "Tell them you're almost done and flush the toilet."

She did.

"Now turn on the faucet and let it run."

I had the driver pull up to the curb in a red zone a few doors down from the coffeehouse, far enough away that no one inside would be able to see the car. Lauren was on the sidewalk and I could see the patrol unit around the corner on Termino. I walked toward it and motioned for Lauren to follow.

To the driver, I said, "Go around the block and cover the other side."

"Got it," he replied, rolling away.

"Kayla, how you doing?"

"I'm okay," she said.

"We're right outside, so everything's all right. I want you to unlock the door and go back to where you were sitting and just pretend like everything's fine. Can you do that for me?"

"Yes?"

"Good," I said. "I'll be coming inside in just a minute. I'll let you know when I'm moving. We're almost done with this. There's nothing to worry about."

Lauren said, "You don't think the guy who's following her will think something's up with her twenty-minute bathroom break?"

"Maybe. We'll just have to see how he plays it."

I told the two officers—a man and a woman—that I'd be sending Kayla out and that I wanted them to take her back to the station and wait for me.

There was a silver Golf in a loading zone across the street from the coffeehouse. "That's your VW, right?" I asked Lauren.

"Yes," she replied.

"Get in it and see if you can tail the guy when he comes out."

"I've never tailed anyone before," she said.

"That's all right. Do your best. If you can get a plate number, we'll call that a win."

I started around the corner. "Kayla?"

"Yes?"

"I'm on my way inside. You're going to see a tall guy with brown hair. That's me. Pretend like you don't notice me."

"Okay."

"Wait until I get a coffee and then I distract the guy who's following you," I said. "As soon as you see me get tangled up with him, grab your stuff, go outside past the yoga studio next door and around the corner. There will be a police car waiting for you. Get inside and they'll take you to the station and I'll meet you there. Got that?"

"Yes."

"Good. Here I come."

Viento y Agua was pretty much everybody's favorite coffeehouse in Long Beach. At least everybody that I knew. It had a Día de los Muertos vibe to its decor and did triple duty, serving also as a performance space and an art gallery. Walking inside, I spotted Kayla at once, but I was careful not to look directly at her. On the right side was a lounge area with sofas and easy chairs. She was in the corner by the front window with her feet up, staring at her phone and moving her thumbs as if she were typing. She didn't look up at me. Good girl.

The other side of the room was all tables and chairs, with a small stage in the back. Kayla's tail was sitting with his back against the white wall that served as the primary gallery display space. I didn't look at him as I headed straight back to the service counter in the corner opposite the stage, but I did manage to snap a few photos with my phone. If he noticed, he didn't give me any indication.

"Just a regular coffee, please," I said to the barista. He had dreadlocks and a thick beard with a waxed handlebar mustache. I didn't allow myself time to try to figure out the odd combination.

"For here or to go?" he asked.

"To go."

He didn't seem to approve of my choice. I paid him and took my bad-person disposable cup over to the other side of the shop and began looking at the art on the walls. The paintings were all of human figures with animal heads. They were actually kind of cool, whimsical images that looked like watercolors or pastels, but I didn't really look too closely at any of them because I was keeping my peripheral vision trained on the man in the light-blue shirt. He had a laptop open on the table in front of him, but I couldn't see what was on the screen.

The third time I caught him glancing at Kayla, I started moving closer to him, all the while pretending to study the art on the wall. I was looking at a walrus man with a baseball bat who had just taken a swing and was finishing his follow-through when I made my move.

Only a few feet away from the blue shirt, I pretended to stumble and poured half my coffee on his shoulder.

He screamed and stood up. "Jesus!" he yelled. "What the fuck's wrong with you?"

Before I could pretend to apologize, he shoved me back into another table and I stumbled, almost falling over. As I turned back toward him, I glanced at the door and I saw Kayla slipping outside.

When I looked back at him, I must have been smiling because he said, "What's so funny?"

I showed him my badge. "You just assaulted a police officer."

As that realization was sinking in, he looked across the room and saw that Kayla was gone. He sat back down and buried his face in his palms.

• • •

Patrick had two new witnesses to question when he got back to the station. As much as I would have loved to help, I knew I'd already stepped way over the line. When Ruiz heard, I expected consequences. I honestly didn't see any way around what I did, though. It needed to be done. We could have sent a patrol unit to pick Kayla up, but in all likelihood we would have lost the man who was following her, who we soon found out was named Avram Novak. Lauren could have gone with the patrol unit, but she had even less experience than the other officers who wound up at the scene. There was also the ticking clock that had left me no time to bring anyone else up to speed. And the fact that Kayla had my number and might have been hesitant to talk to anyone else.

I didn't have a choice. I had to respond.

And the road to hell is paved with extenuating circumstances.

"Why can't I just talk to *you*?" Kayla asked when I told her that Patrick would need to interview her.

"Because it's not my case."

"Then why did Ryan's neighbor have your card?"

"I was investigating something else."

"What?"

"His landlord was killed."

"Oh, no. Ryan really likes him." In her expression I could see the realization as it happened. "Do you think that's why Ryan disappeared? Does it have something to do with that?"

"It might."

"Do you think something happened to Ryan?" The worry was creasing the skin around her eyes and making her look older.

The lie I needed to tell her was too much to handle at the moment, so I withheld as much as I could. "Maybe," I said. Before she could ask anything else, I said, "Let me check with the detective who needs to talk to you, all right?"

She nodded and I went back into the squad room. I called Patrick. He told me he was southbound on the 710 and he'd be there soon. Jen was still in court, so I left her another voice mail.

The familiar twinge of anticipation and excitement that always came with a break in a case was humming through me. My mind was racing with the possibilities, the questions I wanted to ask, the connections I wanted to make, the new threads I wanted to pull. But I forced myself to stop, to try to let go.

Kayla was still in the conference room. It was getting a lot of use this week. "He'll be here in just a few minutes. Can I get you something to drink? Coffee, water, iced tea?"

"Just water?"

"Are you hungry?"

She shook her head.

Lauren was in the break room with a cup of coffee and a toasted bagel. "I missed lunch," she said. "What do we do now?"

"Wait," I said. "Patrick should be here any minute." Usually, I was good at waiting. It comes with the job. This was different. I wasn't waiting for my chance at the big play and my opportunity to score. No, this was waiting to hand off a ball I shouldn't even have had in my hands. Holding it, I discovered, and fighting every impulse that told me I should run for the goal, was worse than not being there at all.

Kayla was all right when I gave her a bottle of water, so I headed back to my desk. As I passed the lieutenant's office, Ruiz called my name.

"The girl's okay?" he said as I stood in his doorway.

"Yeah."

"Good."

I waited for him to tell me to sit down so he could rake me over the coals, but he didn't. When he realized I was still standing there, he said, "We'll talk about it later."

While I was relieved he decided to let me off the hook, at least temporarily, a small part of me almost wished he hadn't. Then at least I would have felt like I was still involved. The feeling reminded me of my days in uniform. I'd wanted to be a detective even before I joined the force, even before I'd taken my first criminal-justice course at CSULB. My father's job as a deputy sheriff, and his death when I was so young, left me with a fascination for both police work and homicide. I didn't understand until I spent a good amount of time with a therapist after Megan's death that I'd spent my whole life trying to fill the void he'd left in my life when he was killed. There was no mystery to his case, it was literally open and shut. The people who killed him were convicted and served their time. Justice was done. Still, I wondered why. Not "why" in the sense of the motive, that was clear enough. But the big why. The why of poets and philosophers and scientists.

When I was a younger cop and making my way up the ranks, I was continually frustrated by the everyday occurrence of responding to crimes, especially homicides—experiencing the acts and their aftermath, becoming enmeshed in them, and then having to let the cases go to the detectives who would arrive and take over, as we were sent on to the next crime and the next, always witnessing, but never being able to ask the questions that might lead to answers. Even after my first detective assignment, it still took years to understand that it wasn't the answers that filled the void. No, they were never enough, they never provided enough knowledge or satisfaction or closure. It wasn't the answers. It was the questions. As long as I could ask more questions, I could cope with the emptiness. They were what I fought with. I knew I'd never win, never understand the big why, but I knew that as long as I could keep questioning, like someone treading water in a vast ocean, I could keep myself afloat.

After I told Patrick everything I had to tell him, he said, "That's great, Danny. Why don't you call it a day? We've got it now."

On the way home I told Lauren I needed to stop at the store again.

"Gelson's again?"

"Doesn't matter," I said.

"You okay?"

"Yeah, it's just hard to be out of the loop."

"Tell me about it," she said.

I wondered how much Jen had told her about what was going on. About the two cases—the bombing of my car and the Denkins murder and how they had come together. She certainly hadn't gotten very much from me. "What do you know about all this?" I asked.

"Just that someone's after you and that it's somehow connected to the case you're working."

For days we'd just been telling her what to do and when to do it. And she had. No complaints. No questions asked. How had I forgotten what it was like to be a new patrol officer, just following orders, always in the dark, always wondering?

When we hit the Ralphs parking lot, I asked, "What do you want to know?"

She pulled into a parking spot, looked me in the eye, and said, "Everything."

I was still detailing the crime scene when we got to the checkout lane with a fifth of Grey Goose and a half gallon of fresh orange juice.

Before she turned the key in the ignition, she asked, "What would have happened if the gun had been in his right hand?"

"You'd be wearing your uniform right now and I'd be sleeping in my own bed tonight."

While she drove, I told her what I knew about the bombing of my car, the South African land mine, and the Serbian crew that might or might not have a connection to it.

In the kitchen, while I poured myself half a glass of vodka and topped it off with the juice, I was still talking about Kobe and his Post-it note and the discovery of his body. I asked Lauren if she wanted a drink.

"On the clock," she said, getting herself a Diet Coke out of the refrigerator.

"That's right." I lifted the glass and took a sip. "Victims don't get overtime."

"What?" she asked.

I explained it to her. She didn't think it was funny. We went outside and sat at the table under the pergola and I told her about Joe and Lucinda and the failed restaurant and the mystery investor. Then I refilled my glass and went on to Jen's interview and what we'd just done, speculating about Kayla and Novak and their possible connections.

"You left out the part when you got abducted," Lauren said.

"I thought you knew about that. Besides, I was unconscious for most of it." I hadn't had anything stronger than an occasional beer or glass of wine for a few months, and I was surprised how much I was feeling the effects of the vodka. The dull throb in my head began to soften, and only as it eased did I realize how strong it had been. Lifting the nearly empty glass off the table, I said, "At least my head feels better."

"Should you even be drinking? With the concussion, I mean."

"If I'd known how much it would help, I would have started as soon as I left the hospital."

"Seriously, how are you? Are you having any symptoms other than the headache?"

"No, I don't think so."

She studied me.

"Why?" I asked.

"You seem different."

"Different? How?"

"Well," she said. "A week ago, could you have imagined hanging out with me for two hours and telling me every detail of a case you were working on?"

That made me think. Could I imagine that? No, not really. But what did that mean? Was I behaving differently?

"I'm not working on the case anymore."

She laughed. "That's even worse. You would have taken a junior patrol officer to the liquor aisle at Ralphs and laid someone else's investigation on her? Come on."

Even though I didn't want to acknowledge it, Lauren had a point.

"Something is different," I said. "But I don't think it's the head injury."

"Jen?"

"I've never seen her like this. I think maybe I went too far over the line this time for her to try to pull me back." As I said the words, I found myself surprised that I was willing to admit this to her. And even more surprised that I was willing to admit it to myself.

Lauren didn't say anything, and I took her silence to mean that she thought I might be right.

After finishing my drink, I put the glass down on the table and stood up. My legs were unsteady and I had trouble finding my balance.

"She always pulls me back," I said, but I wasn't sure if I was talking to Lauren or to myself.

• • •

It was after eleven when Jen finally came home. The alcohol had worn off and left me feeling worse than I had before. My head was aching, and it had triggered my chronic pain. It felt like an electric fire was flowing up from the tips of my fingers all the way into my spine and exploding upward into my head.

I got up off the couch when I heard her close the front door and throw the deadbolt. She came into the kitchen and put her bag down on the table. The recognition of my pain flashed briefly in her eyes, but her voice was flat when she said, "Let's go sit in the living room."

She brought her notepad and sat in the leather club chair I'd helped her pick out at Crate & Barrel, while I went back to where I had been sitting on the couch. It was still warm.

I was afraid of what she was going to say about what I'd done earlier. Only a few days after my breaking protocol had resulted in an incident that put the department on high alert and terrified everyone I cared about, I'd broken the rules again. My right hand was shaking, so I clasped it in my left and lowered them both into my lap.

She sighed and I felt the muscles in my neck and jaw tighten in anticipation of what was coming next. But she surprised me. "I'm not sure if you did the right thing today, but you got the right results."

"What do you mean?" I asked, trying not to allow too much hopefulness to show.

"Looks like Avram Novak is a bad guy. We don't think it would have worked out well for Kayla if we hadn't brought him in today."

I resisted the impulse to ask questions and forced myself to let her talk.

She started with Kayla. She and Kobe, whose real name was Ryan Wong, had an on-again, off-again relationship that had begun when they'd both worked for Joe's restaurant, Winter. She'd been hired there as a server, but Ryan convinced her to join him and a few others on the delivery crew because the money was better. She found that hard to believe until he told her the reason why—they weren't just delivering mediocre gastropub food, they were also delivering pot. Kayla didn't know the extent of the dealer's network, but she liked Ryan and she trusted him, so she hesitantly agreed to him and the two others involved in the ring. She was C. Shepard on Kobe's Post-it note and burner.

When Jen mentioned that, I remembered the Wikipedia page I'd read. Gamers could play Commander Shepard in Mass Effect as either a man or a woman. I wondered if that meant that S. Wise and B. Darklighter were both guys.

The delivery service was a huge success. Ryan told her that even though he was the tacit supervisor of the delivery crew, Joe had set the whole thing up. Customers who wanted more than food would have to type a special code into the Comments section of the Winter website's online ordering page. To Ryan's surprise, though, they weren't successful enough to keep the restaurant afloat. Kayla said that Joe and Ryan wanted to keep things going after Winter had to close its doors. They managed things with the website for a while, but when that became too problematic, Joe had someone create a simple smartphone app that would do the same thing the online ordering system had done for them. That's where the aliases came from. Ryan got the burners so they'd have a way to communicate independently if they needed to.

Kayla didn't stay with them for long, though, because delivering a little pot on the side was one thing, and being a full-time drug dealer was something else. So she went back to serving, while Ryan and the others kept at it with the deliveries.

She had still been hooking up with Ryan pretty regularly, until he disappeared. Not long after that, she saw Novak for the first time. She spotted him at the gym. Then at the supermarket. Then on Second Street after one of her shifts. Then in a BMW that passed by while she was riding her bike along Ocean Boulevard. Ryan stopped returning her calls and text messages, so she went to his house and talked to his neighbor, found out he hadn't been there for days. She tried not to worry. Chalk it up to paranoia. Long Beach wasn't that big a city, right? You see people you know all the time. But when he showed up at Viento y Agua and it was clear he wasn't leaving until she did, it got to be too much. She thought about calling 911, but she wasn't sure it was an emergency. As she sat there longer and longer, she got more and more afraid. So she fished out the business card and made the call.

Jen kept speaking. Maybe it was because it was getting late, or because I was keeping my mouth shut and letting her talk, but I couldn't shake the feeling that she would rather not be telling me all this, at least not now, and that it was coming more from her sense of obligation than from a desire to address any need on my part. Even so, I didn't say anything and let her go on.

"You remember the guy Lucinda mentioned? Goran?" she asked me.

"Yeah, Joe's other investor."

"Well, his last name's Novak, too."

She told me the Organized Crime Detail had a file on him. He was medium fish in the big pond of Orange County, drugs and prostitution, mostly, and he was known to use a number of restaurants in which he invested to launder the income from operations. Patrick was now looking for support for a new theory—that the failure of Winter left Joe so indebted that he was desperate enough to not only try to continue the drug-delivery business but also, eventually, to kill Bill for the inheritance in order to get out from under Novak.

"Novak," I said. "Is that Serbian?"

Jen shook her head. "Croatian."

My eastern European geography was rusty. "That's close, though, right? Could there be a connection to the Serbian crew in the valley?"

"Patrick's looking into it," she said.

"Sounds like he's got a full plate."

"He does, but he's getting help from Organized Crime and the ATF guys. He's on top of it."

"When is he planning on putting Joe in the box?"

"Not until he knows more. Kayla's helping us find the other two from the contact list. And Dave's on board too because we know Kobe's murder is connected. We've got it covered."

I tried not to read too much into that, but the subtext was clear enough. They were doing fine without me.

She asked about my head and I told her it was fine.

"That's not what Lauren thinks. Go to the doctor tomorrow."

I didn't argue with her. "About Joe, when Patrick interrogates—"

"I already asked Ruiz. You can watch the video feed."

She got up and headed toward the hall. She wasn't looking at me when she said, "Good night."

● ● ●

I hadn't gotten a decent night's sleep—unless I counted my twelve hours of unconsciousness in the hospital—since the explosion, and I was feeling the dull weight of insomniac exhaustion pressing down on me. Sleep wouldn't come for hours, though. My mind was racing with all of the new information Jen had shared with me. There's a rush that comes with a big break in a case, and, even though I was not technically a part of the investigation anymore, I still felt it. I wanted to sit down with my notebook and start writing, trying to trace the connections between everyone involved in the investigation. I wanted to make lists and outlines and diagrams to make sense of it all. I wanted to do my job.

In the kitchen, I poured myself another glass of Grey Goose and orange juice and texted Julia. You still up? Sitting at the table, I sipped slowly and watched my phone, waiting, hoping for a message or a call. None came.

The *I Was There Too* theme song found its way back into my head.

> *Napalm smells best in the evening*
> *It's not worth believing what you heard . . .*

Without even trying, I'd somehow managed to memorize the lyrics.

Hoping to chase it out of my head, I went back into the living room and opened the Spotify app on my laptop. I clicked on the "Discover Weekly" tab, looking for something new to distract me. Nothing really caught my attention, though, and I thought of the old playlist I'd made a few years ago while I was recovering from my injury and trying to climb up out of my depression. In the haze after my concussion, I had remembered *Songs For My Funeral*, and it had been floating around in the back of my mind ever since. Switching to iTunes, I scrolled down until I found it.

As I looked at the list, I felt an unexpected sense of relief wash over me. I couldn't really explain it, but somehow looking back and remembering the darkness I'd been drowning in when I created the playlist seemed to make the darkness now less overwhelming. The hours I'd spent laying out the tracks, then revising the choices again and again, and the days I'd spent listening, still tweaking things, making adjustments here and there, had been a kind of boon for me, a way of figuring out how to climb out of the hole I had been wallowing in.

I could still remember the look on Jen's face when I'd accidentally left it open on the desktop. The concerned sadness in her eyes when she thought I might be contemplating suicide. I'm not sure if I had been at that point. I don't think I ever seriously considered it. Though I had thought it might not be that bad to die. But once I saw how deeply finding the playlist affected her, I stopped thinking that way. I knew it wasn't just myself I was hurting, it was her too. It wasn't that I didn't realize my death would affect her, of course I did, but looking at her then made me feel it in a way I never had before. She tried to joke it away, but I knew. And that knowledge, more than anything else, was what gave me the strength to fight my way back.

After a bit of consideration, and knowing that I was likely to wind up changing it anyway, I decided to start the new, improved version off with Tom Waits. And I changed the name in case anyone saw it. I didn't want to have that discussion again with Jen or anyone else. *Songs for My Funeral* became *Come Twilight*.

CHAPTER SEVENTEEN

DON'T THINK TWICE, IT'S ALL RIGHT

On the way to the hospital, Lauren asked if Jen had given me any news about the case when she got home. I gave her a brief rundown.

"Looks like things are coming together," she said.

"It does," I said. "Looking forward to getting back to regular duty?"

"Are you kidding?" she asked. "This is the most fun I've had since I got out of the academy."

"I'll try to get kidnapped and assaulted more often, then."

She grinned. "You know what I mean."

"I do."

"How long did it take you to make detective?" she asked.

"It seemed like a thousand years."

"That's not what I heard."

"I beat the average by a year or two," I said, "but I had a couple of lucky breaks on big cases that sped things up."

"Never heard that before. Everybody always talks about how hard they worked for it."

"Well," I said, rubbing the scar on my wrist, "if you're able to work hard, you're pretty lucky."

. . .

The neurologist's office was in a separate building across Atlantic from the main hospital. The doctor who'd evaluated me wasn't available, so they'd squeezed me into the schedule of one of his partners, an Asian woman who seemed surprisingly happy to see me.

"Hello, Detective Beckett," she said. "I'm Dr. Lee. You probably don't remember, but I saw you in the ER."

"Oh, hi," I said awkwardly. "I don't remember. I'm sorry."

"That's all right. You're several days early for your follow-up. What brought you in early?"

"My colleagues are telling me that I don't seem to be behaving normally."

"Do you think you're behaving normally?"

"It seems like it, but I don't know."

"What do they say you're doing?"

I didn't know exactly. Jen didn't tell me what Lauren said to her. Was I being more talkative? Less guarded?

"Well, I didn't argue with my partner when she suggested I come to see you."

Dr. Lee chuckled at that. "What else?"

"I guess I'm talking more, being more open, less resistant." As I spoke, it occurred to me that maybe what was really happening was that I was being less of an asshole, but I didn't mention that.

"Any other symptoms you're noticing? Confusion? Dizziness? Mood swings? Forgetfulness?"

"No," I said. "I still have a headache."

"Let's take a look, okay?"

She gave me a full neurological exam, checking my eyes, my reflexes, my balance, and my memory, and a doing bunch of other stuff that I didn't really understand the purpose of. When she was finished, she said, "Everything looks okay."

"That's good," I said.

"Tell me about how you're feeling. You said you didn't object to coming in today. That's something you'd normally be hesitant about?"

"Yes."

"Why?"

"Because I usually feel like I know what's best for me and I don't like people telling me what to do."

She chuckled again. "Well, that sounds normal. What's different today?"

"You know I was abducted before the assault, right?"

Dr. Lee nodded.

"Well, I did something very careless when I knew I shouldn't have. If I hadn't done it, the attack wouldn't have happened."

"You shouldn't blame yourself."

"I'm not, but my partner is. It did a lot of damage to our working relationship and I don't think she's going to let me off the hook."

"You had a serious injury and you're reevaluating the actions that contributed to it. You're behaving differently, but I don't think it's because of the injury. If I gave you a referral to psychiatry, would you use it?"

I might as well have told her about the playlist I'd worked on all night. "Yes," I said.

• • •

The visit had taken less time than I expected, so Lauren wasn't back to pick me up yet. I sat in the lobby and called Jen.

"What did the doctor say?"

"She said everything seems okay physically. I don't need another CT scan or anything. Told me I should get more rest."

"You didn't go to bed until after four last night."

192

It surprised me that she knew how late I'd been up. I was certain she had been asleep when I finally turned in. "I was thinking I might take a sick day today."

"That's a good idea."

"Let me know if you need me for anything, okay?" I said.

"Of course. I don't think we will, though. Have a good—"

"Patrick still looking at tomorrow to go at Joe?"

"Yeah, or maybe the next day. A lot of things are panning out."

"What about Novak?"

"He lawyered up."

"That's not surprising. I knew the assault beef wouldn't hold—"

"Danny."

I stopped.

She let the silence hang for a moment. "The Glenlivet bottle in Denkins's apartment? The third set of prints was Novak's."

• • •

"You sure you don't want something to eat?" Julia asked.

"No, I'm okay," I said. It was past lunchtime and I'd skipped break-fast to get to the doctor on time. "Why don't I call down to Michael's and order a take-out calzone for you? I can go pick it up." We were sitting at her table drinking French-press coffee that I was too agitated to appreciate. She had her hair pulled back casually, with a few strands hanging loose. The way I liked it. There was an assortment of flowers in a vase on the table that looked a few days past their prime.

"She wasn't even going to tell me."

When Jen had ended the call in the lobby of the medical building, I was still stunned that there had been such a major development in the case and that she'd thought it better to withhold the information than to share it with me. I tried to see it from her perspective. But I couldn't. I called Julia and asked if she was busy, could I come by and see her. I think she lied when she said she wasn't. Lauren drove me downtown, parked in a loading zone, walked me into the lobby of Julia's condo building, and told me she'd be waiting when I was ready to go.

"She was right not to," Julia said.

"What?"

"Look how upset you are." There was a level calmness in the sound of her words. I imagined it was her therapist voice, the one she'd used in her old job when she counseled people or led support groups.

"That's not why. It's because she was intentionally trying keep me out of the loop. I worked that case. It was mine."

"But it's not yours anymore. There's nothing you could have done today except stay home and worry or go to the station and get in their way. I know it feels shitty. But wouldn't you have rather had a day off and gotten some rest instead of feeling like you do right now?"

"You're on her side."

She laughed at that and I got even more angry. "You think that's funny?"

"No," she said. "I think it's sad."

That shut me up.

"There's only one side, Danny," she said. "And everybody's on it."

"What side is that?"

"Yours."

• • •

After I finished the calzone, Julia told me she needed to get back to Trev's gallery to continue planning the workshop she'd told me about. "Why don't I come to Jen's tonight?" she said as we rode down in the elevator.

"I'd like that."

We said good-bye in the lobby, where Lauren was finishing a slice of pizza.

"Where'd you get that?" I asked.

"Your girlfriend bought it for me. She's good people."

In the car on the way back to Jen's, Lauren said, "So, you think Novak did it?"

"Not my call," I said.

"But you're thinking about it."

"You want to be a detective," I said. "You even went to law school. Do you think he did it?"

"His prints on the bottle put him in the apartment along with Joe. They both had similar motives. Collect money from Denkins to square the debt. So unless one of them left before the murder, they're both culpable."

"Right," I said. "But how do we find out which one pulled the trigger?"

She thought about the question. "If they're acting in concert, it doesn't really matter."

"True, but that's weak. What would happen if it went to trial? Would the jury buy that?"

Lauren knitted her eyebrows and checked the cross traffic before turning off of Broadway onto Ximeno. "Maybe."

"Is 'maybe' good enough?"

She didn't need to answer that one. "So it comes down to the interrogation?"

"I think this time it does, yeah."

"But Novak's lawyered up, so what will you get from him?"

"Probably nothing, but maybe his attorney will try to turn him against Joe to get a better plea deal. Then what?"

She smiled. "Then Joe's screwed."

"Joe's already screwed."

"Tell Joe," she said, thinking as she spoke, "that Novak is selling him out, get him to go all in with his statement." She tossed the idea around a bit more, then added, "But what's to stop him from trying to put the whole thing on Novak?"

"Nothing at all. He's almost sure to try to do that. He might even have something on Novak that's worse than Denkins."

"So how do you deal with that?" she asked, turning right onto Colorado.

"Mostly, you try not to ask any questions you don't already know the answers to. They taught you that in law school, right?"

"Yeah. The difference between an interview and an interrogation." She paused for a moment. "That doesn't answer the question, though. How do you figure out the truth?"

"Sometimes you don't," I said.

We drove in silence for the last few blocks, then Lauren turned left into the driveway. "That was fun," she said. "Right up until the part at the end when you depressed the shit out of me. I thought you had the answers."

"If only."

• • •

The nights were growing warmer as we got closer to the end of summer and the miserable heat that came with it. The weather forecasters were telling us to expect the average high temperature to set records and that we were likely to have more one-hundred-plus-degree days than in any year since they started keeping records. But we probably still had a few weeks of bearable temperatures ahead of us before the hotpocalypse arrived.

Julia invited Lauren to join us watching TV, but when she found out we were planning to continue our *Downton Abbey* marathon, she declined.

I assumed she turned us down for the same reason that I'd been initially reluctant to watch, so I said, "It's really not as lame as you think it's going to be."

"Lame?" She seemed genuinely offended. "If it was 'lame' would I have watched the whole thing twice?"

Julia thought that was hysterical.

A few episodes later, when I started complaining that I didn't buy the procedure the police were using to investigate a murder, she thought we'd had enough. "Will you do me a favor?" she asked.

"Of course."

"Can I borrow your laptop for a minute?"

"Sure," I said, heading into the kitchen where I'd left it earlier that day. I was glad I'd changed the title of the *Songs For My Funeral* playlist.

"Here you go," I said, sitting down next to her again.

She opened a browser window, typed something she didn't want me to see into the search box, and clicked on a link before handing it back to me. I started to close the cover, but she said, "No, that wasn't the favor. This is." She showed me the screen. On the screen was a "Which *Downton Abbey* Character Are You?" quiz.

"Really?" I said.

"Humor me."

I picked a color, a movie, a song, and a bunch of other things. When it told me it was calculating the results, I handed it back to her, pretending not to be curious.

"Ha, I knew it!" she said, grinning broadly. She spun it back around for me to see. It said I was Mr. Bates.

I took the computer away from her, closed it, and put it down on the coffee table, all while trying to hide the fact that I'd gotten exactly the result I'd been hoping for.

"We got him," Dave shouted from the other side of the squad room. I looked up and saw Patrick and Jen rush over to his desk. The lab had matched fibers from the back of Avram Novak's SUV to trace evidence found on Kobe's pants in the Dumpster. Not Kobe, I corrected myself, Ryan Wong.

With Kayla's help, they found S. Wise, whose name, in what could only have been a fundamental error in his understanding of alias theory, did in fact turn out to be Sam. He corroborated Kayla's story, although he hadn't stuck around much longer than Kayla. When Joe told them he wanted to "grow the business" from pot to include harder drugs as well, that was where he drew the line.

Despite the information provided by Sam and Kayla, though, B. Darklighter was nowhere to be found. His apartment appeared to have been quickly vacated just as Ryan's was and he didn't answer either his regular cell phone or the burner linked to the contact list.

"So," I heard Patrick ask, "did Novak kill Ryan because of his involvement in the drug ring, or because of his proximity to the Denkins murder?"

"Good question," Dave said. "If we could answer it, we'd know whether we're looking for a runner or for another potential victim."

Patrick wheeled another chair over to my desk and sat down.

"Good news," I said.

He nodded. "How are you doing? Jen said everything looked okay at the doctor yesterday."

"It did, yeah. Head still hurts. That's to be expected, though."

"How about the other stuff?"

I wondered what other stuff he was referring to and what Jen had told him. "The doctor didn't think it was anything to worry about."

"I'm glad to hear that," he said.

"Me too."

"Jen's been keeping you in the loop, right?"

I nodded.

He looked down at his hands. "Danny, I'm sorry about the way—"

"Don't be. I understand. It's okay."

He let out an audible sigh and I could see the relief in his expression.

"So," I said, "you find any connection between the Novaks and that Serbian crew with the South African hardware?"

"Not yet. But I know it's there."

"What's the relationship between Avram and Goran?"

"Avram is the nephew. Grew up with Goran. Nobody knows what happened to his father. Probably never made it here from Yugoslavia."

"I thought they were Croatian."

He rolled his eyes at me. "You can Google that later. The important thing is that the bombing totally fits Goran's MO. The biggest reason no one's ever made a case against him is that everybody who's ever been willing to testify, and there weren't many, has either disappeared or died."

"Any car bombings?"

Patrick nodded. "Two of them."

And just like that, the suffocating weight that I had felt crushing me ever since I was first informed about the explosion, that morning in Ruiz's office, lifted off of me and floated away.

Patrick put his hand on my shoulder and said, "You can go home tonight. You're in the clear, buddy."

• • •

I caught Ruiz just as he was about to leave for lunch. "Must be a hell of a relief," he said.

"It is. Okay if I take some more sick time this afternoon?"

"You feeling all right?"

"Yeah. Just have some personal business to take care of. Going to keep Lauren with me for another day, too."

He nodded. "How's she doing?"

"She's a good cop. She'll be working for you in a couple of years."

"Too bad she's not ready yet. Just got the word from upstairs. The funding came through. We're going to be adding one more to the squad roster."

"A rising murder rate lifts all boats."

He almost grinned at that.

I got up, but stopped at the door and turned back to him. "You should keep Lauren on reassignment until Patrick closes this. It'll do her good."

Ruiz looked me in the eye, and when he said, "Okay," I knew it was as much for me as it was for her.

At my desk, I packed up my messenger bag and got ready to go. Jen was talking to someone on the phone and the conversation looked serious, so I didn't disturb her. On my way out, I looked over my shoulder and caught her eye. I smiled and lifted my hand to wave, as if to say *It's all good, see you later.* She raised her hand in return, but even from twenty feet away, I could see the sadness behind her smile.

After we left the station, I told Lauren I needed to go home. We were only a few blocks from Jen's house when I realized I needed to clarify that I meant the duplex on Roycroft.

My home.

We parked across the street and I dug the iPad out of my bag and opened the app that would let me check the surveillance footage from Patrick's cameras.

"Do you still need to do that?" Lauren asked.

I thought for a second and realized that I didn't. Looking at her, I said, "Can't hurt." She waited patiently for several minutes while I scrolled through recordings. Some of the cats were starting to look familiar, as was the mail carrier. The possum was still frequenting the backyard, too.

"Looks like the coast is clear," I said.

She followed me inside. It was the first time she'd been there.

"So that's the famous banjo," she said, looking at the Saratoga Star in its stand by the sofa.

"How do you know about that?"

"Everybody knows."

That was news to me. I imagined uniforms at crime scenes making banjo jokes behind my back and was surprised I hadn't got any crap about it.

"What's the difference between a banjo and an onion?" I asked her.

"I don't know. What is it?"

"Nobody cries when you cut up a banjo."

I left her in the living room and went into the office, smiled at the cow jumping over the moon, and opened the file cabinet. In the top drawer, where I kept my financial stuff, I found the file with my paycheck stubs and pulled out the last six and last month's bank statement.

As I joined Lauren in the living room, an odd feeling washed over me like a wave of cold water. He'd been in the kitchen, waiting for me. My kitchen. In my home. It had only been days, but it seemed like something that had happened much longer ago.

She reached down and strummed a fingernail across the strings, and the rich twang of the Deering pulled me back into the moment.

"Let's go," I said.

"Where?" she asked.

• • •

"So this is the end of the line for my reassignment, huh?" Lauren said as we walked down another row of Imprezas and Crosstreks and Foresters at the Subaru dealership. I knew what I was looking for and imagined I was trying to pick a suspect out of a lineup.

"Not quite," I said. "Ruiz is keeping you on until the case is closed. Probably until after Patrick interrogates Joe."

"Really? Sweet."

Two rows back I felt the tingle of recognition as I spotted the one I was looking for.

She followed me as I cut between two Outbacks. "Why is he doing that?"

"Because I asked him to."

I ran my hand over the fender of the Legacy. It was the Lapis Blue Pearl I'd picked out on the website. Cupping my hands and leaning down, I looked inside through the driver's-side window and saw the Warm Ivory leather. This was the one.

A young Latino salesman in a white oxford with a maroon tie approached us. "How are you folks doing today?"

I looked him square in the eye and said, "I want to buy this one."

Less than an hour later I was sitting in the driver's seat basking in the new-car smell and listening to Ramon explain how to operate the car's features. There was a lot more going on than there had been in my fifteen-year-old Camry. He synced my iPhone and hooked it up to the new charger. I had him set the audio system to E Street Radio.

Lauren had been in the backseat, and when Ramon was finished I told her to move up front.

"This is nice," she said.

"I want to buy you lunch."

"Okay," she said. "Tell me where. I'll meet you."

"Let me drive you. We'll pick up your car later."

I turned out of the dealership and into the right lane. The Legacy wasn't much bigger than my old car had been but it felt solid and stout, and more secure in its performance than my Camry ever had. I liked it already.

Lauren was fiddling with the touch screen in the center of the dash. "So this is an all-Springsteen station? Seriously?"

"Awesome, right?"

The next song in the rotation was "Atlantic City." When the Boss started singing, Lauren said, "Hey, I know this song."

"That speaks very highly of your character."

"Dude," she said. "You were almost the chicken man."

• • •

After we had lunch at the Lazy Dog I took Lauren to pick up her car, and then drove to Jen's house. On the 405, I activated the adaptive cruise control, which adjusted the speed to maintain the right distance behind the car in front of me. With all the new technology on the Subaru, it was apparent I had a steep learning curve ahead of me before I'd be able to figure it all out, but I was already wishing I'd made the leap a long time ago. It would be a long time before I realized that what I was feeling about my new Subaru didn't really have much to do with the car at all.

When I got back to Jen's, I gathered up all my dirty clothes that were scattered around the guest room and pulled the sheets from the bed. After dividing everything into lights and darks, I started the first load in the washing machine. Then I vacuumed and cleaned the bathroom. When the sheets were ready to go back on the bed, everything was cleaner than it had been when I arrived.

Lauren found me as I was packing the clean laundry into my duffel bag.

"Staying at your house tonight?"

"Julia's probably."

"Good. You didn't seem too comfortable when we were there."

"It was that obvious?"

She nodded. "Jen wouldn't mind if you stayed here a while longer."

"Are you kidding? She'll be glad to have me out of here."

"You're wrong."

I smiled and nodded. "I hope so," I said. No matter how much I wished that what she was saying was true, I knew it wasn't. "See you in the squad room tomorrow."

The hug surprised me. I hadn't seen it coming, but fortunately I was quick-thinking enough to return it.

"Thanks for the last few days," she said.

"You're welcome."

• • •

The new blue Legacy was parked in one of the visitors' spots in the parking garage under Julia's building and I was leaning against the fender with a bag of takeout from Bigmista's Barbecue—her favorite pulled chicken and my favorite pastrami, along with sides of barbecue beans and pineapple coleslaw—when she pulled her Forester into the spot with her apartment number on it. She almost missed me, so I said "Hey" loudly enough for her to hear.

"Danny?" she said. "I wasn't expecting to see you." She kissed me and looked at the car. "Is this a rental?"

"Nope."

"Nice," she said. "They closed the case?"

"Not yet, but apparently I'm in the clear." I'd been thinking about Patrick telling me I was safe. There'd been no doubt in my mind when he first said it—the relief I'd felt was palpable. But the truth was that there wasn't a solid link between the Novaks and the bombing of my car. Everything was circumstantial. *Let it go,* I told myself, *you're just being paranoid because of the concussion.*

That wasn't hard to do when Julia put her arms around me, and I returned the embrace one-handed while I held the bag of food awkwardly out to the side so no stray sauce could get on her clothes.

"I brought dinner," I said.

"Oh, it smells good. Bigmista's?"

"Yep."

She leaned against me as we rode up in the elevator. Inside, she said, "Put the food down in the kitchen."

When I did, she kissed me deeply, took my hand, and pulled me into the bedroom.

By the time we finally got around to eating, everything was cold. Except the coleslaw. That had gotten warm.

Later we took the new car for a drive down PCH. I was already getting used to the feel and finding myself more and more comfortable behind the wheel.

The Camry was the first new car I had ever bought. I was still young enough then to look into a low-end BMW, but Megan and I were barely beyond the newlywed phase and talking about starting a family, so I knew the way to impress her most was to demonstrate my sensible maturity with a fine new midsized Toyota sedan.

I don't know how long I would have held on to the Camry if I hadn't been forced into the change. Probably until it was too worn down by time and miles to keep going. Maybe it was a good thing I'd been forced to move on. Cradled in the heated, five-way power-adjustable ivory leather embrace of the driver's seat, I glanced over at Julia as she looked out the window at the moon glinting on the Pacific and was glad for the NHTSA five-star safety rating of the choice I'd made.

CHAPTER TWENTY

HEAD FULL OF DOUBT / ROAD FULL OF PROMISE

"I'm not doing it until Monday," Patrick said when I asked him about Joe's interrogation.

While I no longer needed a babysitter, I was still on limited duty due to my concussion. I wouldn't be back in the case rotation until the doctor cleared me to return to active duty, which I was hoping would be at my next follow-up visit.

"Why did you decide to postpone?" I asked.

"He and Lucinda are meeting with the probate attorney this afternoon. I want him to feel like he got away with it for a few days before we go at him."

I thought that was a good move. Once Joe had a taste of the relief that would come with the inheritance from his father-in-law, Patrick could use it and the threat of losing it to his advantage. It was a smart move, but there was a risk. "What if he hears about Novak?" I asked.

"I don't think he will. We've got the phone records. There's only been limited communication between them, and it doesn't look like Joe's been talking to anybody else."

"Not even Goran? They have a history."

"It's worth the risk. We're watching. He's not going anyplace."

How would I have handled the interrogation? I thought about it. Patrick's strategy was good, but I didn't know if I would have made the same choice. Sure, Joe would be relieved and probably feeling overconfident, but if we brought him in before he knew for sure about getting his hands on Bill's money, we could work his anxiety. The more I considered, though, the more I leaned in the direction of Patrick's choice. And besides, it wouldn't be that detrimental to the case if Joe did find out that Avram was being held. The biggest risk was Joe invoking his right to an attorney before he talked to us. Even if he did that, the case against him was still solid. Patrick had made the right call.

I asked him if he'd found anything else that might connect Avram to the car bomb.

"Not yet," he said. "But we will. No doubt about it."

After Patrick left, Lauren and I sat in the squad room. My plan had been to walk her through a few of my open cases, just to give her a stronger sense of the breadth and complexity of the homicide detail's work. I'd worried a bit about starting at the top of the investigative food chain. Most patrol officers never become detectives, and most detectives never work homicide. But I knew she was hungry for it. Our conversation about the Denkins case, and all the time I'd spent with her, proved to me that she had not only the desire but also the perceptiveness and intelligence required. When I talked to her about it, she had seemed interested and enthusiastic. And besides, most cops never went to law school.

It surprised me, even though it shouldn't have, how much progress I was making with her going over the cases. I thought I'd be doing little more than explaining things to her, but she fired back a question or two for every explanation I offered her. And they were good questions, smart ones, that even helped me reframe my perceptions and assumptions on a few cases. On one, a domestic murder in which a battered wife had killed her husband, Lauren studied the half dozen family photos we'd included of the couple, then even more images of the victim and the crime scene. "Look at that watch he's wearing," she said. "It's got to be a

Rolex or something. It's in every one of these." She pointed at the family pictures. "But he's not wearing it in the crime-scene shots. She take it off him before we got there?"

"I don't know," I said. "But that was a good catch."

She grinned.

We kept on like that, case after case, until lunchtime. Jen was at her desk, so I asked her if she wanted to eat with us.

"Can't," she said. "Have to get this finished." She went back to work on the warrant-request template on her computer screen.

Because we weren't pressed for time, I took Lauren to Enrique's, which was literally on the other side of town. Most days, it wasn't a viable option because it just took too long to get there, wait for a table, eat, and get back, but I decided to milk the flexibility we were enjoying for all it was worth.

Of course we took my new car.

As I drove, she asked, "Why are you so quiet?"

"What?" I pretended like I didn't know what she was talking about.

"You were hoping with the case coming together and you not being in danger anymore, Jen would come around. Let you off the hook."

"She didn't even ask us to bring her something back. If somebody's working through lunch, we always bring something back."

"Bring something for her anyway," she said.

"I don't think that will fix anything."

"Sometimes things don't get fixed. But who doesn't like free tacos?"

When we got back to the squad room, though, Jen wasn't there anymore. Dave told us she was out running something down for Patrick.

I gave him the take-out container with the Number Nine Taco Trio combination inside.

"Enrique's?" he said.

I nodded.

"Thanks, man. I'm starving."

• • •

It felt weird to be home.

Before I went inside, I still followed the ritual of sitting out in the car and checking the video recordings on the iPad. I hadn't planned on it or even thought about doing it. I'd been too distracted by my shiny new car to think about it.

There was nothing unusual on the camera footage, but I decided that if I kept checking it, I was eventually going to have to name the possum in the backyard.

I'm not sure what I expected to feel. Before the abduction and kidnapping, I'd felt like a prisoner, constricted and captive, anxious for independence. Since the hospital, though, I hadn't minded the constant presence of others. I thought I had been looking forward to a night of freedom and independence, to having time to do what I wanted without having to consider anyone else.

In the kitchen, I opened the freezer and searched for something to have for dinner. I should have stopped on the way home. None of the frozen meals looked appealing. Well, they never really looked appealing, but now they weren't even looking tolerable. I found a can of chili in the cupboard, emptied it into a bowl, and put it in the microwave. There were spots of mold on the bread, so I dumped it in the trash and took the chili into the living room to watch *Jeopardy!*

Half an hour later, feeling pleased with myself for knowing that the first author to have both fiction and nonfiction *New York Times* number-one bestsellers was John Steinbeck—the mention of his poodle made it too easy—I turned off the TV and practiced banjo for a while. Mostly just scales and finger rolls. It felt like I was starting from scratch. I knew what I wanted to do, but my hands wouldn't cooperate. I'd fallen into a pattern of practicing every day for a few weeks and starting to feel a bit of progress, then not playing at all for a month or two, only to pick up the banjo again to find that I felt even more awkward and incompetent than I had at the beginning of the last cycle.

The heat of the day had broken when I locked up and set out on a long walk, my first in weeks. I took Appian Way past Colorado Lagoon and cut over on Paoli Way to get closer to the water of Marine Stadium, then did a big loop around Belmont Shore and came back home. Almost two hours.

It felt good to walk again, but I didn't feel the sense of liberation and freedom I'd been hoping for. Instead, when I got home I felt a pang of loneliness. It wasn't something I was used to and I didn't know how to process it. I thought about calling Julia. She would have come if I'd asked her. But I didn't want to do that. In an odd way, it seemed to me like picking up the phone would have been a capitulation, a way of giving in and admitting to a kind of weakness that I'd never really had a problem with before.

No, I told myself, it was just the concussion. The injury had left me feeling vulnerable and off center. I was a lot of things, but I wasn't the kind of guy who got lonely.

There were only a few episodes of *I Was There Too* that I hadn't heard yet. Soon I'd be relegated to new episodes like everybody else. That was my biggest complaint about podcasts. I'd find one I liked, binge-listen to all the old episodes, and then when I was completely hooked, I'd be left to the whims of lazy podcasters who somehow think an hour every two weeks or so is an acceptable level of output.

I thought about fast-forwarding through the theme song so it wouldn't be stuck in my head all night, but then I realized that just thinking about skipping it had already planted the earworm.

> *It's been said you can't handle the truth.*
> *But that ain't so.*
> *How do I know?*
> *I was there too.*

In bed, trying to sleep, I listened to Dwier Brown talking about playing Costner's dad in *Field of Dreams*.

I had almost nodded off when I heard a noise in the backyard. Sitting up, I reached for my gun, which I'd left on the nightstand instead of in the safe on the closet shelf, and got up.

Past the edge of the window shade, I could see a sliver of the yard. I nudged it with a fingertip to get a better view.

The yard was dark and filled with shadows.

Nothing moved.

I left my bedroom, went through the hall and kitchen and into the laundry room. Flipping the light switch next to the back door, I watched as the hundred-watt bulb illuminated everything from the back porch to the alley fence.

It didn't look like there was anything outside that shouldn't have been there, so I made sure the door was deadbolted and went back into the kitchen. Out of habit I reached up on top of the refrigerator for the bottle of Grey Goose, forgetting it hadn't been there for months.

When I went back to bed, I took the iPad with me, opened the video-surveillance app, and propped it up on the nightstand. The live feed of the backyard filled the room with a soft gray glow.

• • •

The temperature peaked in the midnineties, but it had dropped a few degrees by the time I got to Julia's, so we decided to leave my Legacy there and walk to Buskerfest. She'd gone to the music festival for the first time the same week she moved downtown and hadn't missed one since. She'd even showed me a few photos she'd taken that year in the portfolio on her website.

They closed off a block-long stretch of First Street between Linden and Elm, just a few blocks away from the gallery where Julia's show had been, and set up a makeshift multistage performance venue by parking large flatbed trucks every fifty yards or so for the musicians to use as stages. I'd been before, but I wasn't a regular. Not because I didn't enjoy myself, but because I never liked being an off-duty cop in a crowd of people drinking and partying. It's way too easy to wind up back on duty.

Everything was supposed to get rolling at five and last until eleven or so. We could hear the first band playing as we turned the corner from Broadway onto Elm. There were three LBPD patrol cars parked on the other side of the street and I wondered how many uniforms were assigned to the event. As we got closer and the music grew louder, I could see that the crowd was still sparse. It never got too packed until around sundown. As we neared First, I slowed a bit and then stopped. I felt a twinge in my stomach.

"What is it?" Julia asked.

"Just a few butterflies," I said. "This is my first time in a crowd since the thing."

She took my hand. "You okay?"

"Yeah. Just a little surprised. I didn't expect to feel weird."

"We don't have to go," she said.

"No, I want to. I'm fine."

"You sure?" she said.

We walked around the corner and I was glad we had gotten there early. The band was on the first stage at the west end of the block, and although they were already into their set, the crowd hadn't yet materialized. There were a few people in front of the stage, including a contingent of fans who'd clearly come to hear this particular band, Tall Walls, and were enthusiastically bopping up and down with the power-pop beat. The music didn't really grab me until the two-woman horn section joined in and the trumpet and saxophone added another layer to the sound.

We listened for a few more minutes, then decided to check out the rest of the street before it got too crowded. As we walked behind the beer stand, we bumped into Stan Burke. He was in uniform and speaking into the radio mic attached to his shoulder.

When he finished, he said, "Danny. Good to see you out and about. How's the investigation going?" He was referring to the attempt on my life rather than the Denkins murder, although those wound up being the same case.

"Looks like we've got things cleared up."

"I'm glad to hear that," he said. I hadn't told him much about it when we ate lunch together at the Potholder, but he knew me well enough to have seen how much it had been rattling me.

I introduced him to Julia. He hadn't seen me with a woman since Megan died, so I expected some kind of joke or double entendre, but none came. Instead he chatted with her a bit and ended by saying, "Danny's a good guy." His earnestness and sincerity could have only meant one thing. He was still worried about me.

"I know," Julia said, taking my hand.

• • •

An hour later, the crowd had quadrupled, and it was still early in the lineup. There was still room in front of the center stage, though, where a scruffy banjo player in a dark T-shirt, baseball cap, and thick-framed glasses had just started a set with his bandmates. They were called Rosie Harlow & the Tall Tale Boys and had a folky alt-bluegrass sound that I really liked.

I wasn't their only fan. In the area directly in front of the stage, a fifty-ish blonde woman in a gauzy white blouse and long gray skirt was dancing oddly out of time with the music. She was clearly in an altered mental state of some kind. Her cheek had some bruising, and a small scab hung just below her eye. The other people in the crowd were giving her space, and, while she didn't look particularly joyful or even happy, it was clear the music was having a positive effect on her. I looked over at Julia, who was watching her, too, with a shade of concern in her expression. The woman wasn't really bothering anyone, though, and no one seemed to have a problem with her.

Until the drunk asshole behind me started talking.

"What's wrong with her?" I heard him ask quietly. He didn't get an answer, so after a few moments he raised his voice and directed it at the dancing woman. "Get out of there," he said. "You're ruining it!"

She seemed oblivious to him. But he kept it up. I turned to look at him. Trucker hat, sunglasses, mustache, T-shirt, shorts, sandals, and, of course, a beer in his hand. It clearly wasn't his first of the evening. He was as oblivious to my dirty look as the woman was to his voice.

I glanced to my right again as he moved past me on the left toward the stage. When I turned, he was a few feet in front of the woman. He moved toward her, his arms outstretched, as if he were trying to herd a sheep.

The nearest uniforms were at the back of the crowd and I couldn't tell if they were aware of what was going on.

For the first time since I'd noticed her, the woman's eyes seemed to connect with the world around her, and when she looked at him they filled with fear. He took another step forward and this time actually nudged her toward the side of the stage.

I moved, quickly closing the fifteen feet between us, and slid in between them, facing the asshole. His eyes were hidden behind the dark lenses of his glasses, but his posture straightened and his chest expanded and I wanted desperately for him to escalate the situation with a swing or a shove or anything else that would give me license to attack. I knew I should say something to calm him down and back him off, but I didn't. I met his threatening posture with my own and tried to will him to attack.

We eyeballed each other.

I should have badged him, de-escalated the situation.

I didn't.

His neck twitched and his head tilted a few degrees.

Something burned behind my eyes.

Everything slowed down.

He dropped his beer and lifted his hand to shove me.

I saw it coming and twisted my torso so his palm only brushed across my chest. Without thinking, I continued the motion and drove my right elbow hard into his jaw. The impact snapped his head sideways. I put my left hand on his shoulder and pushed him in the direction of his own momentum to spin him around.

With one small step I was behind him and used my shin to pop his knee out from under his hips. Then I pushed him face-first into the puddle of beer on the ground. I planted my knee in the small of his back, yanked his arm up hard, then twisted it back down while I reached for the spot on my hip where for years I'd carried my handcuffs while I was in uniform.

There was nothing there.

He kept struggling and trying to pull his arm free.

I put more weight on my knee and began torquing his wrist up between his shoulder blades.

But before I could break anything, two patrol officers were behind me.

"We got this, Detective," one of them said, grasping my triceps and tugging me back.

I stood up and backed off, trying to catch my breath, feeling like I'd been somewhere else for the last minute.

Before I was fully aware of what was happening, Julia was next to me, asking if I was all right, and the two cops had the drunk cuffed and on his feet and were leading him away from the empty hole I'd created in the crowd.

Still breathing heavily and shaking from the adrenaline, I looked around to find the woman he'd been harassing. She was behind me, huddled with a few others. A much younger woman who was comforting her nodded at me.

"Where's Stan?" I asked.

"I don't know," Julia said. She put her hands on my arms and looked me squarely in the eyes. "Are you okay?"

"Yeah." I tried to look over my shoulder, but she put her hand gently on the side of my face to keep my attention focused on her. "Is that woman all right?" I asked.

She nodded. "She's with some friends. They're taking care of her."

"Good," I said. "Good."

As we walked toward the squad cars on Elm, I noticed something I hadn't seen earlier. Someone had strung a cord from one rooftop all the way across the street to a second on the other side. Hanging from it were three-foot-tall blue and black letters that silhouetted the word "Buskerfest" against the last of the sunset fading behind the Long Beach skyline.

• • •

When we got back to Julia's place, she opened the door and we went inside. It smelled like flowers. There was a vase of roses and lilies on the table that I hadn't noticed earlier. Probably because the air conditioning had been on and I was inside just long enough for Julia to pick up her bag and walk back out with me.

"Those flowers smell nice," I said.

She put her hand on my cheek and said, "Thank you."

I was still amped up from the altercation and she wasn't buying my attempt at casual conversation.

"What happened back there?" she asked.

"You saw the same thing I did. That asshole was harassing that lady. As soon as he touched her it was battery, so I had to do something."

"That's not what I meant," she said. "What happened to you?"

"He assaulted me. I defended myself."

The tenderness in her face slipped away and was replaced by something firmer. "Do you really believe that's all there was to it?"

"Yes," I said, almost buying the lie myself.

She sighed softly and looked away from me. "Danny," she said, her voice barely a whisper.

We stood there.

When she finally looked at me and spoke again, she said, "Are you okay to get yourself home?"

CHAPTER TWENTY-ONE

WINNING STREAK

When the first swallow of Glenlivet hit my stomach and the alcoholic warmth began to spread in waves through my body, I thought, for just a moment, that I might be able to forget.

An hour earlier, I'd sat in my new car in Julia's parking garage, trying to figure out how the evening had gone so wrong. Her sending me home was an even bigger surprise to me than the altercation at Buskerfest. We'd planned on spending the night together and going out to breakfast in the morning, but there I was, alone and confused, with no idea of where to go or what to do.

There was no food in my house, so I needed to shop. I decided to go to the fancy Ralphs at Marina Pacifica even though it was out of the way. Because it was bigger and had a much better selection of fresh stuff in the deli and bakery. Not because of its expansive and well-stocked liquor section. But since I was there anyway, why not grab some Grey Goose?

I was headed to check out, a turkey-pesto sandwich, three frozen entrees, and a fifth of vodka in my basket, when I spotted the bottle on the shelf across the aisle from the craft-beer cooler. It was a surprise to see it there. Single-malt scotch in a grocery store? The location surely had something to do with it. The store was just across from Naples Island, the most exclusive part of Long Beach. Lots of rich people shopped there. It was the only market I'd ever visited multiple times without once finding a shopping cart with a bad wheel. Maybe I shouldn't have been surprised at all.

The Marina Pacifica might not have been on my way home, but once I was there, Bill Denkins's apartment was. I parked across the street from his building, not far from where I'd seen my Camry for the last time before the bomb totaled it. It was getting late, but still I got out, crossed Belmont Avenue, and tried the gate at the side of the building that led to the units in the back. The latch wouldn't open. The mechanism was designed to lock automatically, though I'd noticed on a previous visit that it didn't always work. But tonight it did.

From where I stood, three steps up from the sidewalk, I could see the concrete porch that Bill's unit shared with the upstairs neighbor's. If I stepped to the left and leaned, I could just get an angle on his front door. It looked dark.

I took a shot and walked back down to the sidewalk, then looped onto Second Street and around the building Kurt Acker managed. The gate on the alley was open. I went in. Above the garage, the lights were on in Harold Craig's studio. There was only darkness behind the front window of the apartment that had belonged to Kobe.

There was no light on in Bill's place, either.

I wasn't sure why I felt compelled to visit. What could I have possibly expected to find?

As soon as I'd spotted the bottle of single malt on the shelf at the supermarket, Bill had wedged himself back into my mind. I thought of him sitting in his living room on a night like any other and hearing a knock on the door. His son-in-law and an associate. Had Bill known Novak? I thought about it. Their paths might have crossed with Joe's restaurant business. If I was still doing the interrogation, I'd make a point of trying to find out.

Maybe Patrick knew. I didn't know how far he'd progressed on the investigation, how many of the minor details he'd been able to sort out. How annoyed, I wondered, would Patrick be if I asked him about it tomorrow? It didn't matter. I decided I'd try to find out whether he liked it or not.

I stepped up onto Bill's porch and put my hand on the door. "I'm sorry," I whispered. What I was apologizing for, I didn't fully understand. Letting the case go? Not following through? That I wasn't the one who'd be twisting the truth out of Joe on Monday morning? Each of those was more absurd than the last. Bill had never known me, had no investment in me closing his case. The only thing that mattered was that it was closed, and Patrick was doing at least as good a job as I would have. Maybe better. The apology must not have been for Bill, I thought. But before I could pursue the idea any further, I heard the rattle of someone unlocking the front gate and heels clacking on the walkway. It was a woman. As she got closer, I recognized her as the tenant who lived directly above Bill. She didn't recognize me, though, and stopped ten feet away, clutching her purse tightly to her side.

"Hello, Ms. Clare," I said, pulling the badge holder from my pocket and flipping it open for her to see. "I'm Danny Beckett. Long Beach PD. You spoke to my partner a few weeks ago."

As I talked, the tension drained from her posture and she stood up a little bit taller. "Yes," she said. "I remember."

I smiled at her but didn't say anything.

"Can I help you with something?" she asked.

"No," I said. "I was just driving past and I wanted to stop."

By that time she was on the porch, too, and unlocking the door that led upstairs to her unit. "Okay." She didn't do a very good job of pretending to understand what I was talking about. "Do you know what happened yet?"

I nodded.

"But I'm sure you can't say anything about it, right?"

I nodded again. "No, not really. We do know that there's nothing for anybody else in the neighborhood to worry about, though."

"How do you know that?"

I thought about what I might be able to tell her that wasn't confidential. "There was a very specific motive that doesn't really apply to anyone else."

She thought about it and seemed to relax. "That's good."

"It is," I said. I smiled again and started for the gate.

I was already in my car and turning right onto Broadway when I thought about Harold upstairs, alone and anxious in his tiny studio, and it occurred to me that I should have checked in with him while I was there. A small twinge fluttered in my gut and I felt guilty. I considered turning around and going back but talked myself out of it. Maybe I didn't feel guilty enough.

At home I dropped a few ice cubes in a short glass and poured Glenlivet over them. I'd never really been a scotch drinker, but Bill Denkins and his last night were still on my mind. Very few of the crimes we investigate involve people who expected to die, who had some reason to worry or to suspect what was coming. What had Bill known? Did he trust Joe? Was that enough for him to be comfortable drinking with Novak? Did he have any suspicions about either of them that night? Or did he go with no warning at all? A few pleasant drinks and then lights out? Novak didn't seem like the type to signal his intentions.

No, I thought, *he wouldn't warn you off or even attempt it. He'd just come at you. If he put a bomb in your car, you'd be in the driver's seat when it went off.*

The ice hadn't melted very much, so I poured another glass. When that one was gone, so were the cubes, so I started drinking it straight. It wasn't until I tried texting Julia that I realized how much my tolerance for alcohol had diminished since I'd stopped drinking vodka every day. Or maybe scotch just hit me harder.

My thumbs felt twice as big as they normally did and I was having difficulty hitting the right keys on my iPhone. `sre tiu okya?` I wrote. Eventually I was able to correct it to `Are you okay?` and hit "Send."

I hadn't been that drunk in a long time. When I'd poured the first glass I hadn't intended to wind up where I was. The alcohol wasn't providing any escape or relief, it was only pulling me deeper into the tangle of emotions I'd been trying not to acknowledge for weeks. A deep sense of despair filled me to the point that I could no longer contain it. I thought of Bill. And of the victim before him and before and before. So much death. All the way back to Megan and, eventually, to my father.

A therapist once told me she suspected I'd become a homicide detective in order to confront the loss I'd felt since I was a child. Losing a parent to violence at such an early age wounds you, she said. Investigating murder was my way of facing it head-on, of trying to come to terms with the inevitability we all face and trying to heal. But had I healed? I didn't know the answer to that question. Was I still just that open, bleeding wound or had I become nothing more than a mass of hardened scar tissue?

I tipped the bottle one more time, swearing it would be the last of the long night, then raised the glass to all my dead.

● ● ●

Sunday morning I felt like shit. It was hard to tell where the physical hangover ended and the emotional one began. I couldn't remember going to bed, but that's where I woke up. Somehow I'd even managed to change into sweatshorts and a T-shirt. The clock on the nightstand told me it was almost ten thirty. I tried to remember the last time I had slept so late, but my memory failed me.

Julia had texted me back three hours earlier. `I'm okay. Worried about you. We should talk. Dinner?`

We should talk. What did that mean? How badly had I screwed things up last night?

The asshole who was harassing the impaired woman had been a kind of opportunity for me. Not a good or positive one, but an opportunity nonetheless. He'd given me the chance to unleash the anger I hadn't even realized I'd been carrying since the bombing. He'd given me the chance to feel powerful in the face of the utter impotence I'd been experiencing but refused to acknowledge. He'd given me the chance to explode.

I'd been lucky. In different circumstances it could have been far worse. Because, truthfully, I'd wanted to hurt him much more than I actually had. I'd wanted to grind his face into a smear on the asphalt. But what would have happened without a convenient villain to punish? Where would my rage have gone? Who would it have hurt?

That's what really worried me. How much of that had Julia been able to see? I had no idea what she might be thinking or what she wanted to talk about. Maybe she'd seen who I really was. And maybe that was all she wanted to see of me.

• • •

I found Patrick in the squad room. An hour earlier, I'd called and asked if I could buy him lunch. It didn't surprise me at all to discover he was working. If I had an interrogation on a Monday that a major case hinged on, I'd be at my desk all day Sunday, too. On the way downtown I stopped at Modica's and picked up sandwiches—a meatball and a chicken Parm. When I asked him which one he wanted, he chose the meatball. I should have known.

"I've been thinking about Novak," I said after swallowing my first bite.

"What about him?" Patrick asked.

"He doesn't seem like the kind of guy who gives warnings."

He sucked some iced tea through the straw in his cup. "I don't get what you mean."

"Well, are we still operating under the theory that the bomb in my car was a warning?"

"Not necessarily," he said. "You weren't in your car again after that morning at the crime scene. It could just as easily have been a missed opportunity and he detonated the bomb because he figured it would be found and a lot easier to trace if it hadn't gone off."

That was a good point. But it wasn't enough. "What about my abduction?"

He raised his eyebrows and wiped some marinara from his chin.

"Why even grab me? Why not just put a bullet in the back of my head right there in the kitchen? Doesn't that seem more like his style?"

Patrick tossed the idea around for a few seconds. "Yeah, but I'm not convinced. Maybe he tried to warn you off because there was too much heat from the bombing. Figured it was safer that way. And none of the Novak family has ever killed a cop. That's a whole different game." He nodded, more to himself than to me. "I'm still betting on Avram."

His logic made sense, but it didn't ease my suspicion that there was more to the attempt on my life than we were seeing—though I didn't have anything other than my hunch to back up the feeling.

"Since you're here," he said, "would you mind walking me through Denkins's file one more time?"

We spent more than an hour reviewing the work I'd done on the case before it had been handed off to him. When we'd gone over everything and he'd asked me all the questions he could think of, he said, "So how's the new car?"

"It's okay."

"Just okay? Lauren said you were gaga over it. I'm just about done here. Why don't you show it to me? Maybe take a spin."

"It's just a car," I said.

• • •

At home, I showered and got ready for dinner with Julia, all the while worrying about what she wanted to talk about. I figured this had to be it. She'd seen the real me at Buskerfest. Now she was going to end it. What else could she have meant by *We should talk*?

You're just being foolish, I told myself. She was a social worker. She led support groups for veterans from Iraq. She'd get it. I'd just be honest and open and ask for her understanding and forgiveness. Besides, there was more to her message. *Worried about you,* she'd written. I was jumping to conclusions. It would be all right.

But when I stood on the porch, my hand was shaking so much it took three tries to get the key into the deadbolt.

I texted her. Had to meet with Patrick about the case. Won't be able to make dinner. Tomorrow? I read it twice to be sure I hadn't actually lied, then hit "Send."

Back inside, there was still a third of the bottle of Glenlivet on the coffee table. I went into the kitchen for the Grey Goose instead.

When Joseph Polson came into the squad room on Monday morning, he seemed lighthearted and even happy. He'd shaved off his soul patch. Patrick had been monitoring his phone. There had been no unexpected calls and no indication he'd had contact with anyone who might have had information about Avram's arrest.

"Detective Beckett," he said to me. "I'm so sorry to hear about your injury. I hope you're all right."

"I am, thank you. I'm sorry we had to reassign your case. I know Detective Glenn is doing a very thorough job."

"He seems very professional," Joe said. He realized too late that I might take it to mean he thought I hadn't been. "I didn't mean that you—"

"It's okay," I said with a friendly chuckle. "I didn't think you were implying anything. How's Lucinda holding up?"

"She's doing a bit better. But it's still hard, you know."

"I do," I said. "Detective Glenn is on the way. He had something he needed to follow up on, but he should be here any minute. Can I get you anything? Coffee? Water?"

"No, thank you."

I led him up the hall to the interview room. "Go ahead and have a seat. It'll just be a minute or two."

Just down the hall and around the corner was the door to the observation room. I opened the door and found Patrick, Jen, and Lauren inside watching Joe on the monitor.

We assumed Lucinda would have told him about her interview—how she'd been led into the interview room only to be retrieved by Jen and taken to the much more relaxing conference room. On the monitor, Joe was looking around at the room. He didn't look nervous, not yet, but he seemed curious about why he was in the box when his wife had been in the bigger room with a window and much more comfortable furniture.

"How'd it go?" Patrick asked me.

"Just like you planned," I said. When he'd asked me earlier to be the one to greet Joe, I was hesitant. I didn't want to cross any lines that would make Ruiz unhappy. Patrick told me it needed to be me because Joe had to see that I'd been out of commission and that I was uninvolved with the case at this point. We didn't know how much he knew about what happened to me, but on the chance that he knew everything, Patrick wanted him to think that the abduction had worked, that I'd been effectively removed from the case, that I had, in fact, "stayed away from her" as I'd been told to do. I argued that it didn't matter because Jen went right ahead and interviewed Lucinda anyway, but it was Patrick's case now, so I followed his direction.

"How long are you going to make him wait?"

"For a while yet. Let him stew." He told Jen and Lauren and me that we could go back to work and he'd let us know when he was going to start.

Thirty-five minutes later we were all back in the observation room and Patrick went in to join Joe.

For more than an hour Patrick threw softballs at Joe, taking his time, building a rapport. It looked and sounded a lot like Jen's interview with Lucinda and took a similar line. Everything seemed to be focused on his father-in-law, but bit by bit, Joe was getting closer and closer to talking about himself. It was so gradual that when Patrick started to drop the hammer we wouldn't have noticed it if we hadn't known what we were watching for.

"Just a few more questions and then we can wrap it up," Patrick said.

Joe had been calm and comfortable, but when Patrick said that, there was a hint of relief in Joe's eyes.

Patrick thumbed through his notes as if he wanted to make sure they'd covered everything. "And when was the last time you saw Bill again?"

"The day before he died."

"So that was Wednesday. You stopped by his apartment and hung out and had a drink, right?"

"Yes."

"Special occasion?"

"No. I was just in the neighborhood."

"You had the Glenlivet? Man, I love that stuff."

"Bill did, too," Joe said.

Patrick jotted something down on the yellow pad, then consulted his notes again. "Okay, so that's—wait a second. You said Wednesday, the day before?"

"Yes," Joe said. "That's right."

"Not the day of?"

Joe shook his head.

Patrick went back to his notes and dug through them again, a puzzled look on his face. "You're sure about the day?"

Joe said, "Yes."

Patrick tapped the point of his pen on the pad. "This is weird. There's this sales record from BevMo? You didn't buy the bottle of Glenlivet until Thursday morning."

He looked at Joe.

For just a moment, I thought Joe might not crack, but then he blinked three times in rapid succession and looked down at the table. Patrick had him. I turned to Jen and whispered, "Winter is here."

My phone vibrated in my pocket and I sent the call to my voice mail without looking at the screen.

"Here's the thing I don't get," Patrick said. "Remember those fingerprints Detectives Beckett and Tanaka took the day after Bill died?"

Joe nodded.

The phone rang again in my pocket. This time I checked it. Julia's name was on the screen. She knew I'd be watching the interview this morning, so she wouldn't have called unless it was important. I stepped out into the hall and answered.

"Hey," I said. "What's up? I'm in the—"

"Beckett?" a man said.

"Who is this? Where's Julia?"

"She's here." His voice was even and strangely calm. "I asked her to call you, but she wouldn't." I had heard his voice before but I couldn't place it.

"What's going on?" I said, my voice rising. "Put Julia on the phone."

"No," he said. "You need to come here right now."

"Come where? Tell me what's happening." I struggled to maintain my composure. Something was very wrong.

"She's all right," he said. "So are the others. But they won't be unless you come here right now."

Julia was supposed to be teaching her workshop. Who were the others he was talking about? Her students? What was he planning to do?

Someone yelled something in the background. It sounded like "He has a bomb."

"Shut up," he shouted.

De-escalate, I told myself. *De-escalate.*

"Okay," I said. "I'll come. Tell me where."

"The gallery," he said. "You know which one."

"I'm coming. Don't do anything. Don't hurt any—"

"Just you. No one else. Come now."

"I need more information. How many people are with you? Are you armed?"

"You should have left her alone."

A wave of nausea rose through me and before I could speak again, he ended the call.

• • •

I knew, that night on Signal Hill.

The first time I had been with Julia had ended with awkwardness and embarrassment. For me, at least. I hadn't been in a serious relationship with anyone since Megan died. And apart from a few casual encounters, I hadn't been with anyone at all. That first night, we'd only been together a few minutes when her hand found the premature wetness in my crotch and I fled as quickly as I could. I wanted nothing more than to forget the incident and move on, but Julia wouldn't let me. She called the next day. And when I didn't respond she called again. And again. When I finally agreed to meet her for lunch, I asked her why she kept calling. What made me special?

"Nothing," she said. "But I couldn't leave it like that. Let that be our last memory of each other."

Those first weeks were tentative and hesitant. I felt like a child on a bicycle with training wheels. But she was there, her hand on my back, and gradually I came to understand she wouldn't let me fall.

We were walking down Second Street on our way to dinner at Nick's, and we came across an elderly homeless man near the Rite Aid. He was sitting on the sidewalk, a cup in front of him with a cardboard sign that said "PLEESE HELP." I would have walked right past him, but Julia looked down at him and said, "Elliot?" He looked at her, but there was no recognition in his eyes, only fear and confusion. He tried to say something, but his speech was too slurred to understand.

She turned back to me and quietly and calmly said, "Call an ambulance."

I took a few steps back and called 911.

She sat down next to him, took his dirty hand in hers, and, in the same soft and warm tone, began talking to him. She mentioned the VA and the support group they'd both apparently been a part of. She was still talking to him when I heard the siren in the distance. He didn't seem to understand and his eyes were going in and out of focus, but she was calming him, easing his fear.

The paramedics loaded him in the back, and she told them she'd be riding with him. I followed in my Camry.

It was a stroke, they told us. As we waited for more news, she called the VA to arrange support services for him. She spent more than an hour and talked to six different people before she was satisfied. We sat in the waiting room for two hours until the doctor came out and told us he'd stabilized.

Instead of the expensive dinner we'd planned, we drove through the In-N-Out up on Signal Hill and ate Double-Doubles and fries well done, in the front seat of my car, while we looked out through the windshield at the city lights in the distance.

And I knew.

• • •

I parked around the corner on Linden where he wouldn't be able to see me from the gallery. There was no way I could get a look inside without him also being able to see me.

Julia's phone rang three times before he answered.

"Where are you?" he said.

"Outside."

"Come in."

"No. Not until you send everyone else out." I positioned myself on the corner, in line with the storefront windows. Looking inside the gallery was still impossible, but I'd be able to see if anyone came out of the door.

"If I do that," he said, "why would you come inside?"

"Because I say I will."

He ended the call and soon half a dozen people ran out through the door and hurried down the side. Five women—none of them Julia—and Trev, the gallery owner. "This way!" I called out to them.

Trev recognized me and ran in my direction. He was panicked and rambling. I took him by the shoulders and looked him in the eye. "Trev," I said, as calmly as I could. "What's going on in there?"

He was hyperventilating and his man-bun had come undone.

"Calm down," I said. "Breathe slowly. You're safe. It's going to be all right."

"He has a bomb," he said. "A suicide bomb."

"Who has a bomb?" I asked as calmly as I could.

"The man. He just came in. Out of nowhere."

"What man?"

"From the photo."

"What photo?"

"The photo!"

I didn't know what he meant but I didn't want to waste any more time. "Is Julia still inside?"

His head moved up and down in a vigorous nod.

"Go half a block up there." I pointed north up Linden. "Wait there, okay?"

More nodding. I gave him a gentle push and he started moving.

Walking slowly toward the door of the gallery, I took my own advice and inhaled deeply and let the breath out slowly. Then I did it again and again. A few steps in from the corner, I was finally able to see inside.

The lights were turned off, but I could see two shapes, shrouded in shadow, all the way back in the corner. As I looked, I was gradually able to make out more detail. The bomber was behind Julia. Still unable to get a good look at him, I moved toward the door. I took one last deep breath, reached for the handle, and went inside.

"Julia," I said. "Are you all right?"

"Yes," she said.

I didn't believe her. With the sun shining in through the large windows behind me, my eyes began to adjust to the light, and I was able to see more clearly. But I still couldn't get a good look at the bomber. There was a distance of at least twenty-five feet between us. On the floor inside the door lay an oversized coat. He must have worn it to conceal the bomb.

"Come back here," he said.

"Nope. You let her go, then I come back there. That's the only way this works."

"I'm not leaving," Julia said.

He leaned forward and said something to her that I couldn't hear.

"It's all right, Julia. Trust me, okay?"

"Danny, don't—"

"Trust me," I said.

The bomber said, "She takes one step forward, you take one step forward. Got it?" He nudged her gently and she began to move.

I matched her, step for step. As we approached the center of the room, I thought about grabbing her and breaking for the door. But I dismissed the thought as quickly as it came. There was no way we'd make it.

My eyes were locked on Julia's as we closed the distance between us. I could see her fear and it made me hate him even more intensely.

I wanted to reach out to her as we passed each other, and I could see she did, too. But how would he react?

As the backs of our hands brushed against each other and I lost sight of her face, I heard her whisper, "I love you."

My eyes found the bomber and I was hit with a shock of recognition. It was the soldier with the prosthetic leg from Julia's photo. That's what Trev was talking about. He was standing in front of her section of the exhibit. Behind him I could see the edge of the photo she'd taken of me on her balcony, turned away from the eye of the camera.

"Hi, Terry," I said.

"Stop there," he said. "Don't come any closer."

I stopped. But I was near enough to see the device strapped to his chest. There were six blocks of what I assumed to be C-4 or something similar. He held a triggering device in his right hand. I'd stopped moving about eight feet from him and looked over my shoulder just in time to watch Julia slip out the door. The cold burn of adrenaline flowed down through my abdomen.

"What the fuck, man," I said.

"Why didn't you just stay away from her? This wouldn't have happened if you'd just stayed away." There was genuine pain in his voice, and I could see it was torturing him. He had deep lines in his face and dark circles under his eyes that hadn't been there when I'd met him before at the opening. "I saw you with her, you know. At Buskerfest. I saw you. What you did to that guy."

"I didn't know," I said.

"That lady he was messing with? I would have done the same thing for her if I'd been where you were."

"I'm sure you would have."

"But I wouldn't have lost it. You didn't even see how Julia was look-ing at you when you did that. She was scared. Of you. Why couldn't you have just stayed away like I told you?"

"I thought you were talking about someone else," I said.

"Really?" he said.

I nodded. "Really."

The implication that I would have stayed away if I'd known he was talking about Julia seemed to register with him. It didn't matter that it wasn't true.

He wore a blue T-shirt under the black vest to which the explosives were attached. The tattoo on the inside of his forearm that I'd seen a portion of at the opening was fully exposed. It was the same design that Gonzales had on his biceps.

"You did bomb disposal in Iraq?" I asked.

"How'd you know that?"

"The ink on your arm." He seemed vaguely impressed that I recog-nized it. "Is that a dead-man's trigger in your hand?"

"If I let go of the button, the bomb goes off."

I nodded. "Why don't you deactivate it?"

"No."

"I know you don't want to kill me."

"You're wrong."

"If you wanted me dead, I'd already be dead. You had two chances and both times you warned me off. You don't want my blood on your hands." I watched his eyes, but I couldn't read them. "You're a pro, Terry. You know what you're doing. You don't want it to end like this."

"How do you know what I want?"

"I don't. But I know what Julia wants. It's not this."

He looked down at the floor and closed his eyes. I thought about rushing him, but I'd never be able to get my thumb on the trigger in time to prevent the detonation. There were a lot of explosives on his vest, and even though I was no expert, I thought it might be enough to take down this whole corner of the building.

"I was gonna let it go. I was. When you didn't listen and stay away. I saw how she was with you, thought maybe I was wrong, maybe you could make her happy. She has to be happy."

I took a step toward him.

"Stop! Don't come any closer."

I spread my hands and backed up.

"She was the only one. When I came home. The support group. She understood."

"I get it," I said.

"No, you don't. If you did, you wouldn't have scared her like that. How could you do that?"

"I screwed up. I'm sorry. It won't happen again. I'll stay away this time."

He stared at me and I felt like he could see more deeply into me than anyone I'd ever looked in the eye.

"No you won't," he said. "And she has to be happy."

"She does," I whispered.

"She saved my life," he said. Tears were collecting in the corners of his eyes.

"I know, Terry. She saved mine, too."

He grimaced as if someone had pierced his chest with a knife and I knew I'd made a horrible mistake.

Everything shifted into slow motion and it seemed as if it took minutes for him to raise his right hand and lift his thumb off of the trigger button.

CHAPTER TWENTY-FOUR

WALKING FAR FROM HOME

I felt the concussive blast and heard the thunderous crack and saw the bright flash. Something cut my face, and my ears rang and circles of brightness floated in my field of vision. I was sitting on the floor, disoriented, my head spinning, trying to count the lights in front of me. Were there four or five? I couldn't hear anything but the deafening shriek in my ears.

What happened?

Why wasn't I dead?

I tried to blink away the spots in my eyes. There was a haze of smoke and dust. The taste of it in my mouth made me gag. Terry was on the floor in front of me. His chest was ripped open in a mass of viscera and smoldering black nylon. His prosthetic leg had come off. The wall behind him was painted red.

I wasn't dead.

Someone was in front of me trying to get my attention. His mouth was moving but I couldn't hear any words. Gonzales, I realized, it was Gonzales. He was waving his hand in front of my face.

Someone else lifted my arm and wrapped it around his neck and lifted me off the floor like a weightless ragdoll. His shoulders felt like stone. *Farley,* I thought, *Gonzales's partner.* I was trying to move my feet on the floor, but he was taking all my weight. It seemed like I was floating.

Then we were outside. My feet were on the ground. Farley led me across the street and sat me on the curb. The shock of the explosion was fading.

Jen was there.

And Julia.

I wasn't dead.

• • •

"The blocks on the vest were fake," Gonzales said. We were standing in the shade of the buildings on the south side of the street, looking across Broadway at the gallery. From our vantage point, there was nothing to indicate what had gone on inside.

"I don't understand," I said.

"He just had a tiny charge against his chest. Even had a body-armor plate in front of it to direct the explosion."

"What does that mean?" I asked.

"I don't think he wanted to take anybody else with him. He knew what he was doing. The charge was just enough to blow a big hole in his chest. You would have to have been right on top of him for it to kill you, too."

That's why he stopped me where he did, made me take a step back. I was glad I'd listened to his warning this time.

• • •

Earlier, at the station, as soon as Terry had ended the call, I'd rushed back into the observation room and told Jen that Julia and her workshop students were caught up in a hostage situation with a possible suicide bomber at the gallery. I told her to call SWAT and to keep everyone out of sight until she heard from me.

After, I found her sitting on the curb with Julia just a few yards inside the yellow crime-scene tape that was blocking the street. A crowd had gathered on the other side. Down the block I could see the satellite antenna of a TV news van climbing up into the sky.

Sitting down next to them, I said, "How's it going over here?"

Neither of them answered.

We sat in silence a few moments, then Jen said softly to me, "I need to get statements from the others inside." She looked at Julia. "Are you okay?"

"I will be," Julia said.

Jen stood and touched the back of my head as if I were a child at her hip. I looked up at her and she returned my weak smile before walking back toward the gallery.

Julia leaned against me and put her head on my shoulder. She had been crying and there was still a tremor in her hands. "I can't stop shaking," she said.

"I know. It's the adrenaline dump. It will pass in a while." I leaned my head on hers and breathed in the scent of her hair. It smelled like apples.

• • •

At some point, Patrick had shown up to take over control of the crime scene. I didn't envy his situation. This case kept growing on him. *These cases,* I thought, correcting myself. It had been two separate investigations all along. The bomb in my car had nothing to do with William Denkins's murder after all. I found Patrick coming out of the gallery.

"Hey," he said. "How are you doing?"

"I'm okay. How's it look in there?"

"It's a mess. But Gonzales tells me it's not as bad as it could have been."

"I know." I looked down at the ground and felt the weight of what might have been, if Terry had been who I thought he was when I saw him in the suicide-bomber vest.

"How's Julia?"

"Pretty shaken up. Jen got her statement. Okay if I take her home?"

"Yeah," he said. "That's probably a good idea."

• • •

The last of the day's sunlight was shining in through Julia's balcony door as I put some music on and made us dinner. The omelets were too dry and the sourdough toasted too brown, but I managed to pick us a good bottle of wine.

We finished eating and took the rest of the wine into the living room just as Nina Simone's "Ne Me Quitte Pas" was finishing and Leonard Cohen's "Night Comes On" was beginning.

"I like this," she said. "Is it a mix?"

"Just some songs I like," I said. "I'll make you a copy."

We sat on the couch, my arm around her shoulders, and finished the wine while we listened.

"Ashes on Your Eyes" was playing when she turned her face away from me and whispered, "I don't know if I can do this."

I didn't know what she meant and I didn't want to, so I pulled her closer and pretended I hadn't heard the words.

CHAPTER TWENTY-FIVE

IF I SHOULD FALL BEHIND

The week before the anniversary party for Jen's parents, the temperature had topped one hundred four days in a row. Jen had wanted to move the party inside, but her mother wouldn't hear of it. There was a good turnout. Forty or fifty people. I didn't know most of them, only Jen's parents and her brother, Johnny. The only other cops there were Patrick and Lauren, so we huddled back by the garage and talked about work.

"The plea deal's set," Patrick said. "They're knocking a few years off of Joe's sentence in exchange for his testimony against Novak." After I'd left the interrogation, Joe had admitted that he and Avram Novak had gone to William Denkins's apartment to convince him to offer up more money. Joe claimed he had no idea what Novak had planned, but did nothing to stop him as they plied Bill with more and more Glenlivet until he was close enough to unconsciousness that Novak was able to put the gun in Bill's hand and pull the trigger. Patrick believed him, but it didn't really matter. He was certain Lucinda hadn't known what her husband had done. We never did find out why she hadn't taken Joe's last name. Whatever the reason for her long-ago decision, it might provide a tiny sliver of consolation in the face of her overwhelming grief. The case was closed and the men who'd murdered William Denkins were going away. I thought again about how close they'd come to pulling it off. If either of them had thought to put the gun in his right hand, they would have walked away.

Patrick had already told me what he'd discovered searching Terry's apartment. It looked like a textbook case of an intimacy-seeking stalker. Prior to the photo, he hadn't seen Julia since the support group almost two years earlier, but when she bumped into him on the pier and took his picture, it set something off in him. He read it as her initiating a kind of intimate connection with him and he became obsessed. His web-browser histories showed countless searches for every possible variation of her name. He'd bookmarked dozens of sites with mentions of her name or her artwork. There was a journal that documented his actions and he'd taken candid photos of her, too. Even paid an online investigative company to do a deep search and pull up everything from public records to her credit history. There was no way it could have ended well for him. And even though I empathized deeply with his pain, I couldn't say I was sorry he was gone. I'd seen a lot of stalkers in my years with the department, and things could have been much worse for Julia.

Lauren came back from the drink table with a beer for herself and an iced tea for me. "How was the first week back in uniform?" I asked her.

"Not bad," she said.

Patrick grinned and said, "But I'll bet you figured out when you'll be eligible for the Detectives' exam."

We heard a clinking sound and someone saying, "Excuse me, everyone, excuse me."

It was Johnny, Jen's younger brother, standing under the pergola on the steps leading up from the patio into the kitchen, a bottle of champagne in his hand. "Thank you all for coming. We're so happy you've joined us to celebrate Mom and Dad's fortieth."

Jen and another woman I didn't know moved through the crowd carrying trays of prefilled plastic cups while Johnny spoke. By the time

Jen made it back to where we were standing, there were only two left. Patrick and Lauren took them.

Jen looked at me and said, "Shit, I'm sorry, let me—"

"It's okay," I said, holding up the tea bottle in my hand. "This will be fine."

She turned around just as her brother shouted, "Congratulations!"

• • •

The crowd had started to thin, and the pain was climbing up my shoulder and neck by the time Jen found me back in the corner of the yard, sitting on the bench in the twilight under the oak's bough.

"Julia couldn't make it?"

We'd been together almost every night since the gallery, but something had changed. I didn't know if it was the trauma of that day that had been affecting her or if it was something else, something deeper. All I really knew was that we were finally caught up on *Downton Abbey* and the final season was waiting for us. I hoped we'd be watching it together.

"She's still having a hard time," I said. "Didn't feel up to socializing today."

"Anything I can do to help?"

"I don't know. Maybe take her for coffee or lunch. I think she's getting a little tired of me."

"I'll give her a call."

"Thanks."

We sat there in the shade and I could tell there was something else she needed to say. Something she didn't want to tell me. "Ruiz talked to you, right?"

"About what?"

"Getting a new detective for the squad."

"Yeah." I didn't want to hear what came next.

She didn't look at me as she spoke. "He wants me to train him. Partner with him for a while."

I didn't say anything.

"Until he gets up to speed."

There were still a few stragglers hanging around the patio, laughing and talking to each other. Smiling. Not ready for the party to end.

"Danny?"

"Yeah?"

"Say something."

"Patrick just nailed two big cases. Why not him?"

"I don't know. That's not the call Ruiz made."

I wanted to say something but I didn't know what. A breeze rustled the leaves of the tree above us.

She stood up, put her hand on my shoulder, and said, "I'm sorry, Danny."

As she walked away toward the others, I stopped her. "Jen?"

She turned back.

"Are we okay?" I said.

There was something sad and wistful in her voice as she sighed and said, "Look at those people over there. You know who they are? You know who everyone I invited here today is?"

I shook my head.

"My family."

She walked back toward the house and I sat there under the oak in the shadow of the evening trees.

The pain loosened its grip.

I rose and followed her.

This book wouldn't exist without the generous support of many others. To them I owe a significant debt of gratitude. My most heartfelt thanks to:

Gracie Doyle, Alison Dasho, Jacque Ben-Zekry, Sarah Shaw, Charlotte Herscher, Meredith Jacobson, and the rest of the team at Thomas & Mercer.

David Aimerito, Zachary Locklin, Paul Tayyar, and Eileen Klink.

Jay Chase, Derek Pacifico, and Scott Brick.

Matt Gourley, creator and host of the podcast *I Was There Too*, for not only inspiring a significant portion of this novel, but also for graciously allowing me to use the lyrics to the *IWTT* theme song both in the epigraph and throughout the text.

And to my family—my brother and sister-in-law, Jeff and Kim Dilts, whose heavy lifting allowed me the time and space to work; my beautiful amazing wife, Nicole Gharda, whose unflagging belief in me never wavers; and my mom, Sharon Dilts, whose love, encouragement, and compassion made me the writer I am today.

As a child, Tyler Dilts dreamed of following in the footsteps of his policeman father. Though his career goals changed over time, he never lost interest in the daily work of homicide detectives. Today he teaches at California State University in Long Beach, and his writing has appeared in the *Los Angeles Times*, the *Chronicle of Higher Education*, *The Best American Mystery Stories*, and numerous other publications. He is the author of three previous novels in the Long Beach Homicide series: *A King of Infinite Space*, *The Pain Scale*, and *A Cold and Broken Hallelujah*. He lives with his wife in Long Beach, California.